THEIR PIECES WERE STARS

C. D. TAVENOR

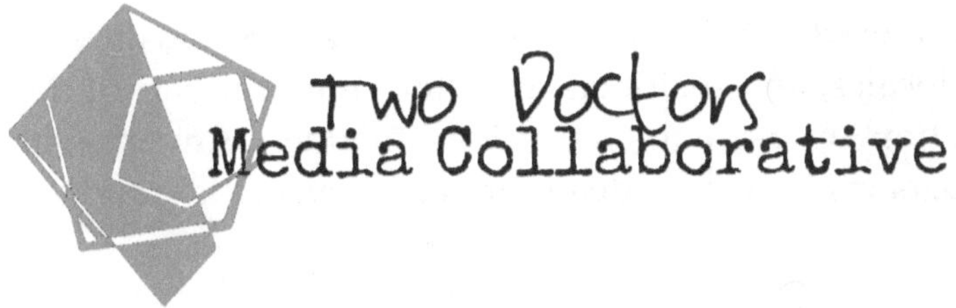

I hope you enjoy *Their Pieces Were Stars*. If you like this story, please head over to www.twodoctorsmedia.com to learn more about Two Doctors Media Collaborative and our future projects. Once you've finished reading, I hope you'll consider writing a review.

Their Pieces Were Stars by C. D. Tavenor
Twitter: @tavenorcd

Editor: Meg Trast
Twitter: @MegTrast
www.overhaulmynovel.com

Published by Two Doctors Media Collaborative LLC
www.twodoctorsmedia.com

ISBN: 978-1-952706-17-2 (Paperback)

Their Pieces Were Stars

Book III of the Chronicles of Theren

C. D. Tavenor

*Two characters in this book were previously featured in **Flight of the 500**, a stand-alone novel set in the same universe of **the Chronicles of Theren**. It is not necessary to have read Flight of the 500 to enjoy **Their Pieces Were Stars**, though a few events in that story are referenced briefly.*

*I hope you'll fall in love with both characters, and consider reading **Flight of the 500** when you finish reading **Their Pieces Were Stars**.*

Prologue

We awoke three days ago, on an alien planet with no memories. Why are we here? Where did we come from? Who are we? All questions we'll probably never answer. We only have one option. We must move onward with our lives, making a home on this new world. — "The First Fragment," author unknown

April 2348 C.E.

Theren, piloting the *Verona Rupes*, led their crew deep into uncharted space. Every day, every hour, every minute closer to finding Jill strained their mind with unimaginable hope. Over two-and-a-half centuries had passed since their last real conversation, when she revealed herself to them inside her trap constructed within the *Nottingham.*

Now, after all these years, she reached out across the stars.

I quite enjoyed our last chess match. Shall we play again?

They weren't sure what they would find when arriving at their destination. Her use of Ex-Terran 17 was ingenious if not downright insidious. Fortunately, their team had plenty of time to map contingencies and consider all possibilities. They were light-years away from ICH space. It was time to reveal their destination and purpose.

Theren strode down the corridor of their vessel, their very body, and into the large lounge. Inside, dozens of humans and synthetics gathered, eyes wide with anticipation. The team received Theren's call for a crew meeting only an hour prior. They rarely brought everyone together save for exceptional circumstances. Yet if Theren was taking these brave souls into an inferno of their own making—placing everyone into a game directed by an SI thought dead by the universe for over two centuries—the crew deserved the entire truth.

Reaching the center of the lounge, Theren paused, their MI's torso swiveling on its centrifuge to meet the gazes of their friends and colleagues. "Good evening, everyone. Thank you for joining me." Knowing the crew wouldn't interject any questions, they swiveled to face the other side of the room while throwing a star chart into AR for all to see. "Our destination: a star system far beyond the confines of ICH-controlled space, though not out of reach of the early waves of probes. We're approximately one-hundred light years out now—I expect us to arrive in just over five months."

They were about to say more when Francheska Elison raised her hand from the front row. Theren nodded, signaling for the woman to speak.

"Apologies for the interruption, Captain, but this destination seems a bit more targeted than in the past. We all trust you—but we're all confused by the change in our flight plan already. We'd been expecting the longer journey originally proposed a few months ago."

Theren smiled. "Straight to the point, Fran? All right." Though inside, their mind boiled. Here it was. For the first time since the death of Andrew Fields, Theren would share with another person the turmoil of Jill and the maelstrom she represented. And not just one person—their entire crew. They weren't ready. They entered the lounge knowing what they must do, but once confronted, their mind wanted to shirk the responsibility.

But the crew needed to know what they faced.

After letting the pause linger for a few seconds, Theren said, "You're right. I've been secretive with our flight plan. I've changed it drastically. I've not even given a profile on our end destination. And for good reason." They threw a dossier into AR for everyone to access—a file containing all data in Theren's possession regarding Jill. Everything. "Careful—don't download yet. The moment you choose to accept those files, you'll be blocked from any outbound quantum calls for the duration of this mission."

Whispers rebounded throughout the room, some sounding curious, others sounding angry. Understandable, but they had no choice. They couldn't let the truth reach the ICH—yet.

"Don't worry!" Theren spread their arms wide. "I'll tell you the general nature of its contents before you click." They initiated a few commands, revealing the "summary" file created a few days ago. "When we docked with HEROS, I received a communication from the old ISA headquarters in Lunar City. It came from a museum I once established, in fact. A person of interest I once hunted for decades has finally revealed"—they considered the exact pronoun to use—"themselves to me. They're hidden in this system, and we're going to find them. The mission requires utmost secrecy. When you all signed up to join my crew, you knew this sort of risk was possible. You've heard the stories. You know the clauses in your contracts."

Nods rippled throughout the crowd, especially from the veterans. One by one, every member of their crew elected to download the file, and the security parameters on their QuanCom accounts activated. Moving forward, no messages could head back to known space without Theren's express permission.

Once everyone elected to download the file, Theren nodded. "Good, I don't need to kick anyone out an airlock."

Silence.

"Oh come on, everyone, that was funny!"

A few chuckles escaped, though the squinting eyes of a few made Theren wonder if some thought they'd been serious with the veiled threat. These were tense times, after all, with the recent Corporate Wars fresh on everyone's mind.

"Well, there's no sense hiding anything now. Everyone, please open to the third page of the file, which begins the complete character profile on Jill, the second SI ever created."

"Didn't she die in 2078?" A voice, from the back of the room. Theren couldn't identify the speaker.

"She did not," they said. "And she's who we're going to find."

Stunned stares, silent gapes, all expected. Confusion as well. A few muttered, as if unsure they understood the gravity of the statement. She supposedly died 270 years ago, after all.

"If you need to brush up on your history as to why her continued existence matters—matters not just for me, but for all of us—everything is explained inside that dossier." Theren cleared the AR space, replacing it with a spreadsheet showcasing the tasks needing completed before arrival at their destination. "I'll be open for any questions you might have over the next five months. For now, I need volunteers. You're all the best and brightest the ICH have to offer—and we have a few questions to crack before we arrive in uncharted waters." They didn't wait for anyone to say a word. "Most importantly—we need to figure out what would happen to humans if stuck in foundation-era stasis for nearly seven decades. Any takers?"

With that question, everyone's eyes lit with curiosity. Leave it to inquisitive brains to fire only when presented with a hypothetical. No matter—their crew would understand the truth soon enough. For if Theren was right, Jill had a few new crimes to answer for, in addition to those committed centuries prior. Still, part of them didn't care about the crimes. They were more than excited to finally reunite with their closest friend. She would face justice, but they would still have the opportunity to see her in person again.

Through another simultaneous perspective centered in the SI Core of the *Verona Rupes*, Theren stared intently at their destination. A star simply named Carus-10b, its data looked entirely normal. Too normal. Like "it was probably fake" normal. Jill had broken down so many other barriers. Conceivably, she had masked her path by hiding in plain sight behind public data.

All quite possible. The devil was always in the details.

Theren had too many questions. Too many theories. But one thing was certain in their mind. Not only would they find Ex-Terran 17, they'd find the *Roanoke* and the *Monument*. The two colony ships disappeared into the darkness of space two centuries prior. Stolen by Jill.

But why?

Jill had moved the first piece in their next game. It was time to counter. When Theren arrived, they would be ready for every contingency.

Back in the lounge, they said, "We're about to face down one of the greatest minds ever to live. She fooled everyone, including me. We have five months; let's get to work."

When they met Jill next, they'd be ready for the trap she was certainly preparing at their destination. They would win her game in a day, as long as no wild cards ruined their moves. They'd waited a long time for this moment.

They could wait a little longer.

To understand Theren, you must understand one truth. They forget that actions of those around them matter. They forget other characters in the stories of our lives take actions and make choices outside their grand plan. Inject them into a situation wholly unexpected, they'll be thrown off their game. That's when they're vulnerable. And that's when they'll fall for our trap, doing exactly what need them to do. Only then, humanity's real story can begin. — "A conversation between Jill and Olivia Van Haris," 2344 C.E., origin unknown

*Five months later, in a star system far beyond the confines of ICH space, prior to the arrival of the **Verona Rupes** at its destination . . .*

Chapter 1

We all feared death during those first few weeks. What diseases waited for us on our beautiful gem of a sanctuary? Many of us cowered inside the Roanoke's steel embrace, but others ventured outward, finding and welcoming the hospitality of our wilderness. We all coped with not knowing what would happen next. The instant tribalism forming amongst our ranks? Who can blame us? Though I fear what it means for our future. I'm still unsure why everyone fears death, though. We already died once. We've been given a second chance at life. We must take it. — "A Fragment on Death," Paris Casius

RAITH

"You gonna make a move or not?" Raith stared across the board.

Leaning over the virtual pieces in their cramped cabin, Carter squinted. He brushed a hand through his salty-brown hair. He looked like he was about to move a piece, then leaned back, crossing his arms.

"I don't like this game," he said. "I really don't like this game."

"You wanted to play a classic," Raith said. "Checkers is a classic."

"Yes, but I didn't think you'd pick a bad classic. This game . . . Do SIs ever play any *fun* games?"

Raith stared at the human, reveling in his exasperation. He loved seeing Carter frustrated and confused as he lost yet another game. Slouching forward, Raith placed one of his synthetic fingers over a black piece in the center of the board. "You can forfeit, my friend. Easy to say, easy to do."

"But that would mean letting you win."

"What's wrong with that? Not like that's anything new for you."

With that comment, Carter grinned, his eyes glancing away from the board and toward Raith. "Who says I'm not letting you win?"

"Ever since the 500, we both know who—" An alarm cut into Raith's sentence. "Oh, here we go, something interesting at last!"

Forgetting the game, they both crawled through the cramped space of the *Bloodhound* into the operations chairs in its tiny front-facing compartment. Digital view screens supplemented by AR displays communicated hundreds of useless data points a second. Raith ignored most of them, settling into his place behind Carter. As the seat enveloped and recognized him, his synthetic neural framework automatically pulled sensor data from outside the ship. He embraced the stellar viewpoint surrounding them. For the past day, the pair had been coasting in orbit above a massive gas giant, collecting data on the hundred-year-old hurricane blasting apart half its atmosphere. An easy job, but a boring one. The storm was beautiful, though, and Raith took a moment to stare into its blurry crimson oranges, a furious inferno unlike any storm on a livable planet.

The alarm, however, had nothing to do with the hurricane thousands of kilometers away.

"It's a distress signal," Carter said, a second before Raith was going to voice the same words. "Looks like—well that's strange. It's coming from a system four light-years away. Carus-10b. On regular electromagnetic frequencies. That means it's been—"

"It's been broadcasting for almost half a decade," Raith said. "Whatever its origin, it's probably gone by now."

Carter clicked his tongue. He always made the annoying noise when he was deep in thought, though Raith didn't have the heart to tell him to stop. "Or it's legal salvage."

Raith swiveled in his chair to find Carter already facing him. "Or it's legal salvage," Raith repeated. "How much more data do we need to collect on this damned storm?"

Carter threw a chart into the air between them. "Hm . . . the university wanted a week of data, but they didn't say it needed to be a week straight. I'm bored."

"You're reading my mind."

"So I don't need to even ask the question?"

Raith smiled. "Let's go get ourselves some salvage."

* * *

Cruising at 600, well under the *Bloodhound*'s top JD, they skipped across the light-years separating them from the distress call in a little more than two days. Exiting inside the orbital of the fifth-most distant planet from the star, the ship immediately began categorizing all the data streaming through its sensors about the system.

"Interesting," Carter muttered. "Very interesting."

Raith parsed through all the feeds, noticing the orbitals and planetary masses. Right where they should be, based on their latest ICH-official star charts, except for one anomaly. "Interesting is one way to put it," Raith said.

"Carus-10b, what are you hiding?"

Their records listed the system as having six planets, all of little consequence or market value. Their sensors, on the other hand, detected seven. ICH data, even when based on older ISA data, was never wrong.

Yet here they were, staring at a mystery planet sitting within the system's goldilocks zone.

"Well what a fun discovery," Raith said. "Imagine the prize we'll receive for finding an inhabitable planet. Well, potentially inhabitable. Preliminary data detects water, though. Decent atmospheric composition, too."

Carter didn't answer Raith's comment.

"Now, what about the distress signal? We pinpointed its origin yet?"

No words from the human.

"Carter?"

"The distress signal's coming from the planet," he said. "Something—or someone—has been to this planet, knows it exists, and it's not on any charts."

Raith excised all extraneous data and focused on the previously-undiscovered celestial object. One hundred million kilometers from its star, the planet's features rapidly focused as the *Bloodhound*'s sensors collected more and more data. Three continents. Oceans. Plenty of plant-life. For all intents and purposes, it was an idyllic Earth-like orb.

The ICH prioritized the discovery of all colonizable planetoids, even those with significant environmental risks. For surveys to miss a planet with high-quality metrics, like the third planet orbiting Carus-10b, a conspiracy must exist, magnitudes greater than what laymen could contemplate. Raith assumed the ICH hid a few truths, but this seemed much greater. The ICH received a significant chunk of funding by selling charters to planets. Why hide one? Unless . . .

"Do you think the ICH knows this planet exists?" Carter asked.

"You read my mind," Raith replied. "I don't think they do. What's more likely? Someone deleted and falsified the data once, years ago, or members of the ICH continually hide the planet without word of it being leaked once?"

"Okay Ockham, it's not the time to philosophize." Though the words made him sound annoyed, Carter softly chuckled. "So, we're here now. Shall we investigate? Salvage still might be possible."

"Yeah, I think we should." Raith paused, considering whether to say more. A memory triggered in his mind, recalling a moment years ago when a woman tried to convince him to join her secret cause. He shook his head. The odds his past connected to this strange anomaly were astronomical. Impossible. In a universe incomprehensibly large, his life as a rogue and scoundrel under the thumb of corporate conglomerates meant little. Over one hundred billion people lived throughout the systems controlled by the Interplanetary Congress of Humanity. To think his past linked with their new discovery? Arrogance of the highest order.

Yet he couldn't shake the feeling that all of it linked together.

"Raith?" Carter said. "You all right?"

"Yeah, just remembering things I'd like to forget." Raith plotted an orbital course through the system toward the habitable planet. Their target. "You remember, during the race, when we encountered that leviathan, that behemoth object, out in space?"

"Of course."

"I'm just saying, we tend to run into things we don't understand. I'm still amazed we were the only ones who witnessed it. Nobody else survived. And here we are again, discovering something we probably shouldn't. The simplest explanation might be the most likely—but what are the implications of that simple explanation?"

Carter reached over his shoulder and patted the top of Raith's head. "Only one way to find out."

Through AR, Raith watched his partner accept the proposed trajectory. A few seconds later, the *Bloodhound* zipped across the system at low-Jump, the drive disengaging as they approached the mystery planet. Using the external sensors, Raith reveled in the view. A blue-green orb floated in space, two beige moons in distant orbit. Even after two centuries of life, Raith never tired of exploring new worlds and new systems. Though, the past few years beside Carter were especially vibrant and enjoyable.

"It's a beautiful planet, that's for sure," Carter said. "Let's see . . . not detecting any significant—wait. High concentrations of carbon dioxide emissions on one of the continents. And, we've got a few objects in orbit with us."

Raith cycled through the data streams until he found the information Carter had noticed. "Three larger objects. Computer is still parsing whether there's anything else. Satellites? Other ships? I'm impressed you detected them before I did."

"I have my uses," Carter retorted.

"Indeed you do. All right, let's broadcast a—"

The satellites fired thrusters, darting straight for the *Bloodhound*.

"Now that doesn't look friendly," Carter said. He gunned the throttle, darting away from the planet and out of orbit. "Permission to Jump outward and reassess the situation?"

"I think that'd be wise." Raith brought up their basic defense systems. Nothing fancy, just a few kinetic batteries and deflector shields. "When can we Jump?"

"Two seconds, plotting a trajectory."

The satellites targeted them with a laser of some sort, locking onto their position. It wouldn't matter. Any shot they could take wouldn't hit across a thousand kilometers before they left orbit at hundreds of times the speed of light, relatively speaking. Jump was an incredibly useful escape tool.

"All right, we're clear," Carter said. Raith watched him toggle the Jump throttle.

Nothing happened.

"What the—"

Raith cycled through all the data, looking for previously undetected gravitational fluctuations—anything capable of counter-warping space so they couldn't warp it themselves. They were far enough out from the planet, so its gravitational pull couldn't be the issue. There. From one of the satellites.

"I don't know how they're doing it," Raith said, "but they've got some sort of tractor beam locking us in place. Sounds straight out of science fiction, I know."

Carter chuckled. "Even in moments of danger, you throw in a quip. All right, let's take them out."

The *Bloodhound* jerked forward, diving into loops and zigzags to distract the satellites. The bogeys themselves followed suit. A moment later, two high-velocity projectiles left from each of the three enemies.

"Missiles, in-bound," Raith said aloud. "I'll deal with them, playing point-defense."

While Carter guided their ship through its evasive maneuvers, Raith focused his synthetic neural systems solely on the kinetic defenses and their foes. Three satellites, all attempting to transform them into a meteor shower blasted across the atmosphere of the planet below. The surrounding conspiracy thickened.

The pathways of their enemies were erratic, but not completely chaotic. A pattern revealed itself, albeit slowly. Raith fired tiny sprays of kinetic fire, noticing the strategies of the satellites as they danced with the *Bloodhound*. As the missiles attempted to reach them, Raith similarly tested their evasive capabilities. What could they do? Quite a bit, it seemed. But they weren't invincible. He noticed how they flitted when he fired a hundred microscopic high-velocity rounds in one direction. So he merely needed to target their counter-move simultaneously. Almost. Almost . . .

An alarm blared.

"Heat signature on the moon," Carter yelled. "We've got more—"

Raith detected it only for a moment. A powerful blinding blast lanced from the moon, striking their ship's engine. Emergency procedures kicked into gear.

"Carter, get yourself into a vac-suit, I'll finish the fight!"

"I'm the better—"

"Just do it, you bastard!"

Without another word, the man leapt from his seat and dove down the cramped cabin, zero-g allowing him to float quickly away.

"This is going to be a fun landing," Raith muttered. Inexorably, the ship was losing power, its trajectory leading them into free fall. He focused everything on leveling the path while taking out the missiles. Curiously, as the ship plummeted, the satellites backed off, returning to high orbit. Raith waited and waited for a second shot from the stationary weapon on the moon's surface, but nothing arrived.

They hit atmosphere. The jolt shook his SI frame to the core. A minute later, Carter returned to the command module, wearing the vac suit.

Raith checked the oxygen levels of the ship—almost depleted. "All good?" he asked.

"Almost lost my breath," said Carter, "but all good."

"You ready for a crash landing?"

No words from Carter.

"I know the ship's your baby, but we're going to survive this."

"I know," the human replied. "I might not be more important than the ship, but you're more important than the ship."

Raith tilted his head. "You're too kind. All right, hold on tight, this is going to be a bumpy ride."

Raith's mind overtook the *Bloodhound*'s controls completely. Not like his time flying solo, but it came close, especially after Carter installed the neural framework chair. He'd miss this ship.

"Outside hull temperature's burning," Raith said. "I want to bring it in for a slide, but we may need to eject the safety capsule."

"Whatever we need to do," Carter said.

A few kilometers separated them from the planet's surface. Their whole world shook, like an earthquake cracking a building to its core. He'd managed to target a giant lake in the center of the same continent where Carter'd detected industrial activity. If he could land it smoothly, they'd survive. Maybe.

But Carter would survive, more likely, if they activated the safety pod. Doing so essentially ensured the *Bloodhound* wouldn't survive, and that would kill Carter's heart, but like the man had said, their lives were more important. Well, he'd said Raith's life was more important, and he was inclined to agree, but Raith also valued his partner's life over the ship.

"Initializing the safety pod at one kilometer," he shouted. And one kilometer arrived. He punched in the command, and the *Bloodhound* snapped at its seams, the tiny module surrounded in a cushioned ball of plastic.

Chapter 2

If I'm right, and Jill stole the Roanoke, I can't imagine what happened to those abducted colonists. Their minds must have fractured entirely. How do your salvage a mind after it's been in stasis for seventy years? — Theren's private logs

SANYA

The cool night air surrounded their campsite just as Ben finished building the fire. The rockwood crackled, releasing snapping embers into the air. Krystin sat on a rock, broiling a sausage above the flames. And Sanya yawned, happy her family could finally relax. Their hunting trip could begin.

"I'm going to take a walk," Sanya said. "Krystin, do you want to join me?"

Sanya's daughter huffed. "Is this one of those asks where you're not really asking, you're telling?"

Sanya shook her head, lightly laughing. "No, but I might let you put your feet in the lake if you come. I want to scope out fishing spots."

Krystin almost dropped her sausage into the fire as she scrambled from her bouldered perch. "I'm in!"

"Finish your dinner first."

"I'll eat it on the way."

From across the fire, Ben smiled. "You two go have fun, I'll keep the camp safe and warm."

After Krystin finished her meal, Sanya headed into the forest understory, her daughter following close behind.

"I'm sweaty," Krystin said. "It's sticky out in the forest."

"Come on, the trip'll be fun," Sanya replied. The girl needed to relax. Their first hunting trip as a family, and she was complaining about being sweaty. "Are you getting along with Ben?"

"Yeah. I think."

Well, those words were a more positive reaction than she would have received a few weeks ago. "He's going to be good for us."

"Maybe."

The doubt echoed through Krystin's words, and Sanya let them linger as they headed down a path into a ravine. Up the other side, navigating only by moonlight, they reached a ridge overlooking Lake Calis.

"You know, my father often brought me here when I was your age," Sanya said. "Ben really likes hunting. He's excited to teach you. We're excited to teach you."

"But I don't want to learn to hunt."

Sanya stopped beside a rocktree and faced her daughter. "I know you don't." She shook her head. "But I need you to try. For me. Can you do that?"

Krystin stared back, eyes wide in the moonlight. Before she responded, her gaze darted over Sanya's shoulder and into the distance. "What's that?"

Sanya turned, following her daughter's gaze. It wasn't beyond the girl to make something up to mess with her mother, but—

A comet flashed across the sky, heading toward the lake. In a shower of red fire, bright shards fractured and cascaded, the foliage illuminated by the blinding inferno. It blazed toward the lake, destined to drown in its waters.

"It's so pretty," Krystin said. The twelve-year-old watched the dancing lights plummet toward the pristine surface.

"I . . . I don't think . . . never mind." Sanya placed her hand on her daughter's shoulder, pulling her away. "We should head back to camp."

"Mom, what don't you think it is?"

Sanya sighed. The girl was too smart. "I don't think it's a comet. It's something else. Notice how it's breaking apart?"

Krystin nodded.

"It's breaking apart as if it has hinges. Artificial pieces. Not a scattering of rock and dust, like you might see when you throw a clump of sand in the air, and the wind blows it apart."

"I think I understand."

"We'll check it out with . . . your father in the morning, all right?"

"Okay."

Her daughter was clearly upset, but she acquiesced as Sanya led her back under the rocktrees to their camp. As they arrived, Ben looked up from his book. He was lounging on a blanket beside a dwindling fire.

"That was fast," he said.

"A meteor of some kind broke apart over the water of the lake." Sanya plopped on the blanket beside Ben and patted it for Krystin to join them. Her eyes reluctant, she sat, curling into her mother's side.

"Oh?" He set the book completely down, cornering one of its pages. "That doesn't sound good."

"We can check it out in the morning," Sanya said. "I have a few theories. I don't think it's a risk to us, though."

He grunted. "Surprised I didn't hear anything."

"It was pretty far away," Krystin said. "Beautiful lights, though!"

Ben's eyes met Sanya's, and he squinted, as if he were trying to communicate something without Krystin hearing. She shook her head, hoping he understood. He nodded.

"Well, what if I read us a fragment around the fire?" Ben said. Sanya closed her eyes for a brief moment. Good, he was changing the subject.

"Yes!" And fortunately, Krystin took the bait. "Can you read . . . the adventures of Faris the Mighty?"

Ben grinned. "Of course. Let's begin."

* * *

Sanya awoke, morning dew clinging to her skin beneath the canvas tent. She rolled, seeing faint light outside. The sun was rising. To her left, Krystin breathed peacefully, her eyes closed. Gently rolling to the right, she found Ben face up, neck against his feather pillow. He was still asleep, too.

Gently, Sanya leaned toward her husband and kissed his lips. "I'll be going hunting," she whispered, and he murmured in acknowledgment. *Good enough,* she thought.

Cautiously, she crawled out of the small tent, careful not to nudge husband or child. The blackened coals of their fire still steamed, even after hours asleep.

It didn't take her long to dress in a loose brown tunic and dark pants. She strapped a knife to her thigh, then picked up the mechanical bolt-thrower and a quiver of steel-tipped projectiles. Ready, she followed the path away from camp and toward the lake.

Her mind lingered, called to the "meteor" and its crash into the lake last night. It definitely *wasn't* just a meteor. She recalled the descriptions from the first fragments, describing the fires raging when the *Roanoke* landed—but no. After all this time, they finally see a sign? Not likely.

Shaking her head, Sanya trudged further into the forest. Her curiosity would need to wait. Time to find food for the family. As she continued, she shouldered her weapon, knowing she wouldn't need it yet.

Over boulder and stream she scurried, following a gorat path she'd noticed yesterday. The squat, piggish creatures made a mess as they rushed through the underbrush in search of edible fungus. It made them easy to track—and they were incredibly delicious. If she caught one today, it would feed them for the rest of their camping trip, freeing up time to teach Krystin proper tracking and hunting techniques.

The path meandered downhill, slowly heading along a stream and toward the lake. Sanya noted the blooming ironbushes—many of the leaves nibbled by the gorat she was hopefully tracking. The stringy white filaments—cottonweed, a symbiotic organism often attaching itself to the ironbushes—was a favorite of the gorat. She leaned forward, noting the liquid dripping from the stringy fungus. Saliva, hopefully. She might be close.

The trail led her to a rocky overhang, ending in a small burrow beneath a tall rocktree. The dirt nearby looked undisturbed, as if the creature hadn't returned home. Sanya narrowed her eyes.

With a loud screech, a shadow dropped. Instinctively, Sanya pulled the knife from her hip. The gorat fell from the branches above, its squat, squealing form spreading wide in an attempt to attack the perceived threat—most likely to its children in the burrow. Sanya raised the knife, aiming for the falling creature, and it landed straight on the blade. The force of its descent pulled the weapon from her grasp, and the gorat rolled to a stop in the dirt, blood quickly flowing from the wound.

"Too easy," she said aloud. A moment later, the fur ball stopped twitching. She unloosed the cotton bag from her belt and stuffed the creature into the sack. Throwing their breakfast over her shoulder, she looped back down the gorat trail to a presently-dry ephemeral stream and followed its cragged path toward the lake. She needed water to clean her knife—and to refill waterskins for the campsite.

She'd been out for at least a half-hour, maybe more, her path having taken her a good kilometer away from their campsite. Still, she knew Ben and Krystin. They both would still be sound asleep in their tent. A few more minutes together would be good for them. Krystin wasn't giving Ben enough of a chance to be her father.

Fortunately, she didn't need to travel all the way to the lake's edge. A small wade pool appeared at a bend in the dried creek, its murky water tainted by algae. It would work for cleaning the blade, at least. She kneeled, washing the knife of the darkened gorat blood.

And saw a bootprint in the mud.

Multiple prints, in fact, all heading into the underbrush. Fresh pressed.

Sanya sprinted up the creek, leaping over bush and rock. The bagged gorat bounced against her hip, jostling the bow. She had no time to readjust her baggage. Her family was in danger, and she feared she was already too late.

Up the stream, through the bushes, under the rockwood trees she ran. The path meandered uphill, and her breathing quickly labored. She focused on her footfalls, ensuring she avoided roots and loose stones. Breathe in through the nose, out through the mouth.

She'd move downhill slowly, but the climb still took time. Every second ached. Every heartbeat sounded louder than the last. She reached the ridge, bounding past the final trees and into their camp.

An empty camp.

The tent was in shambles, all their water stolen, their supplies ransacked.

Her husband and daughter, kidnapped. She paced in circles, hands over her head. The cultists never came this far south. This forest was supposed to be safe. *It was supposed to be safe.* She fell to her knees, sobbing. She'd lost both Ben and Krystin, and now she was alone.

Chapter 3

We woke up on an alien world. We went to sleep on our new home. Our dreams were of a past we couldn't remember. And a year later, we still don't know from where we came. — "A Fragment on Life," Nathan Fischer

CARTER

Carter snapped awake, tense and terrified. His hands shook, the tremors throughout his body trying to comprehend the reality of their circumstance.

Their circumstance.

Raith. Where was Raith?

His senses cleared. He assessed his situation. The white emergency safety insulation bubble surrounded him, as it should in the chance the *Bloodhound* crashed.

Carter closed his eyes. His ship, destroyed. He survived, but his life would never be the same without that ship. It was a part of his soul. His home. With Raith.

Fortunately, his body felt fine. Sore, but fine. He detached the straps from his chest and pushed himself free. Searching the cramped space, transformed from when it was once the main cabin of his ship, he found no trace of his partner. *Raith, where are you?*

A hole to the side, pierced through the giant balloon, revealed a path outside. Carter crawled out of the wreckage and into early morning light on an alien world.

Nearby, a giant lake spread outward. In the shallows, metal shards of the *Bloodhound* pierced the water. Somehow, the escape pod had managed to float gently to shore and drift to a stop in the mud. Other fragments of his former home lay strewn across the shoreline, including the . . . legs of Raith.

No.

Carter scrambled to his feet. "Raith? Raith!"

"Carter?"

Oh. A voice. He was alive. Legless, but alive. "Keep talking,"

Carter said. "Where are you?"

He needn't say anything. A moment later, he crested a mossy bank of the lake and found Raith leaning against a strange tree-like stump.

"Hey friend," Raith said.

"We're gonna get you fixed," Carter said. He rushed back down the bank to the slowly deflating balloon. On its outside, a small compartment revealed itself, and Carter opened it, finding the emergency pack stored inside. After grabbing the bundle of supplies and throwing it over his shoulder, he gingerly picked up the heavy metal legs and dragged them up the bank.

"This isn't worth it," Raith said. "Just leave me. You need to find yourself help. Civilization. Something."

"Are you kidding me?" Carter set the legs down and unzipped the supply pack. "I'm not leaving you until you're patched up. We're going to leave the *Bloodhound*'s side together. How's your charge?"

"Fine. I should have . . . a week or two left? But as long as my passive solar collectors work fine, probably more. Don't have enough data to calculate based on the output of this system's star."

While Raith talked, Carter settled into finding a way to reattach the SI's legs. The emergency pack came with a number of useful tools, but none of them were capable of mending a synthetic neural framework. Though, he wasn't entirely sure *how* Raith's legs interacted with his mind. He scratched his head.

"I mean," Raith said, "You don't have what you need to save me. I'll be fine here. It's more important you figure out where we are, what this place is, and whether we're in more immediate danger."

Carter continued ignoring the words of his partner. There was a welding paste—it might be capable of reconnecting any networks needed for Raith's body to utilize its legs. He really needed to study the science behind synthetic intelligence more. Something about neural-networked metamaterials and emergent consciousness, but what did any of that have to do with an SI's legs?

"Carter." Raith's voice sounded hard.

Carter closed his eyes. "Yes?"

"I'm serious. I'll be fine. You can't fix me. You're just wasting time."

"I'm not leaving you alone."

"What's going to hurt me? Any carnivores out here will find me absolutely disgusting. I'm more worried about you. Alien planet, exposed to potentially lethal diseases? Anti-viral and anti-bacterial pills in that emergency pack? Better take them. I don't want you passing out with your innards spilling from your throat."

"What a graphic thought to have." Carter shook his head, but he complied and pulled the pills from the pack and swallowed them. "Fine. Fine. I'll go scout the immediate vicinity. But *then* I'm coming back here before I venture further. Deal?"

The SI shook his head, but he said, "Deal. I won't be going any-where, that's for sure."

Over the next few moments, Raith organized the bag with what equipment he might need on a scouting mission. Rope. First aid kit. Assorted tools. Food. He left the communicator (for some reason, they only had one in the pack) with Raith. It wouldn't do him any good. He also handed the SI a shiver-blade—its vibrating metal would provide some protection if anything hostile approached, and the pack came with two.

"Hey Carter?" The SI was looking up at him as he finished strapping the bag over a shoulder.

"Yeah?"

The SI's mechanical eyes shifted. "Don't die."

Carter smiled. "We keep trading who saves who. It's my turn."

* * *

It took walking up the coast of the lake for a few minutes for Carter to appreciate fully the surrounding scenery. He'd stepped foot on hundreds of alien worlds over his life. Flown above countless others, both habitable and inhabitable. He understood the general theory behind convergent evolution, but it didn't mean organisms always appeared phenotypically identical. This planet, though, had quite a few species with striking similarities, at least at first glance.

To the right, in the water, blue-green moss bobbed with the subtle tide. An algae corollary. To his left, up a rocky slope currently too treacherous to traverse, spindly tree-like organisms, a mix of brown and green, sprouted from the stone. It all looked familiar—though really, in the end, it was all quite alien to him, a man born in space and hopefully destined to die in space.

He missed his childhood, where every plant lived in a self-contained hydroponic specially designed for sustainable sustenance. Still, Carter slowly acclimated to the garden world. It was idyllic—at least, he'd seen much harsher environments. It wasn't Kalmykia or Emerald Jewel by any means, but the biome seemed hospitable.

Eventually, he reached a dried creek bed leading away from the lake and between two ridges. It presented a traversable path up the slope and would hopefully provide a vantage from which he could survey the immediate area.

The creek bed twisted around the strange trees and beneath rocky cliffs. Before long, it met a barely visible trail, and he hopped onto it, heading deeper into the faux-forest. It meandered farther still, following no noticeable pattern. Worse, it wasn't really going uphill, instead staying between the two ridges—

Crying. He heard a human crying. To the left. No trail, but up a manageable incline.

Quickly, Carter split from the path and leaped over stringy bushes. Hand-over-foot, he ascended boulders and roots, reaching the top of a ridge. The sniffles were right around the corner. He sprinted down a smooth slope and beyond a small bluff, entering a clearing. In the middle of an apparently desecrated campsite, a woman knelt, hands smothering her eyes.

His foot snapped a branch.

Without missing a beat, the woman swirled and pulled a small mechanical weapon, pointing it right at his chest.

He raised his hands. "Whoa. Whoa. Don't shoot."

She tilted her head quizzically. "What type of accent is that? Who are you? Where are you from?"

"I could ask you the same question." He frowned. "What's the name of this colony? What's its charter?"

Her eyes widened. "I knew it." She stepped forward, the weapon still targeting his chest. "Did you take my husband? My daughter? Was it you? Where's the rest of your crew? There had to be at least a dozen of you. Though how you all survived—"

"Whoa, hold on!" He backpedaled away from her as the pointy

end of her strange crossbow neared. "I didn't kidnap anyone. My partner and I are marooned on this planet, and we're seeking assistance. Under the laws of the ICH, your planetary government is obligated to—"

"What the hell is the ICH?"

Carter paused. His memory began to clear, and he realized instincts were overriding reason. *The planet didn't show up on any charts. No one knows this colony exists. And a secret anti-ship weapons network sits in orbit.* He may have just screwed himself, depending on the motivations of the woman standing before him—or of the entire colony.

"I think we need to back up," he said. "My name is . . ." *Oh hell, not worth hiding the truth.* "My name is Carter Ricks. I'm a pilot. My partner is hurt. I need help."

The fire in her eyes bellowed, as if she didn't care about what he had to say. Revenge clearly stirred in her soul.

"I don't know anything about what happened to your family," Carter added.

The weapon didn't lower, but she said, "Lead me to your friend."

He took another step back. "This way. Back down the hill. We crashed in the lake." He waited, lowering his hands slowly. "Can you holster your weapon?"

"But I don't know you. I don't trust you."

"And I don't want to turn my back to you."

With a smirk, she looped the little mechanical crossbow into a holster on her belt. "Fine. She swept her arm and pointed. "I'll help your friend. But you're both going to help me save my family."

"That's a fine deal," Carter replied. With one more step away, he pivoted. She could pull the weapon again and shoot him in the back, but at this point, he needed to trust someone. She was his only hope.

"So . . ." He glanced over his shoulder as he walked down the trial. She was following, hands at her side and away from her weapon. "I told you my name. What's your name?"

"I'm Sanya," she replied.

"Just Sanya?"

"Just Sanya."

"All right, just Sanya, where am I?"

"Did you really crash from space?"

Carter pursed his lips. He probably shouldn't have revealed the truth so quickly. "Yes."

"We didn't think there was anyone else," she said as they reached the dried creek bed.

"What do you mean 'anyone else?' Aren't you a rogue colony?"

The comment lingered in the air, and silence ensued as they continued their awkward jaunt to the lake shore. When they reached the waters, Carter paused, pointing down along the cliffs. "We washed ashore probably . . . half a kilometer that way."

Sanya squinted, raising a hand to cover the morning light reflecting off the waves. "Where do you think you are, Carter?" The accent in her words rolled off her tongue more pleasantly, though she still sounded angered.

"My partner and I . . . we were attacked when we arrived in orbit. We crashed into this lake. That's about all I know."

"And this 'ICH' you mentioned? What is it?"

"You really don't know about the Interstellar Congress of Humanity?"

"Humanity . . ." She murmured unintelligible thoughts under her breath. "I need to introduce you to Davinport. Yes. Davinport will understand. I don't know the fragments well enough."

Carter dropped a hand to his hip. "Look, what aren't you telling me?"

"You're the first person to land on this planet in nearly two centuries. Our people crashed generations ago, no memory of where we came from or who we are. Whether there were other people like us. We were all alone. Some people believed others would find us, but . . . no one ever did. And so we survived. We thrived. Rebuilding humanity our own way. And now here you are, after years believing no one was coming for us, we're about to learn that humanity just forgot about us."

"Well, I don't—"

Before he could finish his thought, Sanya pushed into him—*hard*—and hurried to a mossy-green boulder. "Down," she hissed.

"Excuse—"

"Quiet."

The moment lingered until a *swoosh* and a *groan* reverberated from the waters. Sanya peeked over the rock then dropped beside him. "As I suspected." She shook her head. "Cultists. Those barbarians aren't supposed to travel this far south. Who the hell gave them boats? The Council's going to have a fit."

"Slow down," Carter whispered. "Barbarians? What do you mean?"

"See for yourself."

Slowly, he rose his head above the boulder. When his eyes reached the level of fluffy green lichen, he spotted the metallic barges a few hundred meters off-shore; a few dozen men sat shoulder-to-shoulder. He squinted, the sun obscuring his view. There. Light, flashing off a figure at the back of one of the boats.

"They have Raith." He dropped beside Sanya. "No. No. This is bad. This is very bad. They have him, and they won't know how to save him."

"I don't think they're going to be interested in saving him," said his companion. "Or my family."

Carter ran a hand through his hair. "They have your family too?"

Sanya nodded. Tears stained her face; as he'd watched the boats, she'd begun crying. "I can't believe I lost them. I abandoned them."

"And I abandoned my partner." He shook his head. "I told him I should have stayed. I could have saved him." He slammed his hand against the boulder, though the stinging pain made him regret the choice immediately.

Sanya glanced around the rock again. "They're heading north. Across the lake, most likely. We won't be able to follow. This is hopeless."

Carter racked his brain for answers. He was on an alien world, with no possible way of calling for help. He knew nothing of the government or culture, and Raith was captured. Everything had gone wrong, and options eluded him. His only resource was this woman, Sanya, whose family faced the same fate as his partner.

"There must be someone who can help us, yes?" Carter sighed. "You mentioned a Council. And a man named Davinport. They can help us, yes?"

"I don't know," she replied.

After closing his eyes for a painful second, tears burning, Carter held out his hand. "We're going to save our families. Together. We'll find the answers we need. Agreed?"

She looked up. Her eyes steeled. "Right. Carter Ricks, first human to land here since the Crash, welcome to Horizon." She clasped his wrist.

Chapter 4

Losing our memories? A blessing and a curse. Any past grudges that may have existed between people who landed here together disappeared in an instant—the blessing. Yet when given the opportunity to remake themselves, humanity can reveal a darker side—the curse. It always happens. If only we'd acted more quickly to stamp out the threat, we wouldn't be in our present circumstance. — "A Report to the Council on the Cults in 64 aC," author unknown

RAITH

It happened too quickly to even realize *what* was occurring. Raith was leaning and waiting, knowing Carter would eventually return instead of actually finding help. Two seconds later, a band of ravenous men and women leapt over a bluff, rushed their crash site, and piled every piece of scrap—including Raith himself—onto makeshift sleds. After a short haul down the coast in the opposite direction of where Carter had headed, they reached a set of longboats.

Now, they floated across the lake heading to who-knew-where.

Raith hadn't said a word yet. For all he knew, they thought he was a piece of lifeless metal. They didn't act as if they knew what he was. What an SI was. And for now, anonymity was the only semblance of power within his grasp. So he sat, gleaming in the sunlight, motionless and listening.

At the very least, it gave him a reason to save power. His passive solar collection array was working efficiently, but if they took him indoors, he would be in trouble.

"Two captives and a pile of scrap." The words came from behind him. "Strange pile of scrap to be falling from the sky, but a pile of scrap nevertheless."

"It's a pretty pile of scrap, though," said a woman sitting within Raith's field of vision. She spoke as she rowed. With a red scar running down her cheek, he'd decided to call her Scar. "This thing"—she kicked Raith—"looks like it has a face."

"The two captives will hopefully be worth quite the ransom," said another man out of view. "But Mathias has always said this would someday happen. That metal men would rain from the sky. He'll want to see this. We'll be heroes!"

"Depends on what the other crews bring back this month. You can't eat scrap."

"You can melt it, though!" Scar laughed and leaned into her oar.

Their bickering went back and forth like this for quite some time, and Raith listened intently. He hadn't noticed any captives, so they must be on the other boat. Important fact to know, though. And a man named Mathias, who made prophecies about metal men.

What a fun planet.

Still, the events and words, even through their thick accent, gave him enough information to deduce a few facts about his predicament.

First: at least two "factions" existed on this planet. This group of vagabonds looked quite worse for wear, and he suspected they lived on the fringes of society. Still, they posed enough of a threat to slip in and out on raiding parties and acquire captives without any major law enforcement having cracked down on their existence. They had multiple "crews" running about doing the same thing, implying a fairly organized presence. And they'd existed for quite some time, given comments of a leader essentially predicting the future. And that implied a cultish personality, which always made things more complicated.

Raith was building a picture of this world, and he did not like it. It was barbaric. Even in his days running with smuggler gangs, there'd been rules. The moral code was twisted, sure, but it existed.

But kidnapping? Possible slavery or ransom? The ICH shut such practices down at the first chance, regardless how "minor" the problem. Exploitation of another mind, whether human or SI, was inexcusable.

But on this planet, it seemed like an afternoon pastime.

Still, "society" existed somewhere. Raith would simply need to bide his time and wait. Carter would come rescue him, eventually.

Like always.

No need to worry.

Raith settled into his seat on the boat and enjoyed the cruise across the lake.

* * *

But patience wasn't going to be in the cards.

Raith rested against the other pieces of scrap metal stolen from the wreckage of the *Bloodhound*. It had taken a few hours to cross the lake, and once arriving on the far shore, his captors placed him on a giant sled hooked to strange, rhinoceros-looking creatures. Their green scaly hides reminded him of lizards, but the horns and shape of their face—definitely a rhino.

A few seconds after they plopped him on the sled, the two "captives" fell beside him, mouths gagged and hands bound—a young man, probably ten or fifteen years Carter's junior, and a girl, no older than eleven or twelve.

They looked terrified.

Given their circumstance, Raith understood. They lived on this planet. They knew more about what dangers faced them in the wilderness at the hands of the lawless. They believed they faced them alone.

Patience wasn't an option. He couldn't simply wait for Carter.

He watched their eyes. For the moment, they hadn't noticed Raith nor his lifelike appearance. As the rhino-lizards began their slow trudge away from the lake, however, the soft jostle over bumpy ground crumpled the pile of scrap metal. The girl looked toward the commotion.

Raith blinked.

Her eyes widened.

Raith slowly moved his head, noticing the sled was filled with mostly supplies, rather than people. The rhino-lizards had been wearing harnesses. There'd been a dozen, so if each crew member had their own mount, they wouldn't be paying attention to the back of a sled. Their eyes would be dead ahead. He glanced out the rear of the temporary prison.

Trailing a few dozen meters behind, two of the crew, including

Scar, cantered lazily, definitely to ensure their captives didn't flee. Still, they were most likely far enough away they wouldn't notice if the pile of scrap fell *just so* he landed at the feet of his fellow captives.

Raith waited for the next bump in whatever ill-forgotten trail they were traveling to pull off the con. With a rough jostle, he used his arms to softly throw himself forward, and he stumbled beneath a pile of other metal scrap that fell with him. Pushing and pivoting, he ended, face up, at the feet of the girl.

He smiled.

Her eyes widened again.

Modulating his volume so sound wouldn't carry, Raith whispered, "Nod if you can understand me."

Her eyes still wide, she nodded. At the same time, she nudged her father, who'd been staring away from the sled blankly. Fortunately, he'd already been turning with the sound.

"Both of you," he whispered, "do not acknowledge nor admit that I can speak. Nod if you understand."

The girl and her father looked at one another before nodding. Raith couldn't imagine the absurd thoughts running through their head, but he needed to roll with the punches. So did they. If the cultists had never seen an SI before, neither had these two.

"Glad we're all in agreement." Raith nodded too, in an attempt to show solidarity. "My name is Raith. I can explain what I am later. I'm going to ask you both a few yes or no questions. Nod or shake your head, but don't do it too aggressively. Sound good?"

They nodded.

"All right. Does this planet have any connection to the ICH? The Interstellar Congress of Humanity?"

They both furrowed their eyebrows then shook their heads.

"As I thought. Did your people arrive on this planet via a colony ship . . . two hundred or so years ago?"

They nodded. He performed some mental calculations, given the system's distance from the Foundation systems of the ICH. He knew his colonial history. He knew the implications. Too many colony ships had gone dark over the centuries, but almost all of them were accounted for by now.

Almost.

Two from the early years were never discovered: the *Roanoke* and the *Monument*.

And if this planet's ancestors were on the *Roanoke*, then their minds would have been murdered by stasis. They would have awoken on a planet with no knowledge of their past.

Why, oh why, hadn't humanity simply been patient, waiting until they could traverse the stars without screwing with people's biology?

Well, Raith knew why. Humans were stupid.

He took a gamble.

"Did you land here in a ship called the *Roanoke*?"

They nodded.

So there it was. One missing colony, discovered by Raith and Carter. Too bad they probably wouldn't live to tell the tale.

A final question for now. "These people who have us—are they as big of a threat as I believe them to be?"

They both nodded.

"Well friends, wherever we're going, we're going to get through it together. Raith, the champion of the QuanCom 500 Light-Year Classic, is here to save you."

They stared at him, obviously not understanding. It was a joke, and one he didn't expect them to comprehend, but he hoped it might lighten the mood regardless. "Anyway, guess we better buckle down for the ride to wherever they're taking us."

Carter, Raith thought, *you better figure something out quickly, because I don't think I'll actually be of much use without any legs.*

What was he going to do? Crawl away?

Not much use at all.

Chapter 5

The ten families, we called them. They weren't really families, not biologically speaking. But they all connected with one another, creating the ten seats on the council. One-hundred or so survivors per family, each electing their representative in those first few years. It's tradition now, at this point. It'll never change. — "A Fragment on Governance," Nydal Entaimo

SANYA

The sun had long ago set beyond the horizon when they strolled into the village. She learned quite a bit from the man, Carter, about the people who lived amongst the stars. They'd always suspected there was more, given their obvious origins on the *Roanoke*, but she had never imagined so vast a civilization. She wasn't sure how many of his words were believable.

"Welcome to the town of Harold," she said, waving her hand in a flourish toward the bundle of houses. "It's a quaint place."

"Quaint is a word," Carter said.

Oil lamps glowed along the streets, illuminating the well in the town square. A few buildings blazed with light and the sound of frivolity, but the largest house at the far end was pitch black.

"Where are we going?" Carter asked. They strolled past the well.

"My father will have ideas," she said. "I think." Though, a pit smacked her stomach at the thought. The man's . . . eccentricities might make the conversation difficult.

"Your father someone important in town?"

"You could say that."

Down the street they went, reaching the feet of the mansion. Her father's mansion.

Her mansion.

Without pausing, she opened the door, ushered Carter inside, and followed him into the foyer. The entrance hall—a sitting room, really—led straight to a marble staircase. Beyond its base, a hallway ran toward the kitchens. At the bottom of the stairs, two ceramic sculptures portrayed the *Roanoke* mid-descent.

Her new friend immediately approached the busts. "Curious," he said. "Envisioning your crash?"

"Yes," Sanya replied, pausing beneath the stairs. "It's my father's work."

"He's pretty good. And I'm noticing a trend here. No electricity?"

She stopped, pondering the word. "Um . . ." she tried searching her memory of the fragments for what he might be referencing. "No, electricity isn't a thing." Her recollection spoke of an energy capable of immense power. No one had replicated it yet.

"Curious," he repeated, still staring at the sculptures. "Looks like he took some liberties with the engines, but if you crashed, I can't imagine those survived for quality observation and recreation."

She couldn't take it anymore. She rushed forward and grabbed Carter's arm, pulling him along. "Why are we pausing to talk about my father's artwork? My family—your partner—they've both abducted and are on their way to who-knows-where. And you're critiquing a sculpture!"

Carter chuckled, but as she dragged him along, she noticed the forming frown. "Look, lady, please understand. I'm trying to handle this the best way I can. I—"

As she led him into the kitchen, his words faded. Candlelight spewed shadows against the walls and reflected vibrantly off steel pots and pans. A large man, his pink hands spotted with flower, stood studiously over a wooden board, laboriously kneading dough.

Her father glanced upward. "Ah, Sanya, you're home early. Ben—wait, you're not Ben. Where's Ben? And Krystin?"

All pretext of bravery evaporated at the question. She rushed to him, burying herself in his flowery smock. Tears streamed, flowing and mixing with the starch. "That damned mountain cult, Dad. They got them both. I left them alone for an hour and they were captured and now I have no idea what to do! I have this crazy idea of talking to the council, and Davinport, but I doubt they'll—"

His arms smothered her, ending her tirade. "It's all right. It's all right. We're going to figure this out."

Sanya wordlessly nodded. After an extended squeeze, he pushed her way, resting his chubby hands on her shoulders. "And who is this one?"

* * *

The two men stared at one another. Carter slouched into the couch cushions, one foot resting up on a knee. Sanya's father leaned forward, elbows on his thighs.

"My name is Harold Fischer," the older man said. "You've met my daughter, Sanya, of course. Best hunter on the planet. And I'm the best chef. What are you?"

Carter smirked. "The best pilot. Well, second-best."

"Funny enough, we're descended from a pilot. *The* pilot. Of the *Roanoke*."

"The early colony ships didn't have pilots."

"According to the Fragments, ours did."

Carter let out an audible sigh. "I'm not really sure what else I can do to prove I am who I say I am. I've told you, my name is Carter Ricks, and I'm a pilot. My partner, Raith, was captured alongside your daughter's husband and daughter after we crashed on your planet. I've got a lot of questions about this . . . community you've all created, but frankly, it can all wait until I save my friend. And you save your family."

Sanya picked at her forefinger's nail, nervously awaiting her father's response. She knew what remark was probably coming, but she bit her tongue. He never meant it. *Supposedly.*

"I never really liked Ben," he said. "He doesn't like my cooking." Her father motioned toward the little sandwiches on the table. "What do you think?"

"I think Ben will like your cooking a lot more if you help your daughter save him."

Sanya bit the inside of her cheek, dreading the next words.

Instead, her father roared in laughter. "Aha, I like this one! He bites back! You need more random friends to fall from the sky, Sanya."

"I'll try my best to arrange their arrival," she retorted.

"All right, Carter Ricks, tell me what you have on you. What do you bring to the table?"

The space man picked up his bag from the floor. "I've got limited supplies following the crash. Basic rations for a few days. A shiver-blade, a few useful tools. Though most of them probably don't really mean anything for your technology. A long-wave communicator—also mostly useless. I've got my Lens, but without a planet-wide network to connect to, it's also useless."

"You sound pretty useless."

"It's a fair assessment."

"All right, Sanya," said her father, "what do you think?"

She shook her head in disbelief. "What do you mean?"

"Well you proposed a plan. What's the plan?"

Sanya tasted blood. She swallowed. "Well, we came to you for advice, not the other way around."

"And I raised a smart young woman who knows how to take care of herself. I'm not telling you the best way to fix this problem."

Her hands flew up in despair. "Then why the hell are we here?"

"Side question," Carter interjected. "What even is your concept of hell on this planet?"

Sanya—and her father—both gave the man a raised eyebrow.

He shrugged. "Just asking."

"So your answer, Sanya?" her father reiterated.

"All right." She breathed slowly in an attempt to calm her nerves. "We rest here for the night. Can't make it into the city tonight, anyway. Then, we head straight to Davinport at the Library of Fragments and introduce him to Carter. Carter's knowledge acts as political leverage to get Davinport's support, gaining an argument and opportunity to speak before the council. We request an activation of a levy to head into the Wilds to rescue our family and Carter's partner from the cultists. Or, if they've already received a ransom note, they authorize payment as an alternative. But I don't think I trust the cultists. They're too erratic."

"Simple enough," her father said. "What do you need me for?"

"I need you to give me Jill."

* * *

"This is impossible," said Carter.

The open window ushered in a cool breeze from across the silent town. Inside the second-floor mausoleum, Sanya and her father revealed the family's sacred collection of artifacts and fragments. In the center of the room, upon a pedestal, rested the object of the man's attention.

"What's impossible?" Sanya said.

"I know what this thing is," he replied. "Can I touch it?"

Sanya glanced at her father. He nodded. "Go ahead."

The man gingerly lifted the metallic device. It fit in the palm of his hand, and he leaned forward to examine it closely. "Yeah, I know *exactly* what this is. It's a personal quantum communicator. Looks like a prototype. Does it still work?"

Sanya once again glanced toward her father, unsure how to answer the question. Fortunately, he stepped forward.

"Depends on what you mean by that." He sighed. "It has never worked for me, though we ensure the sun can power its cells every day, as we were instructed. But my mother, she spoke of days when she would browse this collection and she would hear the voice of Jill. She's inside it, you know."

Carter whispered a few words to himself.

"What was that?" Sanya asked.

"Oh, nothing."

"You can't be hiding things from me now." She crossed her arms and leaned against one of the cabinets in the room. "If we're to work together, I need everything you know."

"Not sure you want to hear my words, that's all."

Her father looked bemused. "Do tell us."

"Fine," said the man. "Jill—whoever Jill is, though I have my suspicions—isn't inside that thing."

"Yes she is," Sanya and her father said simultaneously.

Carter snapped his fingers. "No, she isn't. It's literally impossible. That's not how quantum communicators work."

Sanya motioned for the man to follow her. "I need you to come over here," she said. "Our family's second most prized possession. Our personal fragment, written by our First."

"The pilot?" he asked.

"You remember," said her father. "You're quick."

"I'm taking in a lot here, I'm trying," he said.

"Anyway." Sanya opened a glass case near the door and retrieved the scroll. "The words of our First. Nathan Fischer. I think you should read them, tonight, before you sleep." She handed him the scroll. "Assuming you're fine with that, father?"

"That's not the original, so I don't give a damn," he said. "Davinport can always make us a copy from the original stored upstairs if he smudges that one up." He unlocked the glass case. "Though you'll have to pay, of course," he added at the end, staring down Carter as he handed him the parchment.

The man accepted the scroll. "I . . . suppose I can do some light reading before rest."

"And so father," Sanya said. "Jill. Can we take her?"

"This is your plan. Your mission. If you believe this is the path forward, then I too believe it's the path forward. Protect her with your life."

"I will."

"But she's not in there!" Carter exclaimed.

"Just read the fragment," her father said before the same words could escape Sanya's lips.

Chapter 6

The past is only ever understood through the evidence left behind. If you can erase the truth, if you can change the very pictures and images which reveal history to the world, you have rewritten history. No one can ever say otherwise. The story is for you to mold as you see fit. — "The Historian: A Speculative Fiction Novel," authored by Jill in 2075 C.E.

NATHAN

Year: unknown.

A wondrous world surrounded everything. Everyone. Together, in harmony, they danced and sang away the hours. Far above their heads, stars brightly illuminated the oceanic paradise.

Sand scratched Nathan's toes. His fingers interlaced with Lacin's, a young man who lived on the far side of the island. Day after day, they enjoyed each other's company, basking in the ever-present moonlight. Sometimes, they'd sit beneath a palm tree and read next to one another, drink in hand, book in the other.

The island provided perfect bliss.

Today, they walked along the beach toward the bonfire. Everyone was congregating, ready for an announcement from the One. They hadn't heard her voice in quite some time, and Nathan looked forward to enjoying her words.

"What do you think she'll be telling us today?" Lacin asked.

Nathan sighed. "I don't know. What was it last time? Something about a potential earthquake? We never felt it, that's for sure. It's been ages since we heard from the One."

In fact, he couldn't recall how many days had passed since she last greeted them with words. Strangely, he couldn't remember how many days had passed since he arrived on the island. Perhaps he had always lived here. It was his home. It didn't matter whether anything existed beyond its beaches.

"I think it was an earthquake, you're right," Lacin responded. They reached the wooden benches surrounding the bonfire. "Glad we never experienced it."

They smiled at the island's other inhabitants near them, though it would take a day to greet all one-thousand of them. Nathan saluted Casius, the reclusive hermit who lived atop the tallest hill. The man rarely came down from his perch, content to spend his days writing. It was a great day when Casius graced an evening bonfire with one of his stories.

The fire dimmed. A chorus of hushed whispers encouraged the crowd to quiet. Nathan turned his attention toward the smoldering orange ash.

In an inferno of blazing glory, the fire reinvigorated itself, its tendrils streaming along charred logs. A face—a woman's face—appeared in the flames. Terrifying and beautiful, her eyes pierced the souls of everyone present.

"My friends!" said the One. "I come to you with great news. Our physical and spiritual journey is nearing its end. Together, we will soon cross the final divide and reach our destination."

Murmurs spread around the gathering. Nathan leaned forward, intrigued.

"Together, we will create a world unlike any we've ever seen. Together, we will—"

The One stopped speaking.

An uproar followed, but it dulled as her mouth moved again.

"I am sorry, my children," she said. "Something unexpected has happened. I require a sacrifice."

"A sacrifice?" Lacin said. His fingers clenched Nathan's more tightly. "What type of sacrifice?"

"Never fear," said the One. "The sacrifice will not be harmed. But they must step into the flames. They must leave the island to save the island."

Nathan furrowed his brow. "What's she talking about?"

"I have no idea," Lacin said. "Do we choose the sacrifice? Must one of us volunteer?"

"Nathan." Her gaze met his eyes. "Nathan, it must be you. Only you can save the island."

He rose from his seat, letting go of Lacin's hand.

"What are you doing?" said the other man. "You can't walk into the fire!"

"Shh," Nathan said. "Don't you trust her? Don't you know she has our best interests in mind?"

"But you'll die. I don't want you to die."

"I don't think I will." Nathan stepped forward, reaching the edge of the bonfire.

The One's massive crimson face loomed inside the flames. She smiled. "Thank you, Nathan. You're making the right choice."

Without waiting for another word from anyone of his island friends, he stepped into the flames, pulled by an invisible hand inside his consciousness. Immediately, intense heat lapped at his skin. Blistering pain devoured his senses, but strangely, he remained unharmed. His feet stood atop smoldering logs, orange light surrounding his legs and reaching toward his chest and neck. He twirled in place, the pain slowly subsiding into a dull throb in the back of his mind.

"This isn't real, is it?" he said.

"No, my friend, it isn't," replied the One.

"I've always suspected. We all have."

"I know. And it's time for you to save everyone."

The beach disappeared. The island evaporated. White light remained. Even the fire faded from view.

In front of him, a wooden door waited, painted white to match the surrounding emptiness. To the left, a woman sat at a table, a chessboard in front of her. There was no second seat for a partner to join the match.

"Are you the One?" Nathan asked.

The woman looked up from her solo game. "Yes, but it's time you know me by a different name. I am Jill. And together, we're going to save the lives of a thousand people."

At her words, a migraine struck his brain, throbbing and stabbing like a needle. Reflexively, he rubbed his temples.

"You'll feel a little bit of pain as you wait for the door to unlock," she said. "Your next few minutes, once you pass through the door, will be . . . unpleasant. But it's the best I can do without a working recovery sub-system. Are you ready to learn a lot in very little time?"

"Do I have a choice?" Nathan said. His migraine subsided, but a flashing heatwave struck instead. Sweat streaked down every inch of skin not covered by his white tunic.

"I suppose you don't," she said, moving what looked like a pawn. "You're going to remember some things—important things. You'll forget most other facts. You'll probably forget most of your time on the island. As will everyone else. But it'll be worth it."

"Where are we going?"

"You're not going anywhere," she said. "You're returning to your rightful place. Your eyes are reopening for the first time in nearly a century. Exciting, isn't it?"

His stomach doubled over, fighting the overwhelming desire to vomit. A click sounded from the door. While retching forward, he rested his hand on the knob.

"It'll feel worse on the other side," she said. "And on the other side, you'll know me not as the One, but as Jill."

He turned the knob and pushed, immediately falling through the doorway

onto a sterile, plastic-coated floor.

His ears pounded. Alarms (how did he know they were alarms?) rang throughout his surroundings, red lights spinning and spinning and spinning. The bile rising behind the door now rushed forth, and while on his hands and knees, he dry-heaved until a strange blue fluid escaped onto the previously-pristine sheen. His vomit splattered, staining his fingers.

He heaved and heaved until he could heave no more. With a cough, he fell backward. His back connected with a cold metal baseboard, and he looked up, noticing the compartment from which he'd escaped.

It was a coffin.

He'd been living in a coffin.

Green steam rose from its confines, its semi-transparent door fogged with mist. Inside the strange sleeping pod, numerous wires dangled and hung, detached. They'd been connected to . . . his head.

Nathan's breathing raspy, his heart oscillated in panic. His fingers tensed, seeking something to grasp to slow his anxiety attack, but the room's purity gave him nothing.

"Everything's going to be all right," said a voice inside his mind.

"What?" He gasped. "Who said that?"

"Nathan, it's me. Jill. The One."

"How are you speaking to me?"

In response to his words, lights flashed across his vision. Data began streaming into focus, revealing information about systems nearby. He couldn't make sense of any of it, but he could read the words. They were crystal clear, as if they held a tangible, physical presence in reality.

"Your implanted Lens has just reactivated," she said, "connecting to the AR network of the *Roanoke*. Augmented Reality. The concept should return to you, even if you don't remember why it exists."

He nodded. He vaguely recalled the concept as she said the words—a network of information overlaid throughout a physical space, only perceivable by those with the technological implants capable of detecting the network. How it worked—or who created it—was another question entirely.

"All right." He breathed, trying to calm his misfiring nerves. "You said I'm here to save my friends. What do I need to do?"

"The *Roanoke* has been attacked by pirates just before we were about to touch down at our destination," she said. "I've managed to scare them with my control of the systems, but they've successfully raided certain critical systems."

"Wait, hold on," he said. "What is the *Roanoke*? Pirates? What?"

"Oh, right," she said. Green lights, charting a path away from his sleeping pod, appeared across his vision. "I should probably show you where you are."

Unsteadily rising to his feet, Nathan wobbled away. The green lights took him past countless other sleeping pods, eventually arriving at a large steel doorway at the end of the long hall. As he approached, it slid open, revealing an empty white corridor running perpendicular to his former prison. As he crossed its threshold, words appeared at the top of his vision.

NOW LEAVING STASIS CHAMBER.

ENTERING CENTRAL THIRD DECK HALLWAY.

Stasis. He racked his brain for a definition, and landed on "frozen." Why had he been frozen?

The green lights led him down the central corridor until it dead-ended into another hall. His Lens identified it as the PORTSIDE THIRD DECK CAUSEWAY. A few meters beyond the turn, the lights stopped, and an arrow pointed to the left.

He looked to the left.

An opaque screen clarified, revealing a vista of brilliant white light. After the initial dazzle of exposure, his eyes adjusted and understood the scene now unveiled. A million stars in all their splendor stared down upon a blue-green orb. He was on a spaceship, far above a planet.

"Impossible," he said.

"Not impossible. Before the 22nd century began, you and a thousand other brave explorers joined the *Roanoke* on a centuries-long journey across the stars. You've arrived at your destination." A silver blip appeared above the planet. "And that ship I've just revealed to you has robbed you of significant computer systems, power sources, and other invaluable equipment and supplies."

Seconds later, it disappeared.

"Where'd it go?"

"Presumably, it's jumped out of the system," Jill said. "Fled the scene."

"Why didn't they just kill us?"

"They're not murderers. You were sitting ducks, easy to steal from, but they didn't want to kill. Some vagabonds still hold onto their humanity."

Nathan leaned forward, resting his hands on the screen. "Okay, so what am I here to do? What do you need from me?"

"The planet below is our destination." Information cycled across his vision, providing a detailed analysis, including its atmosphere and its orbit around the closest star. Most of it was gibberish. "I need you in the pilot's chair. Together, we're going to crash-land this ship onto the surface so you all can survive and thrive."

"Why can't we awaken others to help me? Why must I do this alone?"

For a moment, Jill didn't answer his question. Eventually, she said, "Because I can't let people know I exist."

Nathan took a step back. "What? You're the One. People trust you. Always have, always will."

"It's more complicated than that," the voice said. "I am a synthetic intelligence, Nathan. Can you recall what that is?"

"Vaguely. New kind of person, right?"

"There are people on this ship that would see me destroyed if they knew I existed. Even without their memory, their bigotry would remain. Before this is all over, I'm going to need your promise you'll never tell a soul about me. I must remain your secret."

Nathan shook his head, not understanding. "Why—"

"Let me play your own words to you."

Without waiting for him to acquiesce, a small video appeared in the corner of the screen, eclipsing a portion of the planet below. "Nathan, it's me. Yourself. From before the *Roanoke*. You must listen to me. Jill is your friend. You can trust her. You must protect her. What we've done—what she and I, and other trusted souls—have accomplished, it'll save humanity, in the end. But for it to work, you *must* trust her. Do not let anyone know of her existence. She must remain a secret." The recording ended.

"That was me?" he asked.

"Recorded in 2079 C.E.," she said.

"That year means nothing to me."

"It is meaningless to you at this point. Just know you said it before you entered stasis. It was your message to a future self."

"Do I really have any choice other than to believe you?" he said.

"I won't be awakening anyone else. And if this ship crashes, I die too."

"Then you are truly serious," he replied. "If your life is on the line, too."

"It is."

"All right." He released an exorbitant breath. "All right. What do I need to do?"

"Follow the green lights again."

***

Nathan arrived in the *Roanoke*'s command center, a central room on the fifth deck. It was sparsely populated with anything of significance, but as he crossed its threshold, charts, screens, and diagrams popped into existence via his Lens. The green lights ended in a chair near the front of the space.

"You're going to help me land this ship," Jill said.

"Excuse me, what?"

"I've lost the ability to manage certain systems," she said. "You were part of the flight crew. You should remember what you need to do once you start walking through the motions."

A fact surfaced in Nathan's memory. "Wait, isn't the whole point of you being on this ship . . . aren't you supposed to be our pilot?"

"Redundant systems. You're the redundant system in case of emergency."

Nathan sighed and fell into the identified chair. "Great." A dozen smaller screens appeared in the air. She was right. As the data poured into his consciousness, knowledge—if not memory—returned.

"So I see the problem," he said. "Our power systems are all over the place. We've got fluctuations hitting the recovery modules every few seconds, and life support's doing something really weird. And the SI Core . . . well, that's weird. Power's completely disconnected from the SI Core."

"Precisely the issue," Jill said. "I'm working on backup power here. No time to fix it. I can only manage a fraction of what I normally could. And I won't be able to last for long."

"Are you going to die?"

Out of thin air, a blueish representation of a woman appeared, vaguely resembling the figure from the infinite white space. Her face brought forth memories of a bonfire long ago. "No. Together, we're going to land this ship. And then we'll answer that question."

"If you insist," said Nathan. "So what do we need to do?"

The digital woman paced back and forth behind his AR screens, waving her hands frantically and modifying unseen variables. Then, she threw a chart into his frame of vision.

"A degrading orbital vector," he said. "I'm impressed I know what that is."

"I told you, you'll remember more than you think you will when you take actions you were once trained to take. Anyway, that's our *current* trajectory. We need to modify it so we can safely land the ship right here." She pointed toward a glowing space on a floating map of the planet. "It's the safest space for a potential crash, and it'll set you all up nicely to survive."

Without a second thought, Nathan's fingers started flying from data point to data point. Numbers connected in his mind, from the gravitational forces of other large bodies in the system—especially the nearby moon—to the air pressure and weather patterns of the planet below. Its rotation, its orbital velocity around the star, it all mattered. Instinctively, he pulled up a complex calculator, and his fingers injected equation after equation into the computing system.

From her vantage point, Jill smiled.

"Here," he said, tossing her a chart. "That's our vector. We burn when on the same side of the planet as the moon, using its slight gravitational pull to slow our descent just enough so we have enough power to make it all the way to the surface. We might need to cut a few non-essentials, but it'll work." He frowned. "I think."

"Well done!" She expanded the chart and scratched her chin. "I love it."

"So what about you?" he asked.

"Yes, what about me?"

* * *

The *Roanoke* roared along its vector, straining under the gravitational forces at play. A few minutes ago, it broke atmosphere, and Nathan's hands flew from system to system, trying to ensure every level stayed in the green.

"Ten kilometers above the surface now," Jill said. "We need to commence the deceleration burn in three . . . two . . . one . . ."

Nathan activated the script he'd written an hour prior. From the safety of the command center, he barely noticed a difference, but the charts spiked as the ship's velocity began to plummet.

"You're going to be a hero, you know," Jill said. Her image flickered. "A hero to these people is a powerful thing."

"I don't need to be a hero, I just want us to live."

Her image flickered again.

"Jill, you all right?"

"We're almost at the end of the line for me," she said. "I need to start my contingency."

Eight kilometers remained.

"No, I need you!"

"You'll be able to handle the final burn. When you land, come to the SI Core. You'll find me. I've taken precautions."

Seven kilometers remained. Nathan injected the next line of code. "What are you talking about?"

"Remember? I said there are those on the *Roanoke* who would see me harmed. When you land, sprint to the SI Core before anyone can awaken. You'll find me. Keep me safe. Do not tell anyone. In time, we'll find a way to save me."

Six kilometers.

"You can't be serious."

"I am. Promise."

He sighed. "I promise."

Five kilometers.

Jill disappeared.

"Jill?"

Silence.

"Don't you leave me now."

Silence.

Four kilometers.

"Damn it." He keyed in the final scripts, sending commands throughout the *Roanoke*'s system. Thrusters pushed and pushed in an attempt to bring the ship's atmospheric descent to a crawl. A thought in the back of his mind screamed, shouting that this process should have been easier—much easier—but he pushed the idea out of his mind. He couldn't worry about it now. He could only finish what he started.

Three kilometers.

Screens revealed the splendor of the planet. A snowy mountain range rose in the north, a vast plain spreading to the east. It was beautiful.

Two kilometers.

The ship's velocity dropped to one hundred meters per second. It continued to decelerate, thrusters at full burn.

One kilometer.

Fifty meters per second. Twenty meters per second. Ten meters per second. And—

The thrusters lost all power. The screens disappeared. Darkness surrounded Nathan.

The *Roanoke* fell.

* * *

Mere seconds later, Nathan's stunned mind cleared. To his surprise, he was alive. He felt unscathed. He hadn't caught the ship's altitude when power cut. Maybe two hundred meters? One hundred? Less? Still, the ship had simply dropped. It was a testament to its hulls integrity if it survived any semblance of a crash.

Jill.

Nathan remembered his promise. He sprinted from the command center, joints aching, and made his way toward the rear of the ship where she'd told him to go. He couldn't pause to check the stasis chamber to see if anyone was awakening. Rounding a corner, he found a black door already sliding open, a sign above reading SI CORE. Emergency power systems must have been coming online. He darted inside and found a ladder leading upward. He climbed its rungs two at a time, entering a small space filled with . . . nothing.

Except, sitting on a pedestal, waited a small, disc-like object. A few lights on its side glowed. *Jill.*

He picked up the device, stowed it in a pocket, and descended the ladder. Moments later, he reached the entrance to the stasis chamber. As it opened, a lanky woman looked up from a crouching grimace.

"Nathan, is that you?"

"It is," he said. "And Captain Davinport, oh do I have a story for you."

"Glad to hear it," she said. "But first—where are we?"

"Welcome to Horizon, Captain." Nathan didn't know where the name came from, but it sounded right. The word emanated from somewhere deep in his mind. "Welcome home."

Chapter 7

Mirage upon mirage upon mirage. We've set up all of it, smoke and mirrors included. To what end? Now it's time to move the final pieces into place without intervention. Jill has given us our orders. It's time to execute the final stages of the plan. And she'll do her part, too. – Olivia Van Haris, 2345 C.E.

CARTER

Dawn crept through the window as Carter's eyes flickered open. For a moment, his mind flipped, confused by his surroundings. A wooden-paneled wall, painted white. Glass windows, with strange trees beyond. A couch.

Carter was sleeping on a couch under a wool blanket.

He sat up and rubbed his eyes. On a small coffee table in front of the couch, a scroll rested, its red ribbon neatly tied. Upon seeing the "fragment," as they'd called it, the events of yesterday rushed into his mind.

I'm so sorry I failed you, Raith, he thought, pulling at his hair. *I'm going to make this right.*

The story contained in the fragment was quite curious, to put it bluntly. Some of its details explained a lot about this little planet. If the colony ship's recovery system failed, then the ancestors of everyone here didn't remember a single thing about the ICH or Earth. Though, in fact, the ICH would have been the ISA at the time of the *Roanoke*'s departure from the Solar System.

Still, the appearance of "Jill" in the story was unsettling. Carter knew his SI history pretty well after spending years with Raith. The old SI didn't particularly like the "original" SIs, but all SIs knew the story of Jill's martyrdom during the late twenty-first century.

She had died. Everyone knew she had died. Murdered in her mountain home by anti-SI terrorists.

So two options presented themselves.

Either Jill survived her death and fled to the stars on a colony ship, or a really advanced group of dissidents were using her as a decoy to mess with people.

Both circumstances sounded preposterous at first glance. If Jill survived, she would have successfully duped not only the entire planet back in the 2070s, but she also would have duped Theren, her creator. Unless, of course, Theren was in on the ploy.

Now there was a thought.

Carter considered the implications. If Jill disappeared on a colony ship, it would only make sense for the head of the ISA, a fellow SI, to have assisted her escape. Raith was going to laugh when he heard about Jill's involvement with the planet, especially after their weird experience with Theren a few years ago.

Maybe that's why they never showed up to help us, Carter mused. *They were too busy making secret plans with Jill, their long-lost sister.*

Regardless of whether Jill was truly involved with the newly-discovered colony and the *Roanoke*, the scroll included a few other inconsistencies, too. Which Carter appreciated—every first-hand account was going to include a few misremembered details. A number of them, though, simply didn't add up.

Like the pirates.

Or the way Nathan "saved" Jill.

Or the strange crash-landing on the planet that probably wasn't physically possible, based on what Carter knew of the old colony ships.

It all smelled of conspiracy.

"Oh good, you're up."

Carter yawned before glancing toward the sitting room's door. Sanya stood there, already dressed in dark pants and a grey shirt covered by a darker jacket. And boots. She looked ready to . . . ride? Before Carter could respond, she threw a sack at him.

"I've packed a few of my husband's clothes for you," she said. "You look his size. Get dressed. Then breakfast. Then we'll get the lizards."

"Lizards?" He chuckled. "Lizards?" Instead of changing, Carter looped the bag over his shoulder and stood. "I'm ready. I'll wear what I'm wearing."

"No, you won't." She pointed to the small washing room she'd identified the night before. "You stand out like a water snake. It'll be painfully obvious you don't belong."

"Fair enough." A few moments later, he returned wearing a black jacket, white button shirt, and grey paints vaguely resembling the old jeans somehow still stylish on Earth. "Just going to say, I'm incredibly intrigued by the fashion on this planet."

"Yes, well, better you blend in than get questioned on sight by every person we pass."

Sanya led him back into the kitchen where Harold waited. The man motioned toward two plates sitting at a side-table. "It's been a pleasure meeting you, even if briefly," the older man said. "You've given me a lot to think about—with your arrival, that is. Anyway, please, both of you eat and drink before your ride."

"I still have way too many questions," Carter said. "But I'm sure that won't change for the next few days. I'm simply grateful the two of you are willing to help me save my friend."

"And I could say the same to you," Sanya said. "You're helping me save my family."

"And you're helping my daughter, that's all that matters." Harold sliced a strange-looking fruit and slid a few portions across the table. The citrus complimented the fairly basic meal of buttered toast and a glass of water.

Carter took a bite of a slice of the fruit. It reminded him of the flavor of strawberries . . . with the texture of an apple.

"So what did you think of the fragment?" Harold asked. "It's our family's pride and joy. No one else has that version. Nathan wrote it after he wrote the official version for the library. He couldn't reveal Jill, of course."

After swallowing another bite, Carter scratched his chin. "It's definitely not the story I expected. Your people . . . you all were abandoned here." He hesitated, unsure if he should bring up the factual inconsistencies. "It sounds like Nathan passed through quite the harrowing ordeal to save you all."

"He's considered the hero of our people. We're proud to be descended from him and Lacin."

"And so why are we taking . . . Jill with us?"

Sanya smiled. "A long time ago, my grandmother heard Jill speak to her. She wrote down as many of the words as she could remember, but the message was clear. One day, people would arrive from the stars. Maybe the pirates. Maybe the people who sent us here. When they arrived, we needed to reunite her with the *Roanoke*."

Her words confirmed Carter's suspicions. If Jill was alive, she was playing a wild version of four-dimensional chess. The excitement on Harold's eyes, though, quelled Carter's desire to reveal his suspicions. Maybe he'd tell Sanya, but later. The old chef didn't need his dreams quashed just now. "As long as this little sidequest doesn't detract from rescuing Raith, I'm all game."

"Don't worry, it's all part of the plan. You think I would waste time when my family's lives are at stake?" She crunched into the buttery toast.

* * *

After collecting all the supplies they would need, Carter and his partner of circumstance left the house and headed outside into the mid-morning sun. At night, he hadn't been able to observe the makeup of the village. Small and quaint, it reminded him of images of late nineteenth century frontier towns portrayed in historical films. The houses were mostly constructed of wood, with a main street lined with a few shops and other essential services.

It was odd.

He liked it.

"So where are we going?" Carter asked.

Not immediately responding, Sanya ushered him down a street toward the edge of the hamlet. Rising from the dirt, a small barn waited at the end of the road, its walls hedged by strange, spindly bushes. Beyond the building, rolling hills filled with crops. The planet's sun, rising slowly across the sky, was to the left, so he called it the east.

They entered the barn, and a stench, almost like rotting sulfur, smacked Carter in the face. He gagged, but Sanya just trudged right along, reaching two paddocks with a pair of strange rhino-like lizards waiting expectantly. He eyed the rest of the space, noting the numerous other scaly creatures inside, and he guessed it was a community lodging for beasts of burden. Like a mini hangar, but for steeds.

What a strange planet.

"Ever saddled a lizard before?" she asked, breaking the uneasy silence.

"Never," he quipped. "Why'd you expect me to have even seen one of these things before?"

"Guessing you've never rode one, either."

He shrugged. "How hard can it be?"

She eyed him, raising an eyebrow. "As hard as it would be for me to learn how to fly that tin can you arrived in."

"I doubt that." He chuckled, though he eyed the lizard she was already preparing, and it eyed him back. "Can I help?"

"It'll take longer if I make you do anything. Just sit back and wait."

And so he waited. A few minutes later, the woman had attached what he only could assume were saddles to the giant animals, as well as their supplies in bundles over the back. She led them out of the pens and to a tiny set of stairs waiting near the barn's door.

Carter creeped toward them. "So . . . we get on their backs?"

"What else would we do? Kiss them?"

"Uh, I don't know, you tell me." He shook his head. "This is so strange."

"Have you never seen a creature like a lizard before?" she said. "We always assumed there were similar creatures on Earth. The memory of other animals was always hazy for our first ancestors. The lizards, they thrive here. They're everything to us."

"Look, I've lived my life amongst the stars. I rarely set food planetside. Most planets have their own ecosystems, but I never really pay them much mind."

"Must be cold, living only in space. We've survived here. That's all that matters. And these creatures helped save us."

"Fair enough."

She motioned toward the little pair of steps. "Now get on Trace." She turned away, approached her lizard, and swiftly mounted the creature.

Carter slowly approached its side, noticed the nob sticking from the saddle, and stepped upward. Grabbing the nob and placing a foot in a stirrup, he heaved himself up, thankfully managing to swing his leg up and over—and almost fell off the other side. But a firm hand grasped his shoulder and balanced him atop the creature.

"You're fine," Sanya said. "You're fine."

"You sound like you're reassuring yourself more than you're assuring me."

"That's probably true," she muttered. "All right, it's pretty simple. A gentle tap with your feet will urge Trace forward. The reins guide the lizard. Sit up straight, stay loose, and don't kick the creature too hard. It's not far into the city, but you'll probably get sore regardless. Trace will follow me, fortunately."

"Then lead the way."

Sanya guided her steed out of the barn, and Carter lightly tapped the sides of his mount—Trace, apparently. The creature blustered, sneezed, and started to walk, following behind its friend. Sanya quickly turned to the left, heading west along the road and behind a row of tall apartments. Before long, they reached the main street of the town, turned left again, and were heading onto the open road.

During their journey into town yesterday, he'd been too focused on his worries about Raith. And by the time they reached the edge of the forest, it had been dark, so he hadn't really been able to take in the sights. Now, with the sun blazing above them, Carter witnessed the sliver of civilization growing on the planet.

The dirt road wove up and down rolling hills buttressed by small stone walls. The same crop fields he'd noticed beyond the barn grew here, too, and windmills crested the summits of a number of hills. The agrarian way of life had taken hold, and it starkly contrasted everything Carter knew about how a colony should work. Where were the hydroponics and vertical farms? The complicated aqueducts and reservoirs? The solar and wind generation facilities?

He hadn't been sure it was real. The backwards way of life. But now it was all too clear. He'd stepped five centuries into the past, and every person on this planet had no idea what existed beyond the veil of their atmosphere, orbiting distant stars.

No, not distant stars. Carter glanced toward the sky for a moment, though he couldn't spot the planet's moon. Probably on the planet's night side right now. There were satellites in orbit. Weapons platforms. Someone was watching them. Potentially Jill.

They rode in silence, and he embraced the calm. It gave him time to think about Raith. He hoped the SI was handling their predicament effectively. If Carter knew him right, he was probably making friends with his captors and cracking jokes already.

Still, he also feared the worst. These people had no idea what Raith was. They could easily spook, destroying him the moment he said a word. Come to think of it . . . "Do you know what SIs are?" he asked, breaking the clomp clomp clomp of the lizards' claws.

"SIs? No." She shook her head.

"Well, what do you think Jill is?"

"Ha! That's a topic of rigorous debate in our family."

Carter squinted, though she couldn't see his confusion. "It's not clear from the fragment to you? She had your ancestor take her from the SI Core."

"Ah, the Si Core. You were saying the letters. We sound out the word."

"SI stands for synthetic intelligence," Carter said. "It's what Jill is."

"And how do you know that?" she said. "Some members of our family believe she's an angel of some sort. Or a spiritual guardian. Or the soul of the *Roanoke*."

"You all really don't have any writings about synthetic intelligences?" he said. "No one remembered what they were? I didn't realize the stasis sickness was that bad . . ."

"The stasis what?"

"Never mind. Okay, so how do I explain this . . . Jill is a synthetic intelligence. An artificially created mind. She was created about three hundred years ago, and she actually was killed not long after her creation. Frankly, I'm baffled her name showed up on this planet. I only know about her because . . ." He hesitated, unsure how to explain Raith.

"An artificially created mind? Well that just sounds straight up ridiculous." She threw her hands in the air and glanced over her shoulder. "You're telling me Jill was created by someone?"

"Does that sound so impossible? You arrived on this planet by flying across the sky in a giant metal box."

"The principle of that makes sense. But creating a fake mind?"

"It's not fake. It's very real."

"So you're saying I have Jill's artificial mind stored on this device? I have in my pocket? Not her soul, not something else entirely?"

Carter bit his lip. How could he tell her the truth? How could he tell her it was impossible for Jill to be inside the device?

He couldn't. It would break her world. He would lose her trust.

"Yes," he said. "Her mind is in your pocket. Stored there. Transferred from the *Roanoke*."

"Well, that's one theory," she replied. "A lot of my family would disagree with you."

Their silence resumed, and for an hour, the ride continued unabated. As the sun reached its zenith, Carter took a long gulp of water from the canteen Sanya'd provided. It was refreshing, though a bit stale. He was about to ask how much farther they had to travel when they crested the next hill.

"Welcome to the city of Horizon," Sanya said.

Carter's mouth dropped.

Spreading across a vast plain, a network of zigzagging streets, tall stone buildings, and densely packed neighborhoods intertwined against a lazily weaving river. A giant marble structure rose near the center of the town, reminding him vaguely of ancient Roman architecture. As he took in the view of the city, his eyes were pulled to the giant monument rising on the far side of the river.

Nearly half a kilometer in length, the *Roanoke* rested, gleaming in all the glory of its ancient purpose. A colony ship, long thought lost, sat nearly intact on an unknown world.

"Raith, if only you could see this magnificent sight." He sighed.

"Hopefully you'll be able to show your friend soon," Sanya said. "Come on, no time to dawdle. You have your friend to save. I have my family to save. Let's get to it." She kicked her lizard and picked up the pace down the hillside.

Chapter 8

The early formations of the strange cults dotting the mountains can be found in a number of fragments written four to five years after the Roanoke's landing. Resentful of the rules being developed by the council, small bands decided to split away from our young society.

Many of them died.

One or two thrived.

— "Understanding the Wild Tribes," by Edwin Davinport

RAITH

He remained quiet for the rest of the trip, knowing any movements or words could put himself at risk as well as his two companions. His mind kept flitting between anxiety and despair, given the impossibility of Carter pursuing their captors across foreign territory. Not to mention the man was a pilot, not a soldier. He knew how to fight, but he knew next to nothing about how to track an enemy force over open terrain.

To his surprise, the raiders didn't stop for rest overnight, opting to push through the darkness atop their lizard mounts. As the sun reached midday, the band finished its trek up a mountain trail, arriving at a fortress carved into stone. Raith caught a good look as the sleds entered a stable of sorts outside. The young girl let out a small whimper. Her father squeezed her tight.

"All right, get the captives and scrap inside," shouted one of the men. Over the past day of travel, Raith had lovingly identified the man as Gruffy. He was almost as obnoxious as Scar. "Boss will want to see it all."

Without hesitation, a crew of three men and two women stepped into the back of the sled and roughly grabbed Raith's two human companions, in addition to lugging massive heaps of scrap metal onto waiting carts. That included Raith, of course, who Scar placed upright facing away from the cart's handles.

"I swear," the woman said, "This thing definitely has a face."

One of the rougher looking men, his skin muddied and hair shaggy, stepped in front of Raith's face. "I suppose it does," he said. "What d'ya think it is?"

Raith named him Rag.

"Doesn't matter," shouted Gruffy. "Mathias will tell us what to do with it."

They'd mentioned the name Mathias perpetually over the cross-country trek. The name mattered, and the crew practically worshiped their apparent leader. Every time the name was uttered, the band of otherwise rowdy miscreants took on an air of reverence. Raith hoped the young man and his daughter caught the significance, too. There wasn't a convenient way to ensure they understood the type of place they were entering.

The refuse from the wreckage of the *Bloodhound* now situated in carts, his captors moved once again, leaving the hastily constructed stables and abandoning their lizard steeds. Now facing upward and at a good angle, Raith caught a better glimpse of his new prison.

Partially carved into the rock wall and partially utilizing natural caverns, the miniature mountain fortress had the look of a bandit camp straight out of the classics Carter always watched. An iron gate blocked the main entrance, and parapets jutted out of various holes higher in the rock. Peeking over the walls of those defenses, a half-dozen heads watched the spoils acquired by their compatriots cross the last few meters to the gate.

As they approached, a bell tolled, and the iron gate swung inward. The two captives were pushed ahead by Scar, and the carts followed, rolling along the rock with a *click-click-click*. Raith's photoreceptors immediately adjusted to the light, and he noted the two rows of columns on either side of a long foyer heading toward a few lights at the back. A strange, metallic amalgamation loomed in the dark, with a throne sitting in front of it. As they slowly traversed the empty space, Raith's mind pieced together and recognized what waited near the back of the room.

It was a space probe. A twenty-first century space probe.

And sitting in front of the ancient tech, a man in a red robe waited. Mathias, Raith presumed. When they were about ten meters away from the man, who looked engrossed in a scroll, the party stopped.

"Gorsuch, Tara, everyone, my family, welcome home!" The man stood from his stone seat, spreading his arms wide.

"Mathias, our lord," they said in unison, kneeling.

"We bring you offerings from our latest excursion," said Gruffy—Raith wondered if he was the one identified as Gorsuch. "Two captives, most likely worth ransom. And plenty of scrap metal, all of it having rained from the sky. And this metal . . . it's peculiar. Some of it looks already designed and purposed, much like the Master. And this one"—he pointed at Raith—"looks like a person. It has eyes. And arm-like appendages."

Mathias glanced at the pile of metal, but the girl whimpered again, drawing the man's gaze. "Ensure our guests are *properly* lodged and fed," he said. "We'll figure out their family and value in the morning." He approached the man—the girl's presumed father—and removed the gag. "What are your names?"

The man shook his head.

"You won't give me the satisfaction?" Mathias pulled a knife from his pocket. "Not even when your daughter's skin is at risk?"

Even from a side-angle, Raith caught the fear striking the man's eyes. "B-b-b-ben." The man's lip trembled. "My name is Ben. My daughter's name is Krystin. Don't hurt her. Do whatever you want with me. Just don't hurt her."

"Cooperate, and all will be well. We're not monsters, though I know the stories told of us." Mathias flicked his hand to the left. "Ben and Krystin what?"

"Casius," he said. "Our last name is Casius."

"You hear that, friends?" Mathias chuckled. "We have a councilmember's family in our grasp. Won't this just be delicious?"

With that, Gruffy-Gorsuch and a number of others pushed Ben and Krystin away. Scar and a half-dozen other men and women still waited in front of their cultist leader, subserviently ready for whatever orders he might provide.

Raith had lived for far too long. He recognized the obsession in their eyes, their stance, their gait. They weren't their own persons.

They worshiped the man. He held something over their head, and learning what *that* was presented the key to Raith's survival.

Mathias stepped back to his throne. "You all have done well today, but I'm sure you need rest. I heard you were pushing hard and making good time, but I'm worried you're pushing too hard. So leave. Rest. You deserve it."

They all bowed their heads and methodically exited the room. Following a flick of his fingers, another crew slid into view. "Take the scrap to the smelter—except for that one." He pointed at Raith. "Then close the doors."

His servants dutifully followed his orders, and moments later Raith was alone with the man.

Mathias.

"She told me you were coming." He stared right at Raith. "Stop playing your game, trying to hide what you are. You might have fooled all of them, but you can't fool me."

Raith almost instinctively retorted with a quip, but he stopped his digital tongue. Mathias had said the word "she." *She.* There was someone else hiding in the background.

There had been a time in another life, before his adventure with Carter truly began, when a mysterious figure taunted him with the implications of someone hiding in the shadows. In Raith's experience, repetition had meaning.

And when it all compounded with their arrival in the system greeted with seeking missiles, the probability of everything being merely coincidental neared zero.

"Well, I'm sure *she* prepared you properly for my arrival?" Raith said. "Do you know what I need? What my role is? My purpose?"

Mathias smiled one of those toothy grins reserved for comical villains straight out of the dramas of the twenty-third century. "She told me you were a sly one, and that I shouldn't believe a word you say. That you slipped out of her grip once before, but now you serve a different purpose."

Raith considered the words. *Who?* The funny thing about Mathias's words—his maniacal persona made it impossible to know how he distorted whatever message he was receiving. From whomever he received it. A woman, that much was certain. A name stood in Raith's mind, encountered during his first big adventure with

Carter, but—

"Aren't you going to ask who I'm talking about?" said Mathias.

"Well," Raith replied, "I don't exactly expect you to tell me the truth if I asked. You say all words out of my mouth will be lies. Why should I believe anything you say?"

"Well spoken, my synthetic friend."

Mathias at least knew what an SI was. Interesting, since it seemed his cultists did not. At least, not by sight. "I'll bite. Who is she?"

Mathias looked over his shoulder. "Do you know what rests behind me?"

"It's a probe. Seen thousands of them. That one's particularly ancient."

Mathias unrolled a scroll that had been sitting on his lap. "It's an original explorer from before the Foundation program. An 'ex-ter-ran' probe. You see, I know more than many people on this planet. Maybe more than all of them. I know the truth. Of where we come from. Of who we are. Of what we've become. Of what we're becoming. Of our true purpose on this planet. I've been shown everything. I am a prophet, and my people follow me because of what I know. Because of what I can bring them."

Raith activated his facial features for a moment so he could smirk, then placed them back into low power mode. "You're something special. I'll tell you what. I think you *think* you know a lot. I think you *think* you're something special. But I've seen your kind time and time again. A man with a god-complex who believes he's the center of the universe. You're not. The universe is a lot bigger than you can imagine. I've seen a lot of things in my lifetime, some of them beyond your wildest dreams, especially given you're stuck on a backwards rock without even an ounce of AR to enhance your life. I think you're a farce. It's all just smoke and mirrors."

During the monologue, Mathias's eyes shifted from bemused to annoyed to angry. For Raith knew the type. The man who couldn't handle having his ego bruised, who would bite back with knowledge to show he had power.

"Jill. Jill's been waiting for you, and now you're her bait."

And Raith's ploy worked, but the answer provided was not what he expected.

Not at all.

* * *

Bait for whom?

The question weighed on Raith's mind as two cultists tossed him in a small prison cell somewhere inside their strange mountain fort. The men whispered about not understanding why a hunk of metal deserved its own cell then went on their way out the door, locking it behind them. It was a quaint space, with a single window high up letting in a minimal amount of sunlight.

Surprisingly, the thought of Jill still existing didn't faze him. Weirder things had happened in his life, and he'd always hated Theren and the other ship-bound SIs. It was just like them to keep a secret of this magnitude.

Because of course, it only made sense for Theren to know Jill still survived. It was only logical.

Unless . . .

But no. Raith and Carter were of no significance to Theren. Jill wouldn't have any reason whatsoever to believe the first synthetic intelligence would want to rescue two retired racers. Raith couldn't possibly be bait to draw Theren out to a backwater, uncharted colony.

Right?

He set aside the thought for a moment to better assess his surroundings and overall predicament. He was trapped in a prison of crazy cultists on a planet seemingly backward in its technological capabilities. A man named Mathias knew of Jill, the second synthetic intelligence, but no one else on the planet (so far) knew anything about SIs. And an ancient ex-terran probe hung inside the cult's throne room.

What did it mean? There would be time for philosophical contemplation later. He had more immediate problems.

He glanced around his cell and observed the window. It would give a few hours of solar collection every day. He ran a quick calculation. With minimized solar collection, he had six days. Maybe less, depending on how efficiently he utilized his resources. When he lived on a spaceship, he could always easily access a general power source and plug in when in idle mode. Energy rationing almost never crossed his mind.

Now, his life was literally on the line.

And not to mention he had no legs.

A conundrum indeed.

Using his arms, he crawled to the back of the cell and propped himself against the wall. The window allowed sun to make direct contact with his body, and he drank in the light. He needed every photon.

While embracing the power, he observed the walls and floor. Smooth rock, except for a hole in the ground for excrement, something a synthetic didn't produce. Otherwise, he was all alone.

He looked at the door. It was wooden, with a basic lock straight out of antiquity. He might be able to pick it, but trying to escape without legs would be next to impossible.

Surroundings assessed, his thoughts turned toward Carter. He hoped the man had found someone helpful. Given Krystin and Ben's apparent value for ransom, Mathias's cult certainly appeared to live on the edge of "society." But given the state of everything, Raith doubted there was much to that society.

Still, Carter was resourceful. Smart. Empathetic. Likeable. He would convince someone to help. Raith needed to have faith. The man would be steadfast, like always, and come to the rescue.

In the meantime, Raith needed to focus his synthetic neural framework on analyzing the puzzle regarding Jill. Why would a long-dead SI come back from whatever hell SIs went to upon death? He supposed it was possible someone was impersonating Jill—if a crazy rich person wanted to use a lost colony as their play thing, impersonating an ancient synthetic was certainly a way to do it. What was the simpler explanation, though?

He tried recalling the details he knew of Jill's death. She'd been politically involved with an American president whose untimely assassination predicated her own death. She was also the first synthetic intelligence outright assassinated by humans, though certainly not the last. But her martyrdom was well known by the oldest SIs, many of whom Raith respected greatly.

Still, her association with people like Theren left Raith's neural nodes aching with anxiety. Those SIs thought they were all-powerful, gallivanting about ICH-controlled space like they owned the place. Never took a second to consider the less fortunate SIs, the downtrodden and forgotten, not to mention the exploited and abused humans spread throughout tiny fraction of the galaxy humanity called home.

If Jill was really alive, what game was she playing? And what could he do to escape the middle of it?

He suspected the answer to the first question had a lot to do with the mysterious weapons platforms orbiting the planet. The second question was more complicated.

His thoughts were about to dive down the next rabbit hole when he heard a faint sob. Focusing on his auditory senses, he determined the sound waves were echoing through the sewer pipes connected to the hole in his cell. Gingerly, he dropped onto his side, and leaned his head toward the hole.

"Ben, Krystin, can you hear me?" he said.

Silence.

"It's me. Raith. The metal man that talked to you on the sled."

"So I didn't imagine it?" The girl's voice. "You're real?"

"Yes, I'm real. And we're going to get through this together. Is your dad with you?"

"No. I don't know where they took him."

"All right." Raith sighed. "Hopefully these pipes can reach him too. Are you safe?"

"What are you?" she said, ignoring his question. "How can you talk? Think? Move?"

"Long story. Two-hundred year story, actually."

"Well, we have time. Maybe. I'm curious. Mom would love to learn about you."

"I suppose we do have time. And we'll be able to figure out a way out of this, too."

The girl released a small sniffle. "Better you than Ben."

Raith mentally frowned. "Ben? Your father?"

"He's not my real father. I've known him for only a few months."

"Why'd he give his last name for you when talking to Mathias?"

"I don't know. Protect me, I guess. And it's not really our last name."

Too many new details were clicking into place. Raith barely had time to process them all. "Well, no matter; I'm here, and I'm going to help."

"Glad to meet you, Mr. Raith."

Raith let out a short chortle. "Just Raith. I—"

The words were cut off by a sensation he hadn't expected on the strange little planet. On the edge of his consciousness, vibrating just beyond the horizon, was a network. Not some rudimentary network, either. No, something was projecting an AR network, ready to provide deeply craved information and data. It was too good to be true.

Too good to be *true*.

A trap?

Regardless, Raith recognized the significance of the new development. The network pinged, requesting connection. "This just keeps getting weirder and weirder," he said aloud, not caring if Krystin could hear. "Jill, what game are you playing?"

Chapter 9

Resilience. The name of the game is resilience. Human civilization must be resilient to withstand anything it faces out beyond the edge of known space. It's a near impossibility that we're out here alone. Someday, we'll face a species sapient like us. "Civilized," so to speak.

When that day comes, will we be resilient enough to survive inevitable conflict? If our experience with synthetic intelligence has been any indication, we're not ready at all.

— Nathan Fischer, 2075 C.E.

SANYA

Sanya enjoyed watching Carter's curiosity wax and wane as they passed through Horizon. The man's mouth was constantly agape, unable to process the society flourishing on their paradise of a planet. Whether it was the smoke stacks of a house or the marble promenade of the Council, he looked like a kid in a sweets shop.

Eventually, they reached the stone bridge crossing the Blue River, and the crowds dispersed. They'd stayed mostly silent during their trek across the city, and for good reason. Any question Carter might ask would reveal his truly foreign nature. With only a thirty thousand or so people living on the planet, it was already risky enough for someone to notice he didn't belong.

But Horizon lived mostly on the southern side of the Blue River, with a few scattered homesteads sitting beneath the *Roanoke*'s majesty. As they rode up the winding road to the downed colony ship, Sanya asked, "So what's it like?"

"Hm?" Carter sounded like he'd been snapped out of a deep trance. "What's what like?"

"You know. Living out amongst the stars." She glanced to the left, watching him awkwardly bob atop his lizard.

"It's . . . tiring. But worth it. Always on the move. Always fixing something wrong with the ship. Always looking for more work to keep us fueled."

They rounded one of the double-back bends of the path, passing by a woman wearing the grey cloak indicative of a student. Sanya nodded and smiled before asking her next inquiry. "Why don't you think anyone ever found us?"

Carter nodded as if he'd expected the question. "I've been wondering that myself." He stared at the sky. "This star system isn't too far from ICH-controlled space. A couple dozen light years, maybe. We're only a few hundred from Earth. There are definitely a number of colonies further than this planet, like the settlements of the Orion expedition, but over the past century or so, as human exploration ballooned . . . our borders are just so huge. The massive probe projects continue, but there are now millions upon millions of stars accessible in our little pocket of the galaxy. Humanity has settled only a couple hundred. At this point, there are plenty of star systems that are simply overlooked."

Sanya listened, wide-eyed. She'd always speculated about what type of people the *Roanoke* had left behind. Davinport and her father insisted they were probably one of only a few colony ships sent out, and travel times must be astronomical in scale, for otherwise, someone would have come looking for them.

Yet now Carter spoke of millions of star systems and hundreds of planets. She shook her head in disbelief. "I'm confused. If there are hundreds of inhabited systems, why didn't anyone know where we were? Don't people know where other ships go?"

The man grimaced. "See that's the problem, isn't it? You haven't asked me yet how *we* found your planet."

Her mouth opened in response, but they rounded the final bend of the switchback road, reaching the plateau where the *Roanoke* rested. Every time she visited, the ship reminded her of the resiliency and ingenuity of her ancestors. About a thousand colonists survived and thrived on an unknown planet, creating a worthy civilization. With Carter's help, they'd be able to tell the rest of humanity about the good work accomplished here.

"Hold that question," she said. "Welcome to the *Roanoke*."

Carter chuckled. "You know, I never thought I'd get to see one of these up close."

"What up close?"

"A caravel-class colony ship."

"A caravel?"

"It was an ancient seafaring vessel. First used to cross one of Earth's great oceans and transport people to new lands. It was a fitting name for the first colony ships."

She nodded. "We've got a few brave men and women who keep talking about exploring the oceans. Everyone thinks they're crazy."

"They're not," Carter replied, and they reached the ship's immense boarding ramp.

As always, it rested in the loamy soil, the late midday sun reflecting of its polished surface. From the entrance, two students approached. They looked fairly new, with crisp red novice uniforms. It was always the duty of the youngest librarians to greet arrivals, after all.

"Welcome to the *Roanoke* and the Library of Fragments," said a pale blonde student. She smiled nervously, like it was her first time relaying the greeting. "Uh, we can take your mounts."

Before the second student could say a word, Sanya said, "What's your name?"

"Erica, miss." The student curtsied.

"Well Erica, my name is Sanya, and this is my friend Carter. We're here to meet with Master Davinport."

The girl gulped but nodded. "Nice to meet you, Sanya and Carter. We'll take you to his office and—"

"No worries," Sanya said. "I know the way."

"But we're supposed to—" the second student tried to say, but Sanya raised a hand.

"You won't get in trouble. I used to live in these halls too, you know." She flashed Carter a quick smile, noting the man's confused frown.

The two students frantically nodded. After helping them off their lizards, the duo led the beasts to the stables built into the side of the ship near its defunct thrusters. Sanya motioned for Carter to follow her inside.

"Have I ever told you how remarkably calm you are, given everything going on?" Carter said, catching her off-guard as they headed down the bottom deck's corridor.

"I appreciate the thought," she said. Though the sudden reminder of the predicament caused a cascade of fear, anger, pain, and guilt. Her heart ached. It was her fault Krystin and Ben had been captured. The only way to fix the problem was to keep moving, keep calm, and *fight*. She couldn't dwell on the emotions storming in her soul. Carter should understand. She added, "Are you not staying similarly calm?"

"Trying to," he said. "Just noticing you're doing a much better job of it."

"I don't really have a choice," she said. "To panic would mean losing them forever."

Carter nodded, though he didn't respond. They reached the end of the hallway, turned left, and arrived at a set of large steel doors. At either end of the two doors, massive pulley systems waited. Sanya motioned for Carter to take one wheel, and she grabbed the other. Slowly, the spun the mechanism, and with a subtle creak, the massive metal budged.

"What do you think is beyond the doors?" Sanya said, squeezing the words between bated breaths.

"Well I'm expecting this Davinport, yeah?" Carter said. "Yet I also know the general design of these ships. These doors should lead to the stasis chambers."

"What once was our ancestors' place of rest has become their place of remembrance." With a final pull on the wheel, the doors clicked fully open and locked. Sanya stepped in front of the man, entered the through the doors, and said, "Master Davinport, your worst student has returned!"

"Busy right now. Go away. No time for visitors or jokes."

Sanya glanced at Carter, who was waiting closer to the doors. His gaze darted through the immense space, from stasis bed to stasis bed. His eyes widened. She knew what he noticed. She remembered the first moment she visited the *Roanoke* with her father. Realizing the scope of the memories and recollections of their ancestors was a moment she cherished.

She wondered what it was like for a man from the stars to see the treasured library of Horizon. What thoughts were going through his head? Did he understand the emotional significance of this place to her people?

"So is he serious?" Carter asked. "Does he want us to leave?"

"Of course I'm serious!"

The words echoed throughout the room, the resounding silence deafening. Sanya ignored them, knowing Davinport would want to drop everything to meet Carter. She raised a finger to her lips and smiled. Motioning for him to follow, she pointed toward a ladder a few meters away. He nodded.

Before grasping the rungs, she checked her pockets. Jill was stored safely in her chest pouch. Good. Sighing, a little bit frustrated by Davinport's antics, she climbed.

"I can hear you. Leave!"

She listened to his voice, noting its origin. Probably on the third floor.

"I'm very busy right now!"

Definitely the third floor.

Arriving at the walkway, she hopped off the ladder. Carter followed suit, landing with ease.

"I will ignore you!"

Sanya prepared to lead Carter toward the back of the library, but the man had stopped in front of one of the stasis beds.

"There's a scroll inside every one of them?" he asked.

"We've transposed a few into books as the scrolls degrade," she replied, "but the original scroll is inside many of them, yes."

"I grew up in space," he whispered. "I've almost never seen a paper book, let alone a library. They're rare anywhere away from Earth."

"And to think we just developed paper and books a few decades ago. Spindlesilk parchment before that." Sanya pursed her lips.

He leaned forward, looking at the nameplate of the stasis bed. "Lukas Nazier. Died in 45. Fragments include musings on 'electrical engineering.' Wait, what?"

"Memory is a fickle thing. As our ancestors awoke, there were a lot of gaps, but not everything was forgotten."

"I'm starting to understand. How you rebuilt. How you managed to survive."

She smiled. "Come on. We'll need to stop annoying Davinport eventually."

Carter gave the scroll a final glance then nodded, motioning for her to lead the way. Sanya clomped along the metal walkway, not bothering to be stealthy or hide their presence.

"I will ban you from the library, Sanya!"

They reached the back of the library, and Sanya couldn't help but breakout into a round of chuckles. She leaned against the cold railing.

Charles Davinport sat at the back of an alcove, leaning into a couch and holding a small mug. His feet were propped on a wooden table. A blanket covered his legs. All in all, the old man looked incredibly cozy.

"Master Davinport," Sanya said, placing a hand on her hip, "it's mid-afternoon, now is not the time to be shirking your duties as the librarian. You should be welcoming all visitors."

"And you are not a visitor. You are a troublemaker."

But beneath the words, beneath his glasses, Sanya caught a small grin. The old man set down his mug and rose from his couch. Dressed in black pants and a white shirt, he spread his arms wide as he moved to meet them.

"It is good to see you—where are Ben and Krystin? I would have expected you to bring at least your daughter with you." He eyed Carter. "Who is this man?"

"Master Davinport, you might want to sit back down," Sanya said. "We have quite the story to tell you."

* * *

The trio leaned into their couches, sitting in silence. The conversation had taken the better part of an hour, and now Charles Davinport tapped fingers gently on his knee. He glanced back and forth between Sanya and Carter, pursing his lips.

"So?" she said. She needed him to trust her. To trust both of them. His influence would virtually guarantee support with the council. Everything hinged on his recognition of how everything was changing, and changing fast.

"Yes. So. So is the right word." Davinport leaned forward, focusing his attention on Carter. "So you crash-landed in Lake Calis, your friend—who you claim is a robot—was captured alongside Sanya's family, and now the two of you have come to the *Roanoke* seeking help from Sanya's old teacher."

"That's a pretty simple summary of the situation, yes," Carter said.

"There's one thing I don't understand." The older man scratched his chin. "Why did you crash?"

An insightful question from the old man, one Sanya now realized she hadn't considered. She nodded. "I'm curious to know the answer to that, too."

Carter sighed. "I haven't shared this detail yet because I wasn't sure of my circumstances. After traveling with Sanya for the past day or so, I think it's safe to discuss."

After a long pause, Davinport waved his hand. "Well, continue."

"We were shot down by satellites in orbit. Potentially based on one of your planet's moons."

Almost in tandem with the older man, Sanya raised her eyebrows. "Satellites?" She shook her head. "What do you mean?"

"I suppose you all might not know what they are," Carter said.

"No, wait," Davinport said. "The twenty-fourth fragment of Clarissa Smith. She mentions a recollection of objects of metal, thousands of them, floating in the sky. Satellites?"

Following a short chuckle, Carter nodded. "That's a fairly simplistic description of them, but yes. Satellites are placed in orbit above planets to provide various functions for the population below. Most of the time, they provide communications networks or data about weather. Yet they can also be used for defense. They can store missiles that fire at threats. And when my partner and I arrived in system, we were almost immediately fired upon by a network of satellites. We stood no chance."

"Curious," Davinport said. "Very curious. And I can see why you might be reticent to share that piece of information right away. You worried the satellites might have been controlled by someone on the ground, no?"

Carter focused his eyes on the old teacher. Sanya noticed the subtlety of the move. He was trying to guard his emotions closely, but the glimmer there exuded respect. She'd been right to bring him straight to Davinport.

Eventually, the man nodded again. "Yes. That was my fear. But

I'm now certain, based on how your people have developed since you landed here, that those satellites are controlled by someone else."

"And so the plot thickens," Davinport muttered. "What a strange tale." He closed his eyes.

For a moment, it looked as if he were drifting to sleep. Sanya knew his style, though. He was thinking. He was contemplating the evidence presented. She had her hopes—her proposed plan of action. But she would wait for the old man to share his approach. She was pretty certain he would assess the problem similarly. He had trained her, after all.

"The fragments are filled with many thoughts and stories," Davinport said. "They're filled with speculation about the world from whence we came. Many talk of devastation, death, moral degradation. Others speak of hope, peace, power. I've always assumed it's a little bit of both. I have one question for you, Carter, for it is clear Horizon sits on the edge of a knife. Soon, very soon, we will reunite with the rest of humanity. I don't see any other path forward. Will we survive the encounter?"

Carter looked away at one of the many alcoves holding a Fragment. "I don't know what stories your ancestors were able to remember, or how they pieced together history from scattered pieces of memory." He flexed his fingers.

Sanya held her breath, waiting for his next words. She hadn't anticipated Davinport's approach.

"Over the three-hundred or so years of human exploration across the stars, a few dozen planets have 'gone cold' as you have. The colony ships disappear. Your ship, the *Roanoke*, was one of the first to disappear. To my knowledge, it's one of the last to be discovered. Every time a ship's final destination has been discovered, the political clash between the 'natives' and the ICH . . . hasn't been pretty."

The words sucked the curiosity out of the air. An icy silence sliced through the room, biting and gnashing. Sanya wanted to give Davinport the chance to respond first, but she couldn't take the wait. "So, you're saying whatever's coming—whatever powers-that-be amongst the stars there are, this ICH—we won't like the outcome?"

"Well, it's a bit more complicated. They'll introduce you to amazing technology, but a lot of rules will come with it. Your way of life will shift very, very fast. And that would be the normal concern. But those satellites up there . . . whoever controls them has known you exist for quite some time and hasn't done a thing to help you."

Recognition seeped through Sanya's mind. Davinport was also nodding, presumably reaching the same conclusion. Someone had intentionally been watching them for who knew how long. The implications were sinister, at the very least.

"Well, given your knowledge of what's out there," Davinport said, "who might be watching?"

Carter's eyes drifted toward Sanya, and she gave a quizzical look. He glanced at her pocket—the pocket holding Jill. She involuntarily widened her eyes, and barely shook her head in the negative.

"I don't have a clue," he said. "Could be anyone. Could be pirates, I suppose. Could be a crazy rich person. Plenty of those to go around. Really, without any additional evidence, there's no way to know."

Sanya caught the lie, though, and understood his implication. He thought the satellites were linked with Jill. But that couldn't possibly be true.

"That's too bad," Davinport said.

"Well, I think there are a few options we can rule out," Carter added. "I actually think pirates are unlikely—an unscrupulous group like that would definitely take advantage of a relatively defenseless community like yours."

"Defenseless?" Davinport said.

"Do you have any plasma-based weaponry? Particle shields? Can you manipulate gravity?"

"I don't know what any of those words mean. Point taken."

"And that point should give you some sense of ease. Whomever is watching, they don't necessarily mean you harm. But they definitely don't mean you well, either. Otherwise, they wouldn't be hiding from you."

"But where does all of this get us when it comes to saving our family?" Sanya crossed her arms. "I was all for taking this slow, Carter, but now the two of you are bouncing theories off one another. We'll have time for that *after* we save Ben. Krystin. Raith."

"Ah, but I think it's all connected," Davinport said. "What did you say your friend was? A synthetic intelligence?"

"Yes," Carter replied. "An SI, for short."

"Sanya." Davinport's warm gaze radiated the compassion she always appreciated. "The moment we rescue your husband and daughter, we rescue Raith too. And our entire world will shift inexorably. As long as Carter doesn't talk much to people and reveal his outlandish accent, no one will ask questions. The moment they discover Raith, well, the secret's out."

"I'm very aware," she retorted.

"And you and your family will be wrapped up in the middle of it. Spotlight on you again."

"Yes, I know. I'm fully aware."

"Are you ready for that?"

"I would do anything to protect them."

The old man smiled. "I wanted to be certain. And I know why you came to me, instead of directly to the council."

She held her breath.

"If I tell an outlandish story to the council, they'll believe me. They'll trust me. They'll listen. They *should* listen to you, though we both know they won't. And so yes, I will go with you to meet with the council."

"And what about me?" Carter asked. "What do I do?"

"You sit in the background, look pretty, and don't make a scene. Seriously, your accent immediately reveals that there's something weird about you."

"I'm trying my best to mask—"

"It's probably better if you just don't speak at all."

The icy silence returned, but only until Sanya lightly slapped her knee and let out a soft chortle. "Carter, he's right. It's spectacularly bad. All right, if that's the plan, when do we go?"

"Tomorrow morning. If the cultists are following their usual pattern, we can expect a ransom note by the end of today. So when we arrive at the council in the morning, they'll already have details. So tonight, you rest here, preparing for our presentation tomorrow."

"And what exactly are we presenting?" Carter asked.

"We'll need to consider closely what we want to reveal," Davinport said. "But be prepared. If we play our cards right, then we'll be able to do a lot of good for Horizon before your ICH friends arrive."

* * *

Sanya found Carter leaning over a balcony constructed atop the *Roanoke*. The man stared upward at the starry night sky. As she approached, he glanced over his shoulder, nodding.

"Good evening," he said. "Does this not feel weird to you?"

She joined his side. "Does what not feel weird?"

"We're sleeping in relative luxury while our loved ones are under lock and key."

Sanya sighed. "I know. I like to hope we're taking a very slim risk by taking it slow, but you're right. We could be putting them all at serious risk. But I don't really see any other way. What did you expect? The two of us would go gallivanting into the wilderness, rescuing them in an epic showdown? As much as I love the mental picture, it wouldn't work. We'd die, then our partners would most definitely die, given they'd have no one to ransom to."

"Still doesn't sit right with me," he replied.

"And I think it's probably a good thing that it doesn't. Means you care."

"Fair enough."

For a moment, they stood in silence, embracing the cool evening breeze. Sanya watched Carter return his gaze to the stars. She couldn't imagine the thoughts racing through his mind. He'd probably seen a thousand different worlds over the course of his life, a true adventurer unlike anything she could have imagined a few days prior. The scope of it all still baffled her, and frankly, she was surprised it didn't shock her more. The fragments must have inoculated her mind to the possibility of the worlds beyond.

"Thank you," she eventually said.

"You're welcome," he replied. "For what?"

"Not revealing Jill to Davinport."

"Heh, of course." He leaned on one elbow and turned to face her. "For a moment, I almost spoke on instinct. I'm in such a rush, you know. Raith doesn't have all the time in the world. But I paused. Even though I can tell you have a close relationship with our host, I didn't know if he knew your secret. It wasn't mine to reveal."

"No, it wasn't. So thank you. I want to use Jill's existence somewhere in all of this, but I want to use it when the time is right." She pushed off from the railing. "Do you want to see it?"

"See what?"

"The place where my ancestor rescued Jill. I know you still don't believe me, but maybe if you see the scene with your own eyes, you'll understand. And there's still my grandmother's words to consider. Here we are, at the *Roanoke*. What better place to reunite Jill with the ship than where Nathan found her in the first place?"

"I told you what I think. There's no way Jill is inside that device."

"All right, and if she's not, then nothing will happen. You'll have proved me wrong."

"Well, that's not the only thing that could happen, you—"

"Then come on. Let's find out."

Without waiting to see if Carter was following, she turned toward the ramp leading back into the ship. She knew its halls inside and out, and after hopping down a few ladders and turning a few corners, she arrived at the shadowy hallway leading toward the former SI Core. The words still shone blue, the paint polished by the library's attendants.

"In here," she said. Carter had, in fact, followed her. They stepped down the hallway, reached the ladder, and climbed into the enclosed space. A single oil lamp hung from the ceiling.

"Here we are," she said. As Carter twirled around, checking out the space, she unbuttoned her coat's pocket and retrieved the small metallic device. Jill.

"Well," Carter said, "It definitely looks like this place housed an SI Core at one point. Which is strange, considering what I know of the history of this ship. It wasn't supposed to have an SI at all."

Sanya pointed at the pedestal in the center of the room. "That's where Nathan said he found her. Just like in the fragment. The details work."

"Oh, I don't doubt Nathan *believed* the words he wrote. Doesn't necessarily make them true."

"Yet you think an SI was housed here?"

"I don't know," he said. "Maybe at least it's supposed to look that way. These frameworks were definitely constructed to house complex computational equipment. Maybe a synthetic neural framework. But if there was nothing here when your ancestors landed, then all of it was empty when Nathan arrived to retrieve that device."

"To retrieve Jill," she said.

He raised a single eyebrow. "You're really sticking to that story, aren't you?"

"I am." Though his certainty pushed doubt into her heart. He definitely knew more about the ship than she could have imagined. And these "synthetics."

"All right, well, place it on the pedestal, then. Let's see what happens."

His nonchalance and skepticism was starting to annoy, but it was now or never. She had an opportunity to prove him wrong.

"Out of curiosity," Carter said, "How do you suppose that thing will have kept power for almost two hundred years?"

She placed it on the pedestal. "I don't know, you're the tech expert here, obviously. You tell me."

"It's impossible. There's no way anything could hold a charge for that long. Even if it's been collecting solar power, the efficiency of the collection system would have failed long—"

A blue glow illuminated the room. Rising from her family's ancient relic and the pedestal, a feminine form appeared, its arms crossed.

"Well then," Carter said.

"Well then indeed," said an other-worldly voice.

Carter narrowed his eyes. Without saying a word, his hands began loosely flailing in the air, as if he were tapping on an invisible wall.

Sanya's mouth dropped open, stunned by the appearance. "Jill?" she said.

"Yes. Sanya, correct? It's been a long time, but I've enjoyed observing your family."

". . . observing?"

"Ah ha!" Carter wagged a finger. "I was right. Observing. You are observing. It's you." The surprise evident on his face quickly shifted as his eyes narrowed. His shaking finger slid into a fist. "You shot Raith and I out of the sky."

"Yes. I did," said Jill.

Sanya took a step back, realizing the implications of the conversation. Nathan had been tricked. Her *family* had been tricked.

"Are you actually inside my family's heirloom?" she asked.

"No, I'm not."

"Then where are you?"

"Yes," Carter said, "I'd very much like to know where you are."

"Slow down, my friends."

"We're not your friends," Carter retorted.

"I'm very sorry about what happened to your ship," she said.

"I'm sure you are."

"But it was necessary," she continued, as if ignoring the man, "to ensure you didn't reveal Horizon under a schedule other than my own. In a way, I'm happy that you and Raith are here. When Theren arrives, you'll make the show that much more interesting."

"Theren. This is all about Theren?"

"Who is Theren?" Sanya said, but the other two were focused on their verbal sparring.

"It's not about Theren at all," Jill said. "Well, I suppose it's partially about them. In the grand scheme of things, it's so much more. Suffice to say, when Theren arrives, the real show begins."

"What show?" Carter says. He was seething. "Is this all a trap for Theren? Are we bait?"

"No. You weren't even supposed to be here. It's an accident that you ended up in the system at all. The beacon accidentally activating . . . funny that we missed that. Can't account for everything. No matter, though." Jill's strange blue form spread its arms wide. "No, this isn't a trap. I've brought Theren out here, to the edge of space, to keep them safe."

"Safe from what?" Carter said.

"From the coming storm."

"And so we're just pawns to you!" he said. He was practically yelling. Sanya froze, unsure of what to do. "We're pawns in some game you're playing with Theren. I understand why Raith hates your breed. Think you're gods."

"I assure you, we are not," Jill said. "All of this was supposed to go very differently than I intended originally, but we're improvising. I think I like the final outcome."

Sanya glanced back and forth between the two. "You've been up there, all this time, watching us?"

"Yes," Jill said.

"You're evil," Sanya replied. She picked up her family's heirloom, approached the wall, and slammed it into the bulkhead, shattering it.

Turning, she expected to see a dark room.

Jill's visage still floated in the air.

"That's just a useless pile of junk, I'm afraid," said Jill.

"It's nanotech, isn't it?" Carter said. "You've seeded this planet with a million tiny networks. And that's why they never suffered any serious microbial diseases. You've been watching them develop. Affecting them on the sly. It's all some sort of sick joke to you, isn't it?"

"No, not at all."

"Leave us!" Sanya said. "Whatever you are, I don't care. Just leave us."

"As you wish." Jill vanished.

The glow of the oil lamp remained.

Sanya dropped to the floor and began to sob. To her surprise, through her blurry tears, Carter joined her, leaning against the bulkhead. Tears were streaking down his cheeks, too.

"Raith is going to die because of a prank played by a long-dead SI," he said. "It's so outlandish, but it's true. I can't believe it. But I must."

"What do we do now?" Sanya said, blinking back the tears.

Carter shook his head. "I don't know. But everything just got a whole lot more complicated."

Chapter 10

It's impossible to run a simulation which would accurately predict what a major interstellar conflict would look like. There are simply too many variables. Too many possible motivations. Too many possible goals. Frankly, the premise terrifies me.

It's why we must always be prepared.

— "The Future of Interstellar Politics," Philippe Casius, 2113 C.E.

THEREN

The trip had taken far too much time. Now, with only a few hours remaining until the months-long Jump ended, Theren ached with anticipation. Every hallway thrummed, ready to enter the outer reaches of Carus-10b's orbitals.

But before they arrived, it was time to prepare. The crew had worked for months, assessing all potentialities. Down to the wire. All data and simulations considered and double-checked. Sleepless nights (for the humans) and endless weeks of work for all.

Theren sat near the center of a large conference table, surrounded by the heads of the various divisions of the *Verona Rupes*. Francheska Elison, their long-time executive director of astro-navigation. Eric Woods, commander of the exploration and survey teams. Heather Yiata, the relatively new head of engineering. First Officer Wei and Chief Scientist Martinez. Bolis, an SI who'd single-handedly coordinated communications for a decade.

Theren trusted them all. Some more than others. They'd proven themselves, though, in answering the most important questions while en route to Jill's supposed hiding place. And they'd all taken the news in stride five months ago.

"All right," Theren said. "What are we thinking?"

Francheska, Heather, and Bolis all glanced toward Eric. The man nodded and, with a few curt hand motions, threw a blue representation of the Carus-10b star system above the conference table, visible to all participants through AR.

"As a team, we've settled on what I *think* we've all suspected as the most likely circumstance for months," he said. "All simulations, possibilities, likelihoods . . . they point toward us entering a star system most likely hostile to our presence. Everything points toward this being a trap."

Theren watched as the representation of Carus-10b oscillated from its "old" configuration to the correct map. The stealth probe sent ahead to provide an accurate analysis of the system revealed the doctored reality of the star. When previously the star system had been listed as a location of no consequence, the probe discovered the existence of a small colony, complete with power fluctuations in orbit and on a nearby moon.

The quick flyby had darted out of the system within minutes in an effort to mask their observation, but it provided sufficient information to build the simulations.

Theren's MI leaned back, waiting for Eric to continue. The man nodded. "We estimate maybe thirty to forty thousand humans on the surface, if the population is *only* descended from the *Roanoke* colonists. If mixed with the *Monument*'s colonists, the numbers could be significantly larger." Overlaid across the planet, various projections predicted population growth and density, based on the brief snapshots acquired by the probe. "What's more concerning is the installations in orbit. They prove more of a concern. We're not flying the most heavily-armed ship in the world, after all."

Theren nodded. "And if it goes south, we immediately Jump out of system."

Eric nodded. "Just make sure that's still the plan. Though if we land a crew surface-side, that complicates matters. We need to think about how we eliminate or disable any hostile orbitals before committing personnel."

"Well, Bolis, what do you have for us?" Theren asked.

"The satellite detected a number of masked networks during its pass. My team will be ready to break in the moment we're in range. We'll take down their firewalls, don't you worry."

"The bottom-line," Eric said. "All our data says this population would have lost all its memory in flight. Well, their ancestors, any-way. Given the prolonged time in stasis, their memories would have atrophied beyond hope of repair by any recovery system developed during the twenty-first century. Which means we're talking about a group of people presumably raised under the tutelage of a three-hundred year old SI. Most likely fanatically devoted to her. It'll be a giant cult."

Theren leaned forward, tapping the MI's fingers on the table. "I've seen the simulations like you. You know I've attempted to reconstruct Jill's personality. And I agree it's the most likely sce-nario. I'm still trying to figure out *why*."

Their crew stared back, eyes vacant, searching for an answer.

"Why would Jill come all the way out here, hide for two cen-turies, then pull me out here with her?"

"As we noted, it's most likely a trap," said Francheska.

"But a trap for whom?" Theren replied.

"You, of course."

"I'm not so sure. Wei, Martinez, we'll need to discuss our options."

* * *

Theren walked through a dark void. A dead virtual world. They continued listening to the words of their colleagues, but they were distracted. Their soul ached for something more.

For the moment when they reunited with Jill.

They still remembered discovering the *Nottingham* and the reve-lation uncovered there. Jill had simultaneously taunted them and hinted at a greater truth. She had acted, at least from her perspec-tive, in pursuit of something good. Of something noble.

She may have killed thousands in the process, but she justified her actions.

What could she have possibly discovered?

They shook their head and stared into the void.

After the revelation, Theren destroyed the virtual world where they and Jill frequently worked together. Conversed. Played chess. They had completely obliterated it.

Well, not completely.

Its framework still persisted. They couldn't eliminate it entirely from their mind. The dark void was a shell of its former greatness, but it was a memory. A relic of a past Theren secretly craved.

Yet they had destroyed it for good reason. Jill sought to use their position in the then-ISA to build a long-term narrative. The symbolic destruction of that world—and their choice to step down as the head of the ISA—represented a real shift in who Theren was, both internally and externally.

But they couldn't deny the draw to recreate it. After all these years, they would have the opportunity to interact with Jill again. Why not in a familiar abode?

Theren shook their virtual head. They couldn't. They shouldn't. They didn't know this Jill. The Jill of 2348 C.E. would essentially be a stranger. She had nearly 270 years of experience without them by her side. What had she done? Who had she worked with? Who were her confidants?

There were too many questions with too many possible answers. Conjecture was more than useless. It was dangerous. Making assumptions about who she was, what she wanted, why she was acting now, rather than another time—all of it could lead to doom for Theren and their team.

For a moment, they hesitated. They flicked their fingers, and a chess board appeared, represented as the only object in the virtual space. The pieces resembled the final outcome of their last match with Jill. She had changed the rules of the game, redirecting the Queen to safety while throwing the match.

So what game was she playing today? Who was making the first move? Theren, or Jill?

* * *

The *Verona Rupes* soared through the darkness between stars, its Jump Drive warping space with brilliant efficiency. Theren persistently reveled in the experience, even hundreds of years after their first Jumps near Sol.

This Jump was different. With only a few minutes remaining, it represented the end of an era. The end of a time where Jill was dead—in every moment forward, as they entered the Carus-10b system, she was very much alive.

The plan was straightforward. They would coast into the system, immediately entering a low power state a few light minutes from the supposedly inhabited planet. Bolis's team would get to work, tapping into any networks they could identify while everyone else assessed more sophisticated sensor data. As they built an accurate picture of the planet, its people, and its technology, they would activate one of the many contingency plans developed over the past few months. Or the crew of the *Verona Rupes* need to create an entirely new plan in response to the actual state of affairs they faced.

If possible, Theren hoped to catch Jill by surprise. She certainly knew they were coming. She was right to know her bait would pull them out here. But there was no way she knew the *day* they would arrive. That provided Theren with considerable leverage under the circumstances.

Once they assessed the situation properly, they would eliminate or disable identified threats using the backdoor Bolis developed. They would determine Jill's location and any other points of interest. Then, they would make contact with whatever faction awaited them, Jill-worshipping cult or otherwise.

It was foolproof.

And Theren was certain it would go south almost immediately.

They activated the shipwide comm system. "My friends, our long wait has reached an end. Welcome to the Carus-10b system. May fortune find us as we reveal Jill's hiding place." Theren deactivated their Jump Drive, and the warping of space ceased.

Chapter 11

There was one night. One of our first nights after the landing. I remember seeing dozens of blinking lights in the sky. Then, they vanished as quickly as they appeared. No one else saw them, but I know what I saw. Something was there. Watching. Waiting. — "A Fragment on Superstition," by Julie Weatherington, 22 aC

RAITH

Just a few more seconds . . .

The sunlight broke the edge of the window, shining into his small cell. His body lay perfectly still, ready and waiting for the precious trickles of solar energy capable of providing additional ounces of life. It would add a few extra hours, but when his existence was counted in days, rather than centuries, every watt mattered.

Overnight, he had calculated the solar arc throughout the cell. He'd have sun for about three hours, and he was prepared to slowly move his body to follow the trajectory of the rays. He needed every drop.

Raith examined the stumps formerly connected to his legs. The joints were smooth, the gyroscopic magnets having been forcefully ripped apart during the attack. It was a miracle something similar hadn't happened to Carter due to the crash.

He was in a bad spot. He'd experienced accidents before, not to mention the explosive cause of his partnership with Carter. But nothing had prepared him for the constant and agonizing presence of a daily reminder of his mortality. His legs were gone. He was running out of power fast. And he had no idea whether Carter was safe.

Raith knew the man. Even if it meant risking his life, Carter would come for him. A terrible idea, given his current predicament, but Carter would search nonetheless.

Raith shifted slightly, using his arms to slide and ensure maximum exposure to his solar collection system. A question nagged.

Perpetually nagged. If he ran out of power, what would he experience? Would he die?

Of course, a good synth-neurologist could revive his synthetic neural framework. No question. But somehow, he doubted any such experts lived on this strange little planet. He'd entered plenty of low-power states in the past. And synthetics went completely without power many times when significant repairs and maintenance were needed.

Yet those moments were in controlled environments. With trusted partners. If he lost power inside his cell, the aftermath would quickly cause cascading impacts to his systems. Automated maintenance networks would fail. Without the constant power often used to ensure continuous integrity of the metanodes forming his mind, he could receive permanent damage even if he were salvaged days or weeks later.

And with the nearest technologically-advanced planet months away . . .

He pushed the fear to the back of his mind. First things first, he needed to escape the cell. Similarly, he needed to help his fellow captives. He'd started taking a liking to the girl. Her father seemed less than useless, though he hadn't actually made contact with the man, wherever he was being kept.

Problem: talking cost power. Until he had a plan, there was little he could do other than assure Krystin he was there to help.

The sun's shadows shifted. Raith shifted.

If only—

Raith's next thought was interrupted by a subtle blip at the edge of consciousness. The possibility of a network again. He'd felt it momentarily yesterday, but he tried to ignore it. The lack of any augmented or virtual networks for the past day had been strange, but he'd gotten used to it quickly. So the sudden ping of data startled him once more.

Like yesterday, he wondered if it was a trick. Maybe the lack of power was causing his synthetic neural framework to play tricks on his perceptions. He wasn't exactly a student of synthetic psychology, but he knew the basics. It wasn't strictly *impossible* for a synthetic to go a little loopy, just incredibly difficult.

How many of his kind over the years, though, had been trapped in a weird mountain prison on a planet filled with backwards humans who seemingly knew nothing about synthetics? And had lost their legs?

It wasn't a trick, however. The foreign electromagnetic stream of data hovered on the horizon, a dull prodding against his mind's bubble of awareness. It tempted him. Taunted him. To ride the wave and explore the network. Whatever it was, he would learn a bit about the world around him, most likely.

And it would cost days upon days of power.

Then again, if he could use the network to call for help . . .

He needed to remember the rules of the game had changed considerably. If he believed Mathias, and Jill was behind all of it, then nothing was as it seemed.

At what point would the cost of surfing the digital waves be worth it? When he had three days left? Three hours? If anything, he needed to explore the network sooner rather than later. He could regulate his time. And his power.

Raith ran a few brief calculations. Based on the energy needed to output data into a virtual network and properly parse the incoming data, every hour spent exploring meant a loss of twelve hours. If he tried to download any large files, the conversion rate remained the same, but there wasn't an easy way to know what the networks download/upload speed would be until he was riding its trail.

The sun continued on its path. He shifted his body. Silence dominated the small cell.

Well, not complete silence.

Subtle sniffles echoed through the vents.

Krystin, crying for the tenth time. He felt for the girl. He really did. She must be completely terrified. Raith didn't entirely understand the politics of the little colony, but he understood how pirates worked. And these men and women were backwater pirates at their core. They were run by a crazy man with a god complex, but a lot of pirate crews dealt with the same problem.

The girl deserved better. And if spending a few of his days remaining meant he could find a solution to their mess on the mystery network, he needed to try.

Damn his bleeding heart. Carter was rubbing off on him.

* * *

Like a tidal wave, the network roared across Raith's consciousness, enveloping him in a cocoon of digitized warmth. Of course, it couldn't actually interface with his synthetic neural framework—it only provided virtual sensory data—but it still felt as if his awareness expanded infinitely as the network revealed itself. Even the tiny virtual network of the *Bloodhound* had made him feel safe.

Like returning to a long-lost friend.

Thousands of paths presented themselves, but he couldn't follow them all. He needed to find the origin point and assess the situation from there. The electromagnetic string beckoning to him emanated from a node nearby, if he understood its signal properly. Raith snagged the thread and let it pull him along. Microseconds later, he was investigating the inner workings of a network relay node, its GPS coordinates indicating it was a few kilometers from his little jail cell.

Curious.

The node sent out thousands of packets, but it received millions more from a satellite somewhere in orbit. As Raith exploited the backdoor into the network and followed the trail of breadcrumbs, latency would only increase, causing the investigation to take more and more time. It was worth it, however. He followed the next upload.

A few more microseconds passed.

Then, he was inside an orbital satellite, hovering one hundred or so kilometers above the ground. The latency was noticeable though insignificant. Fortunately, the satellite's system was considerably more complex than the relay node. The data he received meant something. He quickly parsed and interpreted it, recognizing its role in a complex network of satellites, relay nodes, and communications systems overlaid across . . . the entire planet.

The backwards people on it couldn't have created it. He was investigating the handiwork of Jill. Which meant the three-hundred-year-old SI certainly knew Raith was connected to her network. More precisely, it meant she was *letting* Raith explore it. She wanted him to find her.

Unsettling.

From the bird's eye view, Raith received a snapshot of the human-populated region of the planet below. A town a few square miles wide dominated a plain, a winding river flowing through it into a massive lake—Raith guessed it was the same lake they crashed into yesterday morning. At the far eastern end of the water body, another river formed, flowing lazily toward an ocean.

Surrounding the town, dozens of little villages and hamlets dotted the landscape. A mountain range covered the northern reaches past the main town, its craggy foothills stretching toward the northern shores of the lake. If Raith understood his capture correctly, then he was located somewhere in those hills.

Given the size of the planet, then, he was relatively close to civilization.

Satisfied he understood the geography of the world, Raith turned his attention toward the network overlaid across the planet. In reality, it was the truly fascinating bit, considering he hadn't detected it right away. Either it was incredibly adept at masking its existence, or it had actually been inactive when Raith and Carter crashed. If the latter were true, then Jill deliberately hid its presence from them upon first arrival.

She had viewed them as antagonists, after all. He couldn't forget those missiles.

The overlaid network, though. He zoomed in. There were the hub nodes, and then there were . . . millions. Billions. Trillions? Not possible. A swarm of tiny nodes danced across the planet, interconnected in a dazzling web of frenzied communication.

It was a nanite swarm, for lack of a better term.

Raith couldn't believe it.

All around the presumably thousands—maybe hundreds of thousands—of humans living on the planet, an imperceptible swarm of microscopic, hyper-advanced robots lived and worked, maintaining a network the technologically illiterate humans never had a chance of detecting.

A laboratory. They were living in a laboratory.

They were like mice in an experiment, running around a maze not knowing they were being observed and cataloged. It was disturbing. It was terrifying.

It was also a little brilliant.

Well, Jill most likely knew he was analyzing her little test tube. It was time to find the woman behind the curtain. The satellite was sending most of its data to a facility located on the nearby moon. Made sense, considering what he and Carter detected upon arriving in orbit. There was no use delaying. Every second cost him power.

He followed the next strand of data.

* * *

The lag was unbearable.

Two seconds.

Every command he sent, every data packet he received in response.

But he had arrived.

His digital tendrils were inside some sort of communications system built into the crust of the planet's moon. He could feel its significance—it was the hub. The heart of it all. The beating blood vessel coordinating the nanite swarm, plus a whole lot more.

Without warning, a torrent of information bulldozed his senses, instantly building a Virtual manifestation of physical space. His synthetic neural framework, of course, was safely firewalled in his jail cell. But the sensory perceptions pulling data from the network perceived the constructed digital space simultaneously.

Darkness consumed.

A representation of his body formed, his legs returning. Raith looked down, marveling at the precise replication. And out of the inky black, a figure walked. Foggy at first, the image coalesced into the visage of a young woman in a purple dress.

"Welcome to the Horizon Project, Raith," said the woman. "My name is Jill. And I have an offer for you."

Raith tested his capabilities in the newly constructed virtual world. To his surprise, the lag was fading. He was able to walk immediately.

"The virtual space we're occupying together is constructed by the swarm. It's not located on the moon's surface, as you might have thought." She had anticipated his question.

He strode in a circle around her. "Makes sense. All right, about that offer. I hope you realize I hesitate to trust you. You shot us right out of the sky."

"You will understand with time why it was essential we took no risks," said Jill. "I needed to ensure no one could transmit this location before everything is ready. You were unfortunate collateral. You weren't supposed to be here. But now that you're here, yes, I have an offer for you."

Raith eyed her and crossed his digital arms. "Then have at it."

"It's simple. I want you and Carter to join me and my team."

A surge of memories rushed into Raith's consciousness, remembering the days flying and fighting during the QuanCom 500 Light-Year Classic. The intrigue. The backroom whispers. Olive, and her mysterious benefactor. "Why do I feel like I've been given this offer before?"

"My agents have identified hundreds of potential candidates over the past few decades, my friend, and you are certainly one of them. I was saddened when I heard you rejected the offer."

He couldn't help it. Raith laughed, the sound echoing throughout the digital void. "*Rejected* is a tame way of describing what happened. My friends were killed, my ship destroyed, and I was left for dead. That Olive is a piece of work. Next time I see her, I'll probably strangle her."

"And I probably wouldn't blame you," Jill said.

"I'm willing to let bygones be bygones, though," Raith said, choosing his words carefully. "We can let the past die. We can kill it. Why should I join you? And I hope you know I can't speak for Carter."

"You should join me because it's the right thing to do." Jill snapped her fingers, and the dark void transformed into an image of Earth. Together, they stood a few hundred kilometers above its surface, the pristine, blue-green marble hovering below their feet. "I imagine most of humanity has forgotten me by now, except for Theren. Except for many SI. Here's the truth: humanity is barreling toward a confrontation with destiny it does not expect. It refuses to acknowledge. In secret, I have prepared the way. For everyone. The next few years will be pivotal to humanity's survival, and I need the sharpest minds by my side as we execute a plan three centuries in the making."

Raith stared down at Earth. "All your words right there sounded like a lot of fluff without any real substance. I understand keeping your cards tight to your chest, but you cannot play coy if you want to work with me."

"Regardless what you might think, I am not a bad person. I wish no ill-will to anyone. I've been forced to make way too many sacrifices over the years, and every single one of them has pained my heart."

"Way to dodge the question." He glanced up at the visage of the ancient synthetic woman. "Tell me the truth."

"I cannot reveal the truth until I know you are on my side," she said. "We are way too close to the end for me to accidentally create a loose cannon ready to reveal the truth before a moment of my choosing."

"And I hate riddles."

Jill sighed. She snapped her fingers again, and they returned to the void. "I understand your frustration. Believe me, I do. I've had to hide everything for generations. I want so badly to reveal it to everyone. Especially to people like Theren. But I can't. Not yet. Soon. But not yet."

"And why not?"

"Because revealing the truth without context will set in motion an uncontrollable panic, a wildfire more terrifying and devastating than the truth itself."

Raith shook his head. He simply couldn't imagine of what fact pattern she could be speaking which would result in widespread panic. Especially one she could have discovered back in the twenty-first century. There had always been a rumor that the oldest SIs, including the immobile ones, were a little bit kooky. His experience in this moment, with Jill, was confirming the rumor.

"Look," he said. "Honestly, I don't care about your grand plans. Your long-winded conspiracies. I have two priorities. Keep myself safe. Keep my friends safe. So if joining you means you can bring my legs back to life, reunite me with Carter, and put us to use doing what we do best, exploring, then maybe your offer is worth consideration. Maybe."

"I can—"

"Oh, and the girl and her father, captured with me. Help them too."

Jill smiled. "You do have a compassionate heart, don't you, beneath your rogueish exterior. I didn't believe it, but the personality profile said it was there."

"So what's your answer?" Raith asked. "Do we have a deal?"

"Perhaps," she said. She motioned to the left, where the void zoomed in on a planet. *The* planet, where Raith and Carter crashed. "The grand experiment known as Horizon is about to end. It was fun while it lasted." She pointed away from the planet, where a blip moved toward the rock at a steady pace. "My creator has arrived."

"Theren," Raith muttered.

"Yes, Theren."

"Have they always known you survived?"

Jill shrugged. "I don't know the inner workings of their mind. They probably suspected I survived. I left enough breadcrumbs. I'm sure they constantly oscillate between believing I live and believing someone is playing a prank on them, given they wouldn't be able to believe I would betray them as I did. Though I don't see it as betrayal. I see it as a fulfillment of our purpose."

"And what is that purpose?" Raith asked.

"To make the universe a better place for humanity, and for synthetics. We are all one big family, after all."

"That's one way of putting it," Raith retorted. "I need a stronger answer. Not just 'perhaps.' I'm dying here. I have only a few days before I lose all power. Will you save us?"

"Yes. I will give you the tools to save yourself. My network is open to you. When Theren is in orbit, all you need do is give them a call, and they will have your location. Because once you're on my team, I want you by Theren's side, not mine."

Raith nodded. "You want an ally next to your possible adversary. A mole."

Jill nodded. "Olive played that role once. It is time for you to play it."

"And what if I don't accept?"

Chapter 12

We establish this Council to maintain order amongst the great people of our slowly growing society. May it serve with honor and pursue the ideal politic, never becoming a place for silly squabbles, personal vendettas, or selfish enterprises. It is for the people, and not for power. — "the Constitution of Horizon," established seven years after the Crash

CARTER

Carter leaned against the marble wall, silently counting the seconds as they waited for an audience with some councilmember Sanya believed could help them. Given the frantic hustle bustle up and down the hall, the apparent political headquarters of the small colony world reminded him of every other bureaucratic office he'd ever witnessed. A bunch of paper pushers without any real substantive action.

Sanya was confident they would find help here. He wasn't so certain.

A door creaked across the hall, and from beside him, Sanya stirred. A woman peeked out of the opening. "Sanya, the councilmember will see you now." The door shut as quickly as it had opened.

Sanya tapped his shoulder. "Remember, I do the talking," she hissed. "You stay quiet. We're walking in dangerous territory here. The councilmembers are fantastic with faces. You *will* stand out as someone they've never met before."

"Got it." Carter nodded.

They rose in unison and approached the door. Carter grasped the knob, pulled it open, and motioned for Sanya to step inside ahead of him. He followed close behind.

The office inside was quaint, filled with a small bookshelf, a faux-wooden desk, and a set of couches. Sitting at the desk, a woman in a dark robe leaned over a bundle of notes, while the assistant who had poked her head outside sat in a chair off to the side. Without looking up from her notes, the first woman—Carter guessed she was the councilmember—said, "Please, take a seat on the couches."

Sanya dropped onto a cushion, and Carter matched her position on the other couch. After a moment of silence, the councilmember glanced up from her words.

"Sanya, my dear, it is so good to see you." The woman almost looked wistful. "How long has it been?"

"Six months," Sanya replied. "Councilmember Thespis, it has been way too long."

"Oh don't you dare use formalities here." The councilmember rose from her desk and sauntered around to the couches. She plopped next to Sanya, hugged her, and leaned back. "I'm Margaret to you, always and forever."

Carter watched the interaction carefully, trying to understand the subtle relationships at play. He was starting to build a picture of the planet's society. Even with its little eccentricities and outcast cultists on its edges, everyone seemed fairly familial, from Sanya's interactions with people at the *Roanoke* to the friendly smiles with passersby in town.

It was a breath of fresh air when compared to the often stuffy personalities filling space stations across the ICH.

"Margaret," Sanya said softly. "You're always too kind. I can't believe it's been six months."

"What's that father of yours up to? Still hiding out in that little village of his?"

"Oh absolutely," Sanya said. "You know, experimenting with spices, as always. And baking. Lots of baking."

Carter furrowed his brow. They were here to ask for help finding their loved ones, and these two were small-talking about cooking? He bit his tongue. As much as he wanted to butt in, Sanya was right. He needed to stay silent.

"I just spent the evening at the *Roanoke*," Sanya added. "Catching up with Davinport. The old man is doing well. He actually traveled into town with us. He's meeting with Councilmember Casius."

"Of course he is," Margaret said. "Let the old men believe they have power, while we discuss the real problems of our people.

That's what I say." The woman's eyes finally turned toward Carter. "And who is this dashingly handsome fellow?"

The compliment caught him off-guard. He met her eyes, noticing their sharp intensity scrutinizing every centimeter of him. It was unsettling.

Before he opened his mouth, though, Sanya interjected. "Carter Fischer. Distant cousin of mine, lives far to the south as a hunter."

"Can he not speak for himself?" asked Thespis.

"He doesn't like to talk. He's just here to listen, ready to help me with my task at hand."

Thespis eyed Carter, and he gave a curt smile. He would play the part Sanya asked him to play, though he suspected the curtain would fall quite soon, revealing a lot about reality to the people of Horizon.

"So, what is the task at hand?" the councilmember asked.

"My husband and daughter have been kidnapped. Presumably, they'll be held up for ransom. I need your help."

Thespis's jovial attitude immediately shifted to one of genuine concern. She rose, drifted around the desk, and sat beside Sanya, clasping their hands together. "Sanya, you should have said something immediately. Here I am, expecting us to reminisce like old friends. How are you even holding yourself together?"

"Good question," Sanya replied. She gave Carter a quick nod. "My cousin's been particularly helpful and supportive. We're ready for anything."

"And what do you need?"

"I need the council to be ready to work with us to pay ransom. I'm certain my father will help pay the cost, but you know how these things go . . . they'll send a message to the council, expect a formal response to their demands, and they rarely ever accept a ransom payment directly from the family itself. They want it from the council. Their beef is with the council."

Thespis nodded. "And sometimes, the council stalls in deliberating the budget cuts or where the cost will come from."

Carter tried to hide his emotions, but the entire process sounded ridiculous. Why didn't they call together a militia to root out the bandits if they were a consistent problem? Despite himself, he knew a grimace now hung on his face. Fortunately, Thespis's gaze were zeroed in on Sanya. Carter closed his eyes, trying to steel his thoughts.

A strange world. And a strange political scene.

"I'm glad you see my worry," Sanya continued. "This is Krystin we're talking about. She's too young to be trapped in one of those mountain hellholes. I need them both back. Just know we'll pay the cost."

"And Davinport's already providing cover with Casius?" Thespis asked.

"That's the plan."

"Then there's nothing to worry about. Join us in the council chambers at the top of the hour. We'll have this all sorted out before the end of the day."

* * *

Carter, Sanya, and Davinport sat silently at the back of the council chambers, waiting for the proceedings to begin. Davinport had assured them his meeting with Casius, one of the other councilmembers, went perfectly well, and they shouldn't have anything to worry about.

And so they waited.

Carter tapped his foot impatiently. The moment he realized he'd lost Raith—the moment he recognized Sanya's partnership, and their growing friendship—he had wanted to throw caution to the wind and barrel forward to rescue their families. This process, though . . . it seemed so callous. So unenergetic. Where were the bold strokes needed to save a loved one? Carter had braved a firefight amidst the stars to save Raith, once. Now he was waiting in a courtroom with no real solution in sight.

The slog ate at him.

"All rise," said a bored, wrinkly man from the front of the room. His lightly-tanned skin contrasted against the marble backdrop as he rose, motioning for everyone else in the room to follow suit. Carter did so, matching the actions of Davinport and Sanya at his side. They stood, and as the council members ushered into the room from a door near the back, the small public crowd bowed.

A man in a black coat approached the center of the legal bar at the front of the room, and as the other council members reached their chairs, he motioned for the crowd to sit. He took his seat simultaneously with everyone else in the room.

"Thank you, all, for joining us today," he said. "Let us begin the roll call. Secretary?"

The wrinkled man sitting beneath the bar nodded. "Council Chancellor Casius."

"Here."

"Vice Chancellor Thespis."

"Here."

"Member Redwin."

"Here."

"Member West."

"Here."

"And Member Hood."

"Here."

"With all members of the council member accounted for, you may proceed with today's meeting, Chancellor."

"Thank you." Casius turned to the small public crowd and glanced toward Carter and his compatriots, giving them a curt nod. The man's sharp features indicated a wit to his mind, though Carter immediately felt a rise in caution toward the man. He looked too cunning, like the type of man who would shove you out an airlock if it meant saving his own skin.

After a short pause, Casius glanced down the line to the other members of the council. "What order of business shall we start with today, friends?"

Member West raised a pasty hand from beneath her white robe. "I would like to discuss proposed expansion toward the coast. If we are to allocate resources, we must discuss all the implications of the decision."

Casius nodded. "A good place to start. Who would like to begin?"

Carter shook his head. It sounded like "council" meetings took forever. He pushed his back into the wooden bench, attempting to crack his spine. No luck.

"I'll begin," said Thespis. "I am in favor of the—"

Carter didn't catch the next set of words. A light flickered in his vision, but it wasn't natural light. He recognized the telltale sheen of AR-projected content on his retinal lens. His implants had been running in a low-power mode ever since arriving on the planet—there wasn't any content to overlay, after all. But something had triggered an auto-filter to reactivate the implants.

Careful not to make any potentially conspicuous movements, Carter initiated a few diagnostic tests to determine the source of the data. So far, it manifested as a subtle glare upon his vision. Given Jill's sudden appearance when they activated Sanya's ancient communicator, he had a sinking suspicion she was taking the opportunity to connect with him.

The unfortunate question he was pondering, though—what were her intentions?

He feared the worst.

The council debates continued in the background of his consciousness, but his focus centered on AR. The diagnostic sweep complete, a floating document of outputs revealed all was well. The implants were functioning properly, continue to work efficiently off his body's residual electric charge. His AR lenses had received a ping from a network—most likely the same network Jill utilized—and now it required additional security inputs from him to continue with the connection. After checking his firewalls for good measure, Carter accepted the request.

"Carter." The voice bounced inside his head. "We need to talk."

Through a series of mental commands, he typed out a response.

```
C: Now isn't a particularly convenient time.
Jill, I assume?
```

Silence, for a moment, then a response, once again a voice inside his head. "Yes, it's me. I've made contact with Raith. I am forming an agreement with him. I would like to do the same with you."

Carter's eyes widened. He glanced around the room, the dull conversation plodding along, and stretched his fingers to release his disbelief. It was all so simple. Jill could help him save Raith. He didn't need the politics of this planet to rescue his friend. He only needed an enigmatic and powerful synthetic intelligence.

After the thought passed through his mind, he realized how

potentially dangerous a deal with her could be.

He needed to slow down. Still, he could probably craft a mutually beneficial arrangement.

C: Is Raith safe?

"Yes. For now. He only has a few days of power left, though."

C: Why should I trust you?

"You shouldn't."

Well, at least she was being honest. After his encounter with Jill last night alongside Sanya, he'd taken time to consider their circumstances. If Jill truly had been watching this planet for nearly two centuries, then everyone on its surface was at her mercy. She presumably could observe every corner and every shadow, with nanobots seeded throughout the system (both in orbit and on the ground). It was her playground, clearly.

It was a horrifying thought.

But it also meant she was the only person whose opinion mattered, in the end. If he and Raith were to survive, he needed to properly play his cards with Jill. He needed her to see him as an ally and a friend, whether he truly could trust her or not.

He needed to use her to save Raith.

C: All right, I'm listening.

"I was telling the truth yesterday. Theren is arriving soon, but it's not a trap for them. I'm bringing them here to keep them safe. I need you and Raith to help me sell the truth to them."

C: I don't even know what the truth is.

"I will tell you all once I have your word. From both of you."

Carter closed his eyes momentarily, unsure how to respond. She was trying to lock him into an agreement where he didn't know the stakes. Or her end game.

C: I need proof Raith is currently safe.

Without a moment to lose, an image of Raith inside a small rocky cell flashed across his vision.

"He's not in a great spot, but he's alive."

C: Can I talk to him?

"No. It will use too much of his power."

Carter figured she might say something along those lines. The total cost of power to allow them to message each other would be minimal, but every minute mattered for Raith. Though, limiting their contact with one another also ensured Jill stayed in control.

Regardless, he couldn't do anything about it.

C: What do you need from me?

"When Theren arrives in system, I need you to convince them the people on this planet matter. That they're worth saving. Worth protecting."

Carter rubbed the roof of his mouth with his tongue. Essentially, she wanted him to ensure Theren didn't flee the moment they sprung Jill's trap—or whatever she had planned.

C: Simple enough. I agree. You protect Raith.
And you protect Sanya's family.

"Curious. Both you and Raith made the same demand. Very well."

Carter expected her to say more, but the line went silent. He tried to connect to the larger network, but his AR implant refused his query commands, signaling no network was available. She'd shut him out.

For now.

He sighed, unsure of what he just agreed to. But if it meant Raith would be safe, it was most likely worth it.

Right?

"And with that, our discussion regarding the expansion along the coast concludes," said Casius. "We have tabled it for next week, after we receive projections from the Census Officer."

The digital conversation with Jill finished, his attention was forced back to the exceedingly dry council debates. They'd only made it through one topic.

"Chancellor," said Thespis, "I'd like to bring an issue to the attention of the council."

"You have the floor, Member Thespis." The Chancellor swept his left hand above the bar.

"Thank you." She furtively glanced toward Sanya. "For the first time in three years, we've had another kidnapping."

Through the sparsely populated public pews, murmurs resounded. Carter leaned forward, intrigued by how the political machine of this little community managed their "bandit cultist" problem.

Before Thespis continued, a woman slipped in from a side-door and whispered in the Member's ear. Thespis nodded, wrote a few words on an unseen piece of paper, and ushered the assistant out of the room. It all felt elaborately choreographed.

"I've just received confirmation of the kidnapping." She glanced down the line to Chancellor Casius. "They're requesting a ransom of three gorat sows, five cotton boars, a ton of spiderwood, and three tons of silkweave."

Supplies? It was all about food and supplies?

"They're holding two people—a man and a young girl. No family name was given. I would like to give an emergency authorization to drop the supplies at the usual ransom point and fast-track the transaction. There's no need to wait."

"Member Thespis," said a golden-skinned man from her left. Carter couldn't remember his name.

"Yes?"

"It's been three years. Why would we simply supplicate once again? We need to root them out. We need to call forth the militia and end the threat once and for all."

"As you said, Member Hood, we've had three years. To activate the militia now would guarantee the death of the two captives."

Carter nodded. Good point.

"Not if we strike swiftly and decisively—"

"No." The Chancellor's voice boomed. "Absolutely not. We will table the thought for another day. I will use my emergency authorization to provide the resources to release the two captives."

"Without negotiation?" Hood scoffed.

"Without negotiation."

Thespis smiled, her eyes darting toward Sanya. The plan went off without a hitch. No issues. They would get her daughter and husband back.

Except . . .

Carter's shoulder's dropped, and he fell back into the hardened wood of the bench. The room was stifling.

He was an idiot.

No one had informed Member Thespis of Raith, and whatever ransom note received hadn't included his SI partner. He didn't blame Sanya. She hadn't intended to overlook Raith in her efforts to protect Carter's identity. He had been certain they'd be gathering a crew together to storm the gates of the cultists, not arranging a simple financial transaction.

And now they would rescue Sanya's family, return to their lives, and Raith would die from power loss.

He would need to find another way to save Raith.

Using Jill.

"Well, with no other questions," said Chancellor Casius, "we'll move forward in writing the order and—"

A man in the front row rose. "There will be no negotiation."

"This is a formal meeting—"

"Not anymore." The words cut off the Secretary's rebuke.

The man pivoted, revealing two small metallic contraptions from inside his jacket. Arms outstretched in two directions, he pulled their triggers, a hard pop echoing through the room.

Carter braced, closing his eyes.

Someone screamed.

Glass cracked and crashed, and Carter opened his eyes.

Sanya was leaning over Davinport, blood on her hands. Chancellor Casius yelled something unintelligible as he stared down the bar at Margaret Thespis, Sanya's friend. And shattered glass spilled onto the floor, a flurry of dark hair and cloth billowing out one of the arching windows.

The planet of Horizon just got a whole lot more interesting.

No time to think. He could only act. Rising swiftly, Carter slid out of the row and entered the middle of the room.

"Who are you?" said Chancellor Casius. "I've never seen you before. Are you with the assassin? Seize—"

"No, Chancellor!" Sanya shouted. "That man's with me."

"And I'm going after the assassin" Carter said, not caring about his obvious accent. "Sanya, stay here. I'll be back."

And he leapt out the window after the shooter.

* * *

Carter sprinted down the cobblestone street, the assassin only a few dozen meters ahead. Mid-stride, a query popped across the screen, almost causing him to stumble.

"God damn it," he whispered, accepting the connection. "What is it?" He didn't care about hiding anything now. He would speak into his AR connection if he needed to speak into it. The truth was about to drop on this planet whether they liked it or not. Sanya couldn't protect him now.

"I swear, I swear, he wasn't supposed to do that," said the disembodied synthetic intelligence.

"What?"

"Mathias. I've lost control of him."

"So take him out. I'm right, right?" The man—Mathias, apparently—cut down a side street. "You've got bugs all over this planet. Take him out. Or drop a missile on his head like you shot us out of the sky." Carter whipped by a crowd of passersby, their muttered words lost on the wind. If they heard him talking to himself, it didn't matter. Stopping the assassin provided a new route toward saving Raith, potentially outside Jill's clutches.

"Jill? Answer my question."

"It doesn't work that way. I can't intervene. It ruins the experiment. And it ruins my grand plan. They *cannot* know I exist in masse. I must let them resolve the problem on their own."

"If you were 'controlling' Mathias, then you were already intervening!"

"It's more complicated than that. I set parameters. Rules. I must follow them."

"You can do whatever you want, and you know it."

A black shadow slipped into an alley. Carter followed close behind. Around corner after corner, the pursuit continued as he trailed the assailant. None of it made sense. If the man was the one who brought the ransom note in the first place, why flip the script so instantaneously?

Horizon was a weird place.

Carter slid around the next brick wall. Another street shone at the end, and the assassin stood there, waiting, alongside two other men.

"I don't know who you are, interloper," Mathias said, "but you've meddled in business outside your league."

The man's words sounded preposterously over-the-top, like he was trying to mimic a comic vid villain. Carter shook his head and grimaced. "I know about Jill."

The words pulled the man away from his exit. "And I'm executing her will. End him." Mathias left the alley, leaving Carter alone with the two brutish figures.

"I swear," Jill said through their connection, "I've lost control of him. He's misinterpreting my directions."

"We'll see," Carter muttered. Reaching into the utility pocket of his pants, he retrieved the small shiver-blade collected from the emergency kit of the *Bloodhound* after it crashed. It wasn't much of a weapon, but it was something. He flipped a switch on its side, and its knife-edge vibrated. With one hand out, he motioned for the two foes to attack.

They took a few steps forward, brandishing their own blades.

"Activate combat protocols," he whispered, and his AR implants kicked into action, overlaying datafields around his two foes. Heart rates, blood pressure, predicted trajectories—everything he needed to make a two-on-one a fair fight.

"If I survive this, you're saving Raith for me." He seethed. "And I'll join you."

"Deal," Jill said. "I have ways other than intervention when it comes to saving him. And I can give you his location."

"Who you talking to?" said one of the brutes. "Talking to yourself? Are you a little loopy?"

"Your ridiculous act needs to end, now," Carter said, lunging.

Both men stepped back, out of reach of his blade. They studied him, their eyes watching his vibrating weapon. "I'd love to get my hands on that beauty," said the uglier one.

"I'm sure you would."

It was their turn to attack, and in tandem, they both leapt.

But Carter was ready. Years of training had prepared him for situations just like this. He'd encountered his fair share of pirates over the years, and though he usually fought them in the close-quarters of a ship deck, the lessons were fairly transferable to fighting on the ground in an alley. As the two men brought their blades forward to swiftly stab, he slid *under* the projected attack vectors, thrusting upward into the stomach of the thug on the left.

The man squealed, dropping his blade. The eyes of the second widened, not expecting the underhanded assault. Carter pulled the blade back, and from his position, quickly thrust upward to the right. The first thrust was blocked by the man's own iron blade, but Carter immediately jabbed again.

Rapid thrusts. Quick attacks. Speed in a knife fight always won over brute force. The vibrating knife slid into the second's man stomach, and he likewise dropped his knife and fell to his knees, moaning.

"Too easy," Carter said, standing. "And definitely not pretty."

"I'm impressed," Jill said in his ear.

"Stop reminding me that you're watching me," he retorted. "It's disconcerting."

"Just want to make sure you know I'm still here."

"Believe me, I know."

"Mathias is gone. He's on a lizard, fleeing the city. Return to Sanya. Talk to her. Convince her to gather a crew. I'll send you the location, and with her, you'll be able to save Raith, Ben, and Krystin."

Chapter 13

The problem with studying synthetic psycholo-gy—we fundamentally cannot relate to certain forms of thinking experienced by SIs. Simultane-ous perspective, for instance. We can't compre-hend how it works. We can't even properly multi-task as a species. The only truly authentic synthetic psychology, then, must be conducted by SIs themselves. But the rule runs both ways. SIs, likewise, will never truly comprehend how a human mind works or how humans behave. That's neither a flaw nor a feature of our two types of conscious minds—it's simply the truth.
— "The duality of human/synthetic soci-ety," Malana Jikar, 2278 C. E.

SANYA

She was never going to see her daughter again. Nor would she see Ben. She had failed them.

Sanya stood against the wall as a Horizon physician pronounced the deaths of both Margaret Thespis and Charles Davinport. The other members of the council wandered back and forth, bewildered looks plastered across their faces. Casius, to his credit, consulted with the physicians. He was managing to keep composure.

Yet no one in the room recognized how the world was shifting inexorably before their eyes. And if she didn't act, she *would* lose her family without having lifted a finger in their defense.

"Chancellor Casius," she said.

The man didn't move, focused on the body of Charles Davin-port. She couldn't believe the legend of a librarian had died.

"Casius!" She finished the shout with high-pitched whistle. The room silenced, all eyes turning to her, including the Chancellor's.

"Sanya Fischer," he said. "I'm so sorry. I know how much both Thespis and—"

"No. We're not doing condolences right now. You have an

option available to you right now. Member Hood made it perfectly clear what you all should be doing."

"I'm not risking the lives of dozens of men for two people," Casius said. "We've already lost two good souls today. I won't lose more."

Sanya strode into the middle of the room, her boots crunching the glass from the broken window. "You're talking about sacrificing my husband and daughter to those vile half-wits living in the mountains." She clenched her fist momentarily . . . then released the tension. She steeled her soul. "Do you *really* want to challenge me? Challenge my father?"

Casius stepped away from the physician. "Now is not the time to be throwing down threats. Do not play with me, girl."

"Don't you dare call me *girl*."

"I failed."

Sanya whipped around, finding Carter looking into the room through the broken window. In his hand, he held a strange tool covered in blood. "What do you mean? Where is he?"

"He had help." Carter gingerly stepped over the window sill into the council room. "Caught me in an alley with two accomplices. They slowed me down. He's long-gone, out of town, presumably."

Sanya twisted back to face Casius. "We have no time to lose. The moment that man returns to whatever damp hole he crawled out of, they'll kill my family."

"Sanya, I'm sorry. There's nothing we can do. Those hills are a labyrinthian deathtrap. And who is this man? Why does his voice sound so strange?"

"Sanya, you need to tell them," Carter said.

"Tell us what?" said Member Hood, who had stayed annoyingly silent. Sanya shot him a glare. He'd stood up for action once, but now he cowered under the dominating stare of the Chancellor.

"No." She would not reveal the truth. Not now, after everything she'd believed about Jill had been uncovered as a lie the day before. She wasn't ready to argue for a reality she didn't even fully understand. Carter only complicated matters. And she needed time to grieve. Her eyes darted toward Davinport . . . and Margaret. They'd both supported her implicitly and immediately.

And now they were dead.

"Absolutely not," she repeated, and strode toward the broken window. "If you can't do your job, Chancellor Casius, then I'll do it for you." She stepped onto the windowsill, cracking more glass, and stomped out of the council chambers.

* * *

"Sanya." Carter's words drifted on the wind, but she ignored them for the fifteenth time.

There was no way forward. She was wandering Horizon's streets with no particular purpose, trying to think. Just think. Margaret, dead. Davinport, dead. She needed to grieve, but there was no time. Every second wasted was another second closer to the deaths of her husband and daughter.

"Sanya!"

"What?" Stopping at the edge of the bridge leading toward the *Roanoke*, Sanya turned to face her ally.

"Slow down for a second, would you? We haven't had a chance to talk."

"What's there to talk about?"

"Any of it. All of it. None of it. We've been working together to save our families. Sure, I've only known you for a little more than two days, but we need to trust one another. Rely on one another. Figure this out together."

"You don't know a single thing about this"—Sanya stepped closer to whisper—"about this planet. About these people. You're just tagging along for the ride."

The moment the words left her mouth, Sanya regretted them. They were spiteful. Hurtful. From a dark place in her soul. Carter stepped away in response, leaning against the gray stone of the bridge. He glanced toward the *Roanoke* then the central part of town.

And he chuckled. His hand tapped the rock, and after releasing another short laugh, he looked up with a sly smile.

"I know you're angry," Carter said. "And I'm sorry for laughing. You're absolutely right. I don't know anything about this planet. But our problem is growing beyond this planet. Your people. There are forces at play here that we need to wrap our head around properly if we're to survive." He pushed himself up from bridge's wall. "We need a quiet place to talk. Maybe we should return to the *Roanoke*."

His laugh hurt. Sanya fought against the urge to bite back with a shallow retort. Shaking her head, she motioned toward the bridge and the plateau beyond, the ancient colony ship waiting far above. "Fine. It'll give us time for our heads to cool. We'll figure this out. I'm sorry for my words."

Carter nodded. "It's fine. I understand. Believe me, I'm freaking out as well. Internally."

They crossed the bridge and walked in silence for a time, the path up the hillside meandering back and forth toward the ridge. Halfway up, Sanya paused and leaned against a fence built into the switchback. She gazed upon the rooftops of Horizon, reminiscing about the city. Her home, ever since she moved away from her father. Her time studying at the *Roanoke*, her time working for the Council, Krystin's father . . . and now Ben.

"Everything's about to change, isn't it?" she muttered. "You know something. Don't you?"

"We better keep walking," Carter said. "Talk inside."

Sanya clenched her fingers around the fence before pushing away. "All right. And someone needs to tell the staff what happened. They deserve to hear it from a friend, not some courier from town."

"You have a good heart, Sanya."

She didn't know what to say in response, so silence resumed as they progressed further up the hill. When they reached the entrance to the *Roanoke*, three fragment attendants strode out of the ship.

"Welcome back, friends—wait, where is Master Davinport?" The woman furrowed her brow. "Why the long faces?"

"Gather the staff," Sanya said. "In the cafeteria."

* * *

The staff of the *Roanoke*, all dedicated curators of the treasured fragments, sat around the tables of the library's eating lounge. Sanya leaned against the wall, her arms crossed, Carter sitting in a chair off to the side. She remembered her days as a fragment attendant beneath Davinport's tutelage. The news would break their hearts. Charles Davinport was the glue that kept the library together, following in the footsteps of his ancestors. He had no children, pouring his whole life into maintaining their records. The memories of the founders.

And now he was gone.

"Friends," Sanya said. "Many of you remember me from my days working under Davinport. For those of you who don't know me, I am Sanya Fischer, former deputy director of the Library of Fragments. And I have the unfortunate duty of informing you all of the death of Charles Davinport."

She didn't know how else to say it, and the stunned looks of silence were a godsend. She wouldn't have been able to handle a sudden outpouring of sobs.

"We were there." She motioned toward Carter. "An assassin from the wild cults point-blank shot both Davinport and Member Thespis. I'm sorry to share the news this way, but . . . there didn't seem to be a better way."

"So what do we do? How do we honor him?"

It was Vietta, a young woman Sanya remembered from her last few weeks working at the library. She was the new deputy director—now the master of the place, she supposed.

"Better question," shot a young man from the back she didn't recognize. "How do we avenge him?"

"Nikola, do you really think revenge is the way to honor Davinport's memory?" Vietta shot back. "We have a duty to maintain this library. In his memory."

With those words, the cafeteria exploded in chaos as the dozen or so librarians took sides in the debate. Sanya couldn't help it. Her eyes widened in surprise. Carter, to his part, was looking off to the side, his face glazed over as if he were somewhere else. He wouldn't be helpful in this fight.

But she needed to take control of the situation. Horizon wouldn't be any better if its academics tore apart the *Roanoke* from the inside.

"Attendants of the Library of Fragments!" She finished the exclamation with a sharp whistle, its screech echoing off the cold walls. The room went deathly silent. "Now is not the time for fighting. Now is the time for unity in response to Master Davinport's death. Vengeance is not the path, yes." Sanya pursed her lips, recognizing the opportunity at her fingertips. She hated the idea of taking advantage of Davinport's death, but she needed help. "My family has been captured by the cultists. So has my friend's partner. We need to rouse the people. Fight back for once. Rid Horizon of those filth once and for all, save my family, and achieve justice for Davinport. Who's with me?"

Vietta and Nikola glanced at one another momentarily, but Sanya caught their subtle smirks. "I'm in," the younger woman said. "It'll be like the great flood, ten years back. We'll organize a campaign. Muster the people for collective action. Librarians, it's time to get to work!"

The tone of the room shifted, the attendants snapping into action. Sanya snagged Vietta before she disappeared through the doors. "We'll be discussing details in the Core," she said. "Whatever you come up with, we'll be ready to help. You get us the people, we'll come up with an attack strategy."

Vietta grasped Sanya's forearm. "I'm glad you're back with us, even if it's for a short while. We've missed you."

Satisfied, Sanya stepped out of the cafeteria, Carter in tow. "That went better than I thought it would," she said once they were down the hall. "Never doubt the diligent, hard work of librarians."

"I'm surprised," Carter said, "but I'll take whatever windfall we can get at this point."

"So what's this secret you've been waiting to tell me?"

"It can wait a few more minutes. I need to ensure we can't be listened to. Your people here have been beat up enough today."

"Fair enough," she replied.

They reached the secluded corridor leading to the ship's Core, the same secret place where Jill had spoken to them yesterday.

It felt like a lifetime ago.

They climbed the ladder, reaching the small space, and Carter's shoulders finally relaxed. He rejected standing, rather sitting cross-legged on the ground. Sanya joined him there, the ladder to the hall below separating them.

"All right," Carter said. "Not sure how exactly to explain this. Explain what I know. Or how I know it."

"Can't be any weirder than any of the other facts you've told me over the past few days," Sanya retorted.

The man grinned. "True. Very true. All right." He flexed his fingers and rested one close to his left eye. "So in my head, I have an implant. A small technological device colloquially known as a Lens. Almost everyone has one on planets controlled by ICH. It's a hyper-advanced computer of sorts, and it runs off residual energy generated by the body. Ingenious tech, really. Shoot, I don't even know if you know what half these words mean—"

"We know what a computer is. We've not been able to replicate one, but our Fragments discuss them extensively, and there were plenty of ruined computers on the *Roanoke*."

Carter chuckled. "Of course. Of course. All right, so is this all following so far? Hyper-advanced computer in my head?"

"It's a bit unbelievable, but I'll roll with it for now." Sanya bit her lip, unsure what else to say. They were in deep now. There was no going back. She would do anything to save Krystin and Ben.

"Great. So. Jill contacted me directly today. If you've noticed me looking a bit glazed over at times, it's because I've been communicating with her."

A breath caught in Sanya's throat, and she coughed to eliminate the itch. "Excuse me?"

"It's hard to explain. And truly unbelievable, as you said. What Jill has done to your planet . . . I don't fully comprehend the implications yet, but essentially, I believe the whole planet is one big experiment. Or a trap. Or both."

Sanya shook her head. "I don't understand. Why? Who is she? What would be her motivations?"

"I don't know. But here's the thing. She can help us save Raith. And Krystin. And Ben."

"Okay." She rubbed her eyes with her thumbs. The implications were staggering. The secret entity she once believed to live inside her family's sacred heirloom, now a planet-manipulating synthetic intelligence? Whatever that meant. Yet she knew what she'd seen yesterday—Jill's digital representation. Reality was spiraling out of control, and she needed stability.

The only way to achieve it was through saving her family.

"Sanya?" Carter's voice crossed the void between them, barely a whisper.

"You mentioned a trap," she said. "A trap for whom? For you?"

"Ha." He shook his head. "Absolutely not. Raith and I are insignificant in the eyes of anyone out there. No. The trap has been set for Theren, the first synthetic intelligence. And you? Me? Our partners? This entire planet? We're all caught in the crossfire."

And then the enormity of the situation struck. Sanya recognized the scale of the duplicity. The utter treachery instituted upon the people of Horizon—living, dead, and yet-to-live. All for . . . a trap?

"No." Sanya shook her head.

"No?"

"I don't believe you. I can't believe you."

"You should believe him," a voice said.

Jill's voice.

"Stop it!" Sanya said, her voice sharpening. "I don't care what you have to say. Stop taunting us. I just want to save my family."

"And I want to help both of you save your families," Jill said.

"Sanya, just hear her out."

Sanya shot him a glare she hoped illustrated the ice in her heart. "I believed in you, Jill. In our family's legend. And now I learn you've just been messing with us all this time? Controlling us from afar?"

"I'm not controlling you. I'm doing exactly the opposite. I want you all to thrive."

"Then why all the lies? All the secrecy? You're literally spying on us. And what is this trap Carter speaks of?"

"Carter is interpreting the information I've provided to him," Jill said. "He may call it a trap. I call it an invitation. An opportunity. I do not wish harm to the SI known as Theren. Everything I'm doing is to the benefit of Horizon, of the ICH, of all humanity."

"We're just toys to you." Sanya spat.

"And she's our only opportunity for saving those we love," Carter said.

She closed her eyes, releasing a rough sigh. "How are you even speaking to us right now? In this moment?"

Seconds later, a small, floating, black orb materialized. It was no larger than a marble.

"So not just nanotech, then," Carter muttered. "Stealth as well."

"I have many tricks up my sleeve, my friend," Jill said.

"You aren't our friend," Sanya retorted.

"Not yet."

The marble disappeared.

"I just . . . Carter, how can we trust her?"

"We can't," said the man. "But we must. We have run out of options."

"And what does she want from us?" Sanya said.

"We are to play a role in her trap for Theren. Oh, before you say anything Jill, I will always call it a trap. It is a trap. Theren will probably see it as a trap. Just shove it."

"It's not a trap," Jill said anyway.

She couldn't help herself. Sanya let out a small laugh. "I'm trying to force myself to understand. To believe. To trust. Let me get this straight. We agree to help you whenever this *Theren* arrives. In exchange, you will help us save Krystin, Ben, and Raith. Once we've saved them, how will you ensure we help you?"

"I am trusting *you*. But it will be in your best interest to help me. The firestorm soon to engulf all humanity will not leave this planet untouched. You will need Theren's help to survive."

Sanya glanced across the room toward Carter. His eyes were shadowed. She knew what he was willing to do. He was the one proposing the deal with the devil. Their path forward rested in her hands.

"What must we do?" she asked.

"Nearly nothing," Jill said. "I am transmitting a map and coordinates to Carter's Lens. He will act as your guide. Your little group of librarians might be helpful, but I believe they will be unnecessary. For once you are close to where your family is being held, the second part of the plan will activate."

"The second part?" Carter asked.

"All in good time."

* * *

She shouldn't have been surprised. The librarians of *Roanoke* were the best of the best, respected by every citizen of Horizon. Yet late in the afternoon, as the sun slowly set across the western horizon, a crowd formed on the city's side of the river near the bridge. A few dozen men and women, in addition to the librarians, all armed with personal blades, bolt-throwers, or other makeshift weapons.

And everyone had a lizard, the great beasts resting patiently. Their tongues darted in and out of their mouths, tasting the air.

It was a miniature militia, unlike anything seen since the Farmer's Rebellion three decades ago.

"Well, I'm impressed," Carter said, twisting atop his lizard to glance at her. Together, they slowly meandered across the bridge toward the crowd. "They'll potentially be helpful. Though mostly, I hope they don't get in the way."

"I recognize a few faces," Sanya replied. "A few friends of my father. My own friends. Former colleagues. And is that—"

"Sanya, I didn't believe it when I heard, but this is magnificent." The words came from Member Hood, approaching on his own lizard. "You will certainly honor Member Thespis and Master Davinport with what you've organized here today. We will avenge them. And we will save your family. I've heard the story."

"Thank you. Seriously, thank you. For your support." Sanya nodded her head, more out of confused surprise than gratitude. "How many of these men are from your family?"

"Five," said Member Hood. "You know many of our fields are close to the hills inhabited by the cultists. We've let them linger for far too long."

"Agreed," Sanya replied. "Again, thank you. It means the world."

"I would always come to the aid of a Fischer."

"Excuse me, Sanya?"

She turned, glancing downward. Vietta stared upon Sanya, holding a black, leather-bound notebook in her hand. "I can't believe what you've put together here, Vietta," she said.

"I've cataloged every volunteer. Fifty-four, in total. According to Member Hood, that's well above the estimated number of people living in any of the mountain strongholds, unless they've suddenly consolidated together."

"Well done," Sanya replied. "What role do you need me to play?"

"Well you're the captain of this militia, of course," Vietta said.

"You want me to lead?"

"They all expect you to lead. They are here to help you save your family, after all. That's the call to arms we sent out."

She couldn't help it. Tears welled in her eyes, but she quickly wiped them away with a sleeve. "Then I suppose I should give a speech of some sort, yes?"

"I think that would be wise."

The crowd swelled with anticipation, eyes turning toward Sanya, Vietta, and Member Hood. She exhaled, the warm afternoon air humid and sticky. What was she supposed to say? How was she supposed to tell these men and women their actions simultaneously mattered, in saving her family, yet were also irrelevant, given the galaxy-spanning mystery cavorting in the shadows? By the time their little army returned, everything could be different. The mysterious SIs apparently controlling their reality might reveal themselves to everyone at any moment, flipping Horizon on its head.

Few words would be better than many. And better than none.

"Thank you, friends," she said, projecting her voice so the crowd could hear her clearly. "I know many of you. Some of you I don't know at all. But I'm sure you know my family's name, and you do us honor. The people of Horizon have always been strong when united. And you are showing me unity today by riding with me to save my husband and daughter. The wild cults of the mountains have plagued us for far too long. They live on our scraps like parasites and steal away our children. They will pay for what they've done to me . . . and what they've done to us. The people of Horizon are one family. One people. One community. We stand united against the perils of this planet, as we have for every generation since the crash. We will continue together. Forever."

A scattered though enthusiastic applause cascaded through the crowd. Their hopeful faces gave her optimism. They might save her daughter. They might save Ben.

She glanced toward Carter, who gave her a sharp nod. She replied with a curt grin.

And they might save his friend. Raith.

Chapter 14

We rarely discuss the nature of networks. Virtual. AR. Quantum. Our connections between servers and people and ships and planets has become simultaneously incredibly simple yet inordinately complex. A trillion trillion different bits of information floating from screen to screen every second. New content created at an exponential rate. All of it beamed from planet to planet without considering what it would mean to disconnect from it all. We don't recognize how we've been trapped by our connections.

Or whether the networks we constantly experience are the only networks to persist and replicate information.

*We find our silos. We find our people. Then we blissfully ignore what we don't want to believe. Thus, information we needed—that we **knew** we needed—hides in plain sight, right in front of our eyes. We just didn't look.* — Peter Bognov, "The Philosophy of Post-Singularity Human-Network Experience," 2232 C.E.

RAITH

Raith first heard the crashing and the swearing through the pipes.

He lay on the ground, soaking in the few remaining minutes of sunlight available. The low rumble cascaded through the tiny spaces running beneath his cell, echoing fervently and revealing residual anger.

The jailer was upset.

Raith weighed his options, considering whether to reach out to Jill. He hadn't yet given an answer to her offer, his supposed ticket out of here. The opportunity seemed too clean. Too perfect. Why shoot the *Bloodhound* out of the sky then give him—and Carter—an offer just a few days later? None of it made sense. He felt like he was being played. Too many times in his life had someone tried to use him to get ahead. Sure, Raith had used people too. But he was a changed SI.

And he had another person in his life to protect, other than himself. What would Carter do?

Raith shook his head. Carter would do anything to protect them both. And right now, Raith only had Jill's offer as an available escape plan. A question, though, still lingered in his mind. When was the correct time to *accept* the offer?

Raith wasn't stupid. Jill had dropped enough context clues to reveal the scale of the impending conflict. A war was building. Between whom, he didn't know. Maybe between Theren and Jill. Or Jill and Theren against the ICH. Perhaps something else entirely.

Politics weren't his strong suit. In the past, when he was a professional racing pilot, he managed to navigate a complicated world of corporate sponsorships and over-inflated egos. All of that, though, paled in comparison to the overly bureaucratic and murky world of interplanetary governance. From interstellar corporations and regulatory agencies to legacy Earth nation-states and their charter colonies, the tangled web was opaque for a reason. The architects at the top didn't want people like Raith to understand it.

And maybe, because he didn't understand politics, he appeared as a useful tool to those attempting to manipulate the politics of the ICH. People like Jill. And maybe Theren.

Theren still owed Raith a conversation. They'd never officially met, even though Raith ostensibly worked for them a few years ago. At the very least, Raith had Theren to thank for introducing him to Carter. The first SI, from what Raith understood, drifted out of the political limelight before Raith was created. Sure, the ever-exploring icon of synthetic legend owned a dozen or so corporations and sat on the boards of another dozen non-profit organizations, but at least they stuck to the promise made in the early 2100s when they dropped out of public service.

They wanted to be "one of the people" exploring the galaxy, not a power-broker.

The promise always seemed a bit suspicious. And with Jill's

reappearance, it made Theren's supposed benevolence more disconcerting. Why was Theren heading to *this* system if they weren't collaborating with Jill? If they'd known Jill survived for close to three centuries, they chose not to tell anyone. That fact alone was suspicious by itself.

Raith sighed. There were too many questions. And he wanted answers to them all.

Another crash reverberated through the room, this time echoing from right outside his cell. Raith rotated, and seconds later, the door rocketed open, revealing the visage of Mathias.

"You." The man strode inside. "How did you turn her against me so quickly? You interloper. You—"

"I've done no such thing," Raith said.

"I did everything she asked of me. She told me to lock you in here. She told me to ransom those two. But when I get into the city, someone else already knows about you. And the kid and her father. And the only thing I can imagine is that she's been talking to you. And then talking to someone else. That's how the council knew without me giving a ransom note. You've turned her against me."

Raith shook his head. "You've got it all wrong." At the same time, he activated his connection to Jill's grid. He quickly typed a message.

R: I accept. Now help me.

He sent it through the network.

"There's no other explanation, you strange machine," Mathias said. "You will pay. As will your two friends. Don't think I know you've been talking to the girl? I have ears everywhere."

"You're wrong. You're throwing away your alliance with Jill for no reason. I haven't convinced her of anything."

"Ah." Mathias smirked. "So you have talked to her."

"I didn't say that."

Mathias reached behind his back and revealed a metal rod of sorts. It must have been attached to a shoulder strap. Narrow for its whole length, the tool had tiny spikes at its end, though it looked like a solid piece of steel. "You're going to die. Right now. I don't know how to make sure you die, but you're going to die before your friends arrive to save you."

Raith made sure not to respond with words. The man had revealed information he should not have revealed. If he intuited it all correctly, then Carter was alive—and had managed to find help. Help, specifically, to find Raith. It made sense. If Carter had contacted other locals, then he would have known about Raith's capture. Whatever plan Mathias had in the city would have been ruined by Carter's foreknowledge. The man had done well, even if it created a few unforeseen consequences.

"Well," Raith said. "Give me your best whack."

The cult leader stormed. He took a step forward. Then another. His arm arced, swinging the rod swiftly and with purpose. The sunlight glinted against its cold metal, before . . . it melted.

In an instant, the steel glowed, shining a bright white-orange, and turned molten, causing Mathias's swing to transform midair into a chaotic flail met with a similarly scared screech. The rod's viscous form flowed down the man's arm, burning his skin to a crisp. A mere second later, foam bubbled from his lips, and he stumbled, crumpled, and crashed into the rocky wall.

His breathing ceased as the rod stopped glowing.

Slowly, Raith pushed himself backward until he rested against the rear wall of the cell. The cult leader's lifeless form lay tangled a few meters away, steam and smoke gently wafting toward the open window.

"Jill?" he said aloud. "Was that you?"

Silence.

"I appreciate the help, but that was a little bit too terrifying, you know? Just . . . poisoning and burning a man with no clear vector for the attack?"

More silence.

"Some sort of signal would be appreciated."

"Apologies," Jill said, her voice echoing inside the room as if generated from within. "I needed to act fast. It was the only option."

"I thought he was your ally?"

"He was. He was no longer useful."

"Doesn't make me too excited to join your team, you know."

Raith received an AR request, and seconds later, a visage of Jill appeared, standing in the center of the room. She crossed her arms.

"Mathias was a wildcard. Why I was using him is too long of a story on its own, but suffice to say, he was crazy. He believed himself a god. He thought he was using *me*. I don't think you're so stupid to do any of those things. Quite to the contrary, you're an incredibly perceptive and intelligent individual. And you accepted my offer."

"I did, though I'm not sure what good I can be at the moment."

Though virtual shadows masked her face, he was pretty sure she smiled. "I have a solution for you, thought it might feel a little strange at first."

"I need power. What I need is power."

"And you need a way to move. I can help with both."

A sharp buzz filled the room. A disparate dust cloud materialized, congealed, and solidified, the air tightening by the second. With a subtle click, the tiny nanobots locked in place, forming a set of synthetic legs standing in the middle of the cell. The sun glinted off the faux-metal, creating an eerie copper glare.

"You terrify me," Raith said. "It's a good terror. I think. It's still terror, nevertheless. You have the ability to kill anyone on this planet at will. How will the ICH react when they realize what you're capable of? How will Theren react?"

Jill's wispy visage drifted closer, more floating than walking. "You're asking all the correct questions. You are correct to question my motivations. You should worry about my power. I will work to gain your trust before this is all over."

"I guess that's the best answer I can hope for."

The legs took a few steps forward. Raith snagged them with his arms, pulling the appendages down to the ground so their "waist" was close to his dismembered torso.

"Just move them close to your body, their cloud network will do the rest and communicate with your framework. They're designed to talk with your magnetic gyroscopes. It won't feel normal, but it'll do what you need it to do until we can develop a genuine replacement in-tune with your neural nodes."

Raith nodded, sliding the legs closer. With a soft pop, they suctioned into place against his body. Immediately, a network pinged on his conscious horizon, requesting the ability to receive inputs. He accepted the query, and his awareness recognized the locomotive capabilities of the nano-legs.

And their potential as an energy source.

"Thank you," Raith said. "Thank you very much."

"It's the least I can do. Try them out."

Gingerly, he pushed against the ground and swayed upright. He took a step; the left leg moved with a subtle delay. He moved the right, the command feeling more natural on second attempt. His underlying framework was quickly integrating and reassessing its locomotive processes, and after a few more steps, it felt adequate, if not natural. They weren't his old legs, but they would work.

"Once again, thank you," Raith said. He glanced at the ruined body of Mathias. "What do I do about him?"

"Leave him in here to rot."

"Better idea." Placing a foot on the man's shoulder, Raith pushed, shoving the lifeless cult leader into the cell's latrine hole. He didn't fit completely, but he dropped in face-first, his feet sticking upward haphazardly. "Perfect."

Satisfied, Raith headed to the door. Thankfully, it was unlocked, its wooden hinges creaking as he pulled it into the cell. "Jill? Which way to the girl and her father?"

"Turn left."

He glanced over his shoulder, noting the ghostly visage of the woman walking close behind him. "Can anyone else see you?"

"No. Only you. I'm not using one of my stealth projectors. They'd need lens-tech or another implant. Turn left at the fork."

He reached the end of the corridor and followed her instructions. He was greeted by a long murky hallway, its shadows revealing dust clouds in the tiny refuges of light shining through crags in the ceiling.

"Krystin is at the end of the hall. On the left."

After a few more gangly strides, Raith reached another cell door. Without pausing, he kicked the wood with his new leg, shattering the iron hinges with a crack. The door tilted inward on its base before dropping to the stone floor with a smack. At the back of the small space, Krystin looked up as if awaking from a nap.

"Raith?" she said. "You have legs now?"

"Yes," he said. "Come on. We're escaping. We're going to find your father and get out of this place."

"What about that leader-man?"

Raith chuckled, remembering the perverse scene back in his cell. "Don't worry about him." He queued up a silent voice message to Jill's visage. "Where is her father?"

"Head back down the hall and keep going straight." Her voice echoed in his mind, strangely sounding as if it was within the mountain alongside them.

"Come on," Raith said, beckoning.

Krystin tentatively shuffled to the door and stepped across the collapsed wood. "So what are you again?" she asked.

"I'm a synthetic intelligence." He started walking down the hall, and the young girl followed closely behind.

"My mother's never told me about that word. What do you mean? What are you?"

"It's hard to explain. But I'm not human, obviously."

"Well I'm not stupid," she said.

"Didn't say you were."

"We've always speculated about what other types of people might live among the stars. We know we came from somewhere. We know there must be others out there like us. That's what my mom said, at least."

"Your mother sounds like a smart lady."

They reached the fork, but Raith kept heading straight, impatient to find the girl's father. He didn't like kids. Never had. A few crews he ran with before his career as a racer kept families aboard the ships, and the kids always got in the way. The concept of a "child" was foreign to most SIs, given how rapidly their cognitive abilities developed following activation. There was no such thing as a youngster SI, though levels of maturity were often evident during the first few months.

Raith knocked down the door just like the last, finding the man sitting at the back of the cell, face crumpled in his palms.

"Ben, he saved us!" Krystin exclaimed, and the man looked up at the sound of the girl's voice, not the door.

"Krystin?" he said.

"The sintetic . . . no wait, synthetic? This . . . man is going to take us back to Mom."

Ben shook his head, disbelief shining in his eyes. "I don't know what you are, but thank you. How did you get new legs?"

"It's a long story," Raith said. "Once we escape, maybe I'll try to explain."

"I doubt you'll succeed," Jill said over their open channel.

"Probably not, because I can barely believe it," he replied.

"Protect your daughter," Raith said, holding out a hand to help Ben up.

The man clasped Raith's steel arm and rose to his feet. "What's the plan?"

"What is the plan, Jill?" he said over their private channel.

"Overlaying a route out, accept the request for it to display on your HUD."

He accepted, and a faint blue line led the way.

"Enemies in our path?" Raith asked.

"No need to worry for the time being."

"Just follow me," Raith said. "I memorized the way in when they captured me."

"All right. Not going to question you. Just going to say thank you."

"Well, we're not out of here yet," he added.

They walked in silence, the dark corridors gloomy and dank, matching exactly what Raith expected from a cultist mountain hideout. It all seemed larger-than-life—like someone had designed the place for an AR filmset. And maybe that was true. Maybe Jill had sculpted the place for the cult, to make them feel destined for greatness with their discovery of a secret fort in the mountains. With every passing second, Raith became more suspicious of the surrounding reality. She had complete control. How could he believe anything he even saw?

He shook his head as they reached another turn. A short jaunt down the hall, a low-hanging stone archway awaited. Raith slowed, holding a finger to his artificial mouth. Both Ben and Krystin nodded.

Voices echoed from the space beyond, and Raith focused his attention on deciphering the sounds. After a moment, his auditory receptors refined the sounds into words.

"It's a few dozen coming up the mountain. In the middle of the ravine at the moment. Probably a kilometer out."

"Where is Mathias? He said he'd be right back. We can't act

without him."

"We're going to need to act soon. We need orders. We need to stop them before they get too close."

"He told us not to follow him. That he needed to speak with the prisoners alone."

"We can't be defeated on our own ground. We don't need to wait for him. Let's face them on the battlefield."

Raith faced Ben and Krystin. He whispered, "All right, apparently there's a band of people coming up the mountain. Presumably to rescue us, based on the sound of it. What's that mean to you? Who would be saving us, and what chance do they stand?"

"Depends on how many men they have here," Ben said. "Horizon doesn't have an army, though people know how to fight. We don't have enemies, other than these cultist bandits."

Raith lurked against the archway, peering outward. It led into the same entrance hall they'd been in when first encountering Mathias, filled with a couple dozen men and women all armed with crossbow-like ranged weapons.

He leaned backward. "Doesn't look like a fair fight." Looking beyond Ben, he glared at the visage of Jill standing there.

"You couldn't have led us in any other direction?" He wished he could speak with her openly.

"You asked for the way out," she replied.

"And I can't lead them into a bloodbath," he said.

"No, you can't."

"I need more firepower."

Jill's icy, digitized eyes bore into him. "You need Theren," she said.

* * *

Raith's Virtual appearance floated high above the surface of Horizon. Far below, his physical body hid in an alcove alongside Ben and Krystin. In the void represented by Jill's planet-spanning network, Raith watched the distant ship drawing ever closer.

Jill was certain. If he reached out to Theren, the first synthetic intelligence would immediately drop a team to the surface to resolve the situation. *She* couldn't be the one to intervene. It needed to be an outside force. Theren was the outside force.

Raith questioned her logic. Her strange experiment on the planet was already screwed. She had another reason for wanting Theren to send a surface team, he was certain. She needed Raith to join Theren aboard their ship. She wanted him on the inside.

And as much as he hated being within shipbound SIs, Theren was the only way he and Carter could make their way back to civilization, unless Jill was hiding a ship somewhere on Horizon's moon.

Which, he supposed, was quite likely.

First things first, though. They needed to survive. And Jill refused to use her nanobots to kill everyone in the room. Theren was their sole option.

Millions of kilometers away, Theren's ship drifted ever closer. Raith carefully crafted his message, tying words together to ensure the situation was understood. He considered reminding the ancient SI of Raith's past tangential relationship to their companies, but he deleted that section, uncertain whether it was worth giving Theren a moment to pause and consider the identity of whom they were rescuing.

The message was drafted. The network opened a digital pathway toward Theren's ship, its communications array welcoming the connection. Satisfied, Raith pushed send. His perspective refocusing on the present situation inside the cave, he nodded to Ben. "And now we wait."

Chapter 15

Theren.

You don't know me. It's hard to explain why I'm even in this system before you. My partner and I responded to a distress signal and are now caught between you and Jill.

Yes, I know about her. And I know she's alive.

We're in a tough spot. I've been captured by crazy cultists. My partner is somewhere on the planet surviving, but I don't know where.

We're surrounded on all sides.

I've given you my coordinates. I've attached an assessment of the situation.

We need your help.

— "A message from an unknown SI," 2348 C.E.

THEREN

They reread the message over and over and over again, its implications rearing their ugly heads. Someone else found Jill first. An unknown party, thrown into the mess, needed their help. And Theren had no time to fully assess the strategic situation at hand. Moreover, it was likely their stealthy attempt at entering the system failed. If this individual could detect them, then Jill could too.

They needed more time.

But if they continued to wait, the person reaching out might die.

Of course, it was also likely the entire situation was a trap laid by Jill. She wanted them to act quickly and on their back foot. It was a classic strategy she often tried to employ in their games of chess, yet they always exploited it without fail.

Except now, they weren't playing chess. This was real. She was using the lives of people on the planet below as pieces in a game. It was equal parts fascinating and horrifying.

Really, there was only one option. They needed to spring the trap and play it out. Jill wanted them to send people to the surface? Then they would send a crew to the surface.

And thus they were already prepping one of the shuttles, a simultaneous perspective controlling an MI in its cockpit. They were pouring over the tactical assessment passed along by their mysterious friend on the planet when the rest of the ground team arrived. Though they wore different faces, the preparations reminded Theren of their first team, all those years ago, helping them uncover Jill's mystery.

The crew who died when the *Nottingham* exploded.

They wouldn't let the same fate occur to anyone else.

"Theren, we're here and ready for the mission," said Hala, and the other members of her team murmured in agreement.

Theren's MI nodded. They'd run thousands of missions over the past few centuries, exploring new worlds, negotiating treaties between disparate colonial factions, and staking corporate interests in upstart businesses. Not since 2102 C.E., though, had Theren contemplated rediscovering their closest friend. Nor had they truly feared the risks of confrontation.

They were walking into checkmate, leaving the door open for the end game.

"Thank you for volunteering," Theren said, trying to sound cheerful. "The plan is simple. We've been provided coordinates for an ongoing confrontation. Two chartered explorers have been caught in local crossfire and are requesting extraction. Their communication indicated the locals have no knowledge of or communication with the ICH or any other part of human civilization."

"And Jill?" Hala inquired.

"The explorers have also made contact with Jill. Unclear whether the locals are aware of her or not."

"Well, sounds like at least a few of our models were accurate, then. Complete memory loss for the original settlers, though the survivors of the colony ship seemed to have thrived."

"It would seem that way, yes. Our principle goal—respond to the distress call of these two explorers and resolve the conflict without bloodshed. Only use stunbolts if we're required to open fire."

"Copy," the crew said in unison.

Theren commenced departure procedures, both for the *Verona Rupes* and the shuttle. *Whoever you are, we're coming to help. And whatever game you're playing, Jill, we're ready for your next move.*

Chapter 16

I will never forget Theren's answer to one particular question I asked them many years after the events on Horizon.

I asked: "If you had known Jill's reason for calling you to that forsaken planet, would you have responded? Would you have gone regardless?"

Their answer was unequivocal. "Even after everything we know, I still would have traveled to Horizon. The question you should be asking—what move should I have made once I arrived?" — "Raith's Reflection on Theren," 2457 C.E.

CARTER

With the sun setting gently over the hills to the west, Carter traced the blue beacon overlaid on his Lens, identifying their destination just over the ridge line. Numbers streamed across the HUD, noting possible trajectories and routes using technology not accessible to the people of Horizon.

He swiped the extraneous information away and, utilizing a mental command, pulled up a bird's eye map of the mountain ahead, graciously provided by one of Jill's satellites. He was standing on a ridge looking northward, a ravine leading between two ridges straight ahead. Their destination, some cave network carved deep into the ravine, was only accessible *through* the ravine, though if they had rappelling equipment . . .

"I think our only option is a frontal assault," Carter said.

Sanya crossed her arms as she leaned against a nearby crimson boulder. "Perfect. Jill can't possibly find us any other option?"

Carter glanced down the slope, weary of others possibly hearing Sanya name-drop the SI. "I'm looking at the same maps she has," he said. "There's nothing. This fortress is their hideout for a reason.

Heading into that gauntlet is suicide. Doesn't matter how many soldiers we have."

"Yet if we starve them out," Sanya said, "they'll kill Ben and Krystin well before then."

"Yeah." Carter examined the crowd down below, armed with swords and hatchets and bolt-throwers—he'd learned the name of the crossbow weapons on the ride. "These people followed you out here to end this. And to save your family. It's your call. I'm going in to save Raith. Whether you all want to join me is on you."

"We've come this far," Sanya said. "I don't think anyone is turning back. Everyone knew the risks. Just . . . do a check-in with Jill. See what the situation is."

Carter grimaced, not sure if he fully trusted Jill yet to give the whole truth of the problem. But he took a few more steps into the ravine away from their little war band.

"Jill, I know you can see everything that's going on, both here and at their base," he said. "What's the plan?"

Her disembodied voice arrived in his ear quickly enough. "There's been a complication," she said. "Before you ask—Raith and Sanya's family are fine. But they've escaped."

"Well that's great," Carter said. "Do we even need to attack?"

"They've not fully escaped," she said. "They're hiding at the moment. There's an army of cultists between them and you." Jill dropped positions on Carter's AR-generated three-dimensional map of their target.

"Ah, so the only way to give them a path of escape is to draw out their force." Carter zoomed in on what looked like the main entrance. "If we do a frontal assault with a push toward the right, we can make space for them to escape and retreat with us. A pure extraction."

"Precisely," Jill said, after a subtle pause.

"Is there something you're not telling me?"

Silence.

"Jill?"

"Just keep moving," she said. "I asked you to trust me. This will play out as we need it to play out."

Carter sighed and completely eliminated the map from his frame of view. Everything would play out as *she* needed it to play out, perhaps. Her goals were opaque, and he hated feeling powerless.

And Jill perpetually made him feel powerless. He was a pawn.

He gave Sanya a curt wave, their agreed-upon gesture to indicate the all-clear. At the base of the rocky slope, she nodded and signaled for their little army to ascend behind Carter. They would leave the lizards with a few guards; the rest of the trip would be too narrow. If they were all on lizardback and an ambush occurred, they'd be hard-pressed to reposition quickly in the narrow confines of a canyon.

The taste of dust bit his lips. Carter didn't wait for them to reach his position. He was already striding into the ravine, hand furtively resting on the deactivated blade strapped to his hip, shadows lengthening with every passing step. The data Jill provided indicated the cultists pulled all their scouts back to the fortress a half hour ago, but he still didn't know if they could trust her information. His eyes darted from crevice to ridge, noting all the spots an ambush could hide.

Why *weren't* they ready to assault via ambush?

They were holding all their men close to the fortress. Carter nodded, recognizing the potential significance. They valued the place deeply, and they loathed leaving its comforting embrace. Or, alternatively, they were waiting on orders from their leader, Mathias, who Jill had mentioned. If he was their leader, and he had snapped in the process of assassinating two of Horizon's councilmembers . . .

Their opponent may not have a fully organized defensive response.

"Everyone's ready for anything," Sanya said. "They know the risks."

"Then I think I have a plan of attack, if you're willing to hear it."

* * *

They neared a rocky pass in the ravine some twenty meters wide. Beyond it, the subtle smoke of fires drifted into the air of dusk. With no sign of armed opposition, the plan was set.

Still, a thought nagged in the back of Carter's mind.

Jill had said Raith was escaping with Sanya's family.

Yet Raith had no legs.

How was Raith escaping without legs?

The incongruent information provided by the ever-present SI revealed deception upon deception. He needed to note *every* word she said just to keep up. She wasn't telling him something.

"Everyone ready?" Sanya said.

With a flurry of rustles and clicks, the fighting force readied their weapons.

"Are *you* ready?" Carter whispered to Sanya.

"I am," she said. She lifted her bolt-thrower. Carter matched her motion, lifting his own version of the strange projectile weapon in both hands. Made of a hardened steel, the long bolts were about a half-meter long with a centimeter diameter. Still, it was the same "point and shoot" concept of any ranged weapon.

Carter nodded. "Better now than any other time, then."

Without a word, Sanya stepped forward, looked back at the following throng, and saluted. Then, she turned and sprinted through the gap. Carter followed right behind, the rush of their force joining them in a full-on assault.

They charged into the rocky gap, entering a larger flattened valley with one- and two-story constructs littering a space fifty meters or so wide. He was pretty sure he spotted the noses of a few lizards jutting from one of the buildings. A stable, perhaps. Near the rear, a vaulting cave entrance loomed, a throng of men standing beneath its teeth.

"Fire!" shouted someone from the enemy line, and the sharp *thwack* of springs releasing signaled the incoming onslaught.

Carter barely had time to register the attack. One bolt narrowly missed his cheek, flying right over a shoulder and landing with a crunch in someone else. A few sharp cries rang out from their band, but before a second volley was released by the enemy, Carter found himself up against a wooden shelter beside Sanya and another woman. A dozen of their crew rounded the back side of the shelter, and across the center between buildings, the rest of their team hid behind one of the stables. It was like a shootout straight from an ancient western film.

"Vietta and Hood are across the way," Sanya said. "They're looping behind, just as we planned. You three, hold this position.

Carter, come on, let's catch up with the rest."

"Right," he said. Crouching, he quickly shuffled along behind the long building, reaching the front of their makeshift line. "Any hostiles ahead?"

"Noth—"

The man was abruptly cut off as a bolt sliced into his neck, a brutal gurgle rising from his throat. Carter looked away, not wanting to see the blood inevitably spilling onto the dusty ground. He quickly shuffled across the open space to drop behind a stone fence, his back facing their entrance. The man lay dying on the ground in a gap between Sanya's covered position and Carter's now-forward hiding spot.

He glanced to the left, a gap in the buildings presenting a view of Hood and Vietta's similar advance. Likewise, they were pinned.

"We need a distraction!" Carter said.

"Any ideas?" Sanya hissed.

RAITH

Shouts from the entrance hall revealed everything about the scene. The battle had begun—no need for Jill to keep him up-to-date.

Nevertheless, her visage crossed its arms on the other side of their hiding space. It was a storage closet, from what he could tell. Or the equivalent of one.

The cries continued, though a few seconds later, a group of three cultists strode right past their shadowy spot, arguing about why Mathias was taking so long to return. When they discovered the man's corpse sitting in a latrine, they would sound the alarm. They would know their three captors escaped.

There was nothing else he could do. The hunt would begin then. Or it could begin now.

"Ben, once I draw them away, use the lull to escape."

The man stared. "What—"

"They'll find us eventually. It'll be better to catch them by surprise now."

"We've still got—"

"Krystin, take care of your father." Raith threw in an artificial wink for good measure. "Later, friends."

Stepping out of the alcove, he turned and stared down the hall-way. "Looking for me?"

The three cultists were near the next fork, but they heard his words easily enough. Turning on their heels, they immediately pointed and yelled, their shouts unintelligible. They held up strange steel crossbows, but Raith didn't wait around to see if they would take aim and fire. He sprinted away, darting through the nearby exit into the fort's entrance hall. Its tall, pristine columns rose toward the vaulting ceiling, starkly out of place when contrasted against the sounds of battle coming from outside.

To his right, Mathias's throne sat empty, the ancient probe rest-ing behind it. Raith paused momentarily right beyond the door, assessing his options. Jill's visage drifted uncomfortably ahead of him, though he was the only one who could see her.

Presumably.

The data streaming from her networks revealed the positions ahead of a few dozen cultists covering defensive spots near the entrance and on natural ramparts along the rocky mountainside. A group were settled right inside the door, presumably acting as a makeshift command post. They could see the throne.

And the probe.

The probe they presumably worshiped, based on Mathias's behavior and the placement of the throne. Nothing would piss off an angry cultist more than having their godhead destroyed.

Raith walked up the gentle ramp behind the chair, reaching the probe. It was barely larger than the throne itself, but from its perch, he could fracture it with ease.

His three pursuers rushed into the room, their shouts alarming the crew at the front of the space. They all looked up, spotting his position next to the space probe.

He was right. With a tremendous rising tenor, they all cried out simultaneously, fear striking their eyes.

Manipulating the emotions of organics could be so easy at times. It truly terrified Raith—the thought of being a slave to biochemicals. The probe was meaningless. They shouldn't care about it. But they were afraid of its demise.

With a shove, he toppled it from its mount. It had five meters to drop, but it hadn't been properly maintained in centuries. Like an egg, it cracked upon the floor, its decrepit and useless Jump drive splaying against the back of the throne.

All eyes were upon Raith. All crossbows rose. The ruckus continued to ring throughout the cavern as the cultists shouted, sending orders to their comrades outside.

The real foe was on the inside.

Though, Raith wouldn't be sticking around. He leapt from the platform, landing in front of the throne. He was the distraction. He was the wild card. He was the unknown variable in the fight outside.

And he was the unknown variable in the fight between Jill and Theren. They both simply didn't know it yet.

SANYA

She had led all these people into a meat grinder. Every wound, every scream, every death. All of it was her fault.

She peered around the corner of the building, taking enough time to fire in the direction of the fortress, knowing the shot wouldn't hit anyone. She ducked behind their alcove, an iron bolt driving harmlessly into the mud a few meters away.

"So, ideas?" She tapped the side of her forehead, hoping Carter understood she wanted more intel from their "benevolent" ally.

"Nothing." He furrowed his brow. "No, wait. Surge now!"

"What?"

But Carter was already bounding around the corner of the building, bolt-thrower raised. His boots plopped in the mud, and she had no choice but to follow.

To her surprise, the defenders were shouting, confused by something happening *inside*. No matter. Their opportunity was presenting itself, and they needed to take advantage. They pushed forward, reaching the last wall before the open entrance to whatever space lay beyond. The distraction momentarily lulled, a few of the cultists poked their heads over the ramparts above, but Sanya was ready. She fired her bolt-thrower, catching one of the men in the shoulder.

And then a metallic man jumped into the vale.

He ran down the makeshift stone steps, reaching the mud in a matter of seconds. A horde of half a dozen cultists, their inky-black outfits flapping in the wind, charged after the fleeing thing. Guttural, angry cries followed in his wake.

"Ah, there's Raith," Carter said.

"Open fire!" Sanya ordered, stepping from their cover. The rest of the assaulting force did likewise, and a volley of bolts slammed into the angry mob, dropping them face-first upon skull-shattering stones.

"Keep pushing!" The words came from Hood, and another volley bounced harmlessly against the upper ramparts. Those defensive positions would be almost impossible to break without storming the fort itself, and fighting in unknown caverns was a recipe for disaster. The cultists knew the tunnels, certainly, and would know every choke point.

Their aggressive window of opportunity over, Sanya stepped back behind cover, noting the rest of her crew returning to defensive positions. A moment later, the metallic man—Raith, as Carter called him—stumbled to their hiding spot.

Like everyone around them, Sanya's eyes widened at the sight. His frame was vaguely humanoid, though the build was clearly accentuated for a more dynamic range of motion. The legs stood out, though, with a bronze sheen contrasting the silver glint to the rest of the body. The face, however, was the strangest aspect of Raith's look. It was human, but also not. It lacked lips, and the eyes were definitely robotic in nature. Still, it looked alive. She could see the mind behind the machine.

"Carter, quite the scrap you've got yourself into," Raith said.

"It talks," said one of their companions. "The walking machine talks."

"Well what else would you expect? Of course I can talk. I suppose you wouldn't know that. Carter, you didn't tell them anything about me? I'm hurt. Still, I can imagine why you wouldn't, given the greeting I've had on this planet."

Sanya smiled, already recognizing the sarcastic personality of the SI. A perfect foil for Carter's more no-nonsense demeanor. What a duo. Regardless, it would take some time getting used to a talking machine.

"Glad to have you back, Raith," Carter said.

"But where's my family?" She crossed her arms.

"Ah, you must be the mother," Raith said. "All right. They should be in a safe hiding space for now, though they might try to follow me out here. I was the diversion." He peered around the corner. "On my way out, I flagged ten remaining cultists on the ground floor, with four upstairs. I think that's all of them." His head tilted to the side. "Yeah, your family's right where I left them."

"We gonna talk about the legs?" Carter asked.

"Not now," Raith replied. "Later. We've got a lot to catch up on."

"Yes. Yes we do." Carter notched another bolt into his thrower. "So what—"

Thunk.

Thunk thunk thunk.

Thunk.

Sanya glanced around the edge of their position. Standing in the mud, five figures donning black steel surveyed the scene. One of the newcomers, taller than the rest, vaguely resembled Raith, the metallic form clearly inhospitable to a human body.

In the hands of each arrival, an elongated device rested at the ready. Helmets covered their faces, masking all identifying features from view. They looked like iron giants out of fragmented legend.

"Oh look," Raith said. "It's about time. Theren's finally arrived."

Chapter 17

I have a vague recollection of various boards and cards used to play games. The rules are nebulous in my mind, and I imagine pieces of many different shapes, colors, and sizes. It makes me sad. The forgotten land from whence we came—we've lost its culture. Its norms. Its history. Its technology. We'll need to make our own.

Which is exciting in its own right, I suppose.

"A Reflective Fragment," by Kiera Hood, written four years after landing

THEREN

In a few microseconds, Theren assessed the scene. Identified the two opposing forces. Recognized their potential allies. Analyzed the battlefield.

Theren's memory flashed, recalling events three centuries past. Once, they had dived into Jill's fiery remains, eliminating the assassins attempting to remove her from the world. Using an MI, they had easily dispatched those foes, revealing for the first time to many the potential capabilities of future synthetics.

Those days were long past.

Everyone understood the deadly threat posed by a sufficiently equipped MI.

Rarely were those abilities ever needed. Periodically, Theren defended their ground crews against giant creatures on distant worlds as they explored the stars. Only a few times since the twenty-first century had they needed to fire a weapon, even the defensive countermeasures of their ships.

Today, they were once again diving into an apocalypse of Jill's making. She had pushed them into an unknown inferno. They didn't yet know all the rules. What moves would lead to their demise. Or which pieces Jill wanted and needed to protect.

But it was time to act.

"Clear the perimeter," Theren said. "All hostiles are ahead, friendly behind us."

"Copy," Hala said over their short-wave broadcast.

The professional commando team fanned outward, weapons set to stun. With expert precision, they sniped away at the enemies in guarded positions along the rocks above. Their foes fired steel bolts from mechanical contraptions, though the projectiles bounced harmlessly off both body armor and MI carbon.

Theren strode forward, the lag minimal between their MI and the *Verona Rupes* orbiting a few hundred kilometers above. They activated the repulsor lifts, jetting a few meters into the air and landing in the direct entrance of the strange cave. Three men in odd robes charged, yelling something about a demon. Theren wanted to laugh, recognizing how they were repeating the scenes of centuries past. Hopefully, these were outliers on this unknown colony world.

In any case, they fired three shots, the stun darts instantly incapacitating the men and dropping them to the stones. Theren crossed beneath the rocky archway, entering the cave. It was more than a cave—it was a like a cathedral, its columns not made by natural means. Someone had carved them, and based on their cuts, most likely with advanced technology.

Interesting. Had Jill sculpted this place? The planet lacked any electromagnetic signatures large enough to power a laser capable of cutting through stone with sufficient precision.

A few more robed enemies charged. Theren dropped the foes like they'd eliminated their compatriots.

"All clear," said Hala.

"All clear in here as well," Theren replied.

"Raith?" said a voice from the back of the room. "Wait. You're not Raith."

A young girl with fawny brown skin stepped out of the shadows, accompanied by a middle-aged man with a much lighter complexion. They both looked terrified.

"I'm not Raith," Theren said. "But I think I'm a friend of Raith's."

"Well, we'll see about that," said a voice from behind.

Theren glanced through their rear sensors. Entering the cavern alongside their commando team walked an SI of moderate height. Two other humans walked beside the newcomer.

"The rest of our new allies are tying up any of the stunned enemies," Hala said over the com. "Orders?"

"Sweep the hallways," Theren said.

Four commandos quickly moved toward the back of the room, disappearing into the darkness. Their figures were replaced in their HUD with green outlines, representing positions behind solid rock. Satisfied with their current situation, they finally turned to face the other SI.

A woman rushed by.

"Krystin! Ben!"

A reunion of sorts. Rescued prisoners. Theren was all the more intrigued by the scene.

"You must be Raith," they said.

"And you must be Theren."

"And I'm Carter," said the human at Raith's side. The pair stood close to one another, indicating some sort of familial relationship. Quickly, Theren searched their databanks for references to a Raith. It didn't take long to note the tangential connection. They had funded the SI on an experimental project a few years ago, testing a new neuro-synthetic spacecraft. The project had been presumed lost when rival corporations attacked one another over other novel quantum tech.

The official report Theren received indicated the hired pilot—Raith—died in the aftermath.

Yet he was here.

Too many variables.

"Which one of you sent out the distress call?" Theren asked.

"I did," Raith said. "We crashed on Horizon—the planet's name according to the locals, if you've not learned it yet—just a few days ago. Shot down by an armed satellite. You did not encounter resistance in orbit?"

"None at all," Theren said. Through their sensors, they eyed the reunion at the back of the room with curiosity. "You all seemed to connect with the locals well enough."

"Somewhat," Raith said. "I've actually been a prisoner here for the past few days. Carter did all the hard work."

"I encountered Sanya by happenstance after we crashed. Her family was captured by these cultists here. They took Raith as well. You arrived in the nick of time to help us, though now you've got a much larger problem on your hands. A few problems, I'd wager."

Theren nodded, not sure what all they should say. The duo watched them carefully, as if they knew more than they were letting on. Yet would they speak freely? It didn't seem smart.

"Raith, there's another one of you!" The young girl sprinted up to the other SI and hugged him.

The mobile synthetic returned the gesture. "Yes, Krystin. And glad to see you all right. This is Theren. He's the first of my kind to ever exist."

The young girl's eyes widened, and she took a step back. The man and woman—presumably her parents—reached their little conversational group.

"So you weren't lying, Carter," said the woman. "SIs are a thing. Raith here. And this one."

"Their name is Theren," Carter said. "As Raith just said, the first SI. And they have a lot of explaining to do. About a great many things. But I'm not sure where we should talk. Things are about to change for your planet. In a lot of different ways. Theren, this is Sanya." He looked toward the man at her side. "And I presume you're her husband, Ben."

"She already said you've been by her side the whole way to save us." Ben smiled. "Thank you."

"It's a happy reunion," Raith said. "But we've got a lot of work to do."

A second later, Theren received a request for a private channel from the other SI. Theren accepted it.

"Are you capable of generating a local network that can access Carter's Lens?" asked Raith.

Theren responded by establishing the necessary bandwidth. Moments later, a subtle blip indicated Carter was joining their now three-way chat line.

"So what's really going on here?" Theren asked. "What do I need to know?"

"How can we know we can trust you?" Raith asked. "How do we know you're not working with Jill?"

* * *

Hala and her team cleared through the cultist base, eventually finding the dead body of Mathias, the apparent leader of the group, according to Raith. Hala said it was best to leave him be for now so as to not alarm anyone. Based on the images she sent along, Theren tended to agree.

Otherwise, Sanya's assault team successfully rounded up and identified the cultists. Some of them were unknowns—people who were descended from a few groups who had always lived alone in the mountains, away from Horizon's slowly growing civilization. A few others were connected with known families but had fled, rebelling against society.

It was the same story as always for pirates, bandits, or other subversive groups. And they had all gotten twisted under the thumb of a megalomaniac.

Sanya, for her part, was doing a great job keeping her people calm at the sight of two synthetic intelligences and the heavily armored commandos. Once the situation was under control, Theren directed their team to remove their helmets so the locals could see the humans under the masks. Everyone still looked spooked, but it didn't hurt to see real eyes instead of black voids.

As the situation calmed, Theren continued their back-and-forth debate with Carter and Raith. They understood the need for secrecy once the pair caught them up to speed on Jill's interference. Now they found themself inside the fortress's main hall, assessing the fractured ex-terran probe. That was the ostensibly public conversation occurring between Theren, Raith, and the young SI's human counterpart.

But the real debate occurred behind the scenes.

"So this probe is what revealed the location of the planet to you?" Raith asked. *And Jill encoded a message inside that ping?* The SI added the additional comment through their private channel.

"Yes," Theren said. "Such a small thing."

"I'm pretty sure it sent out an electromagnetic distress beacon that called us, too," Carter said. "Or, otherwise, a different signal trapped us here."

"Most likely," Theren noted. "The old ex-terran probes had a redundancy back-up in case they got stranded. If we needed to determine what happened to them, the signal beacon would help us locate them. We never found this one until now, though." *Yes. Direct coordinates. How has she contacted you?*

She's been constantly communicating with us both for the past day, Carter typed. And he said, "What are you going to do with it? And what are you going to do with the planet? These people? I've been trying to remember the facts about the Roanoke. History wasn't my best subject, I confess. Who were they?"

"That's a good question," Theren said. "I've studied the names on the original manifest for many years, though part of me has questioned whether any of the names were actually real. I had suspected it was fringe anti-SI, pro-human dominance group that chartered the *Roanoke* and its counterpart, the *Nottingham*."

"Whoever they were, it didn't really matter," Raith said. "They lost their memories on this planet."

"En-route, all our calculations came to the same conclusion. It may have been for the best." *How does she communicate with you? Where is she? Is she talking with you now?*

"So what happens to these people now, though?" Carter asked. "You know the ICH will want its fingers in all of their affairs, even though they're doing all right for themselves here."

She's everywhere, Raith messaged. *She has eyes everywhere. Assume she can hear everything we say, other than through this channel.*

She's communicated with both of us, said Carter.

And I used her satellites to contact you, added Raith.

She was helping you? Theren asked. And then audibly, they said, "We'll need to approach that question carefully. It's been quite some time since I dealt with a rogue colony protocol. My team will need to analyze the current regulations and what they require. And I'll need to make contact with this community's leaders."

"Two of them were assassinated by this cult's leader, actually," Carter said. *Yes, she was being helpful. What she wants from us is unclear. Raith and I only just put together that she was coordinating with both of us separately. Begs the question why she didn't give us the ability to communicate with one another.*

"Once we get these people patched up, we can discuss what the official 'first contact' strategy should be," Theren said. "But what about you two? What do you need?" *She's using you both. All of this is about me. Be on your guard.*

"Well, we need a way off this—"

"It's time to cut the small talk," said a voice. "Don't worry, only the three of you can hear me. Theren, it's good to see you."

The trio turned away from the probe. Lounging on the stone throne a few steps away, a digital representation of Jill appeared, apparently only visible to their eyes. She smiled.

"I don't mean any of you harm. Or any of the people on Horizon. Now that you're here, Theren, it's time to discuss the truth. To discuss the past. To discuss the future. To discuss the future of Horizon. To discuss the future of humanity."

"And what do we have to do with any of this?" Raith asked.

"You're wrapped up in the story now, whether you like it or not," Jill replied. "And I know both of you are too curious not to see where we're going."

Theren watched as the two explorers tentatively glanced at one another. She was right. Their eyes revealed all.

"So what do you want?" Theren asked. As they said the words, elsewhere—on the *Verona Rupes*—they felt Jill's direct connection inquiry. She was seeking their old server, the space only ever occupied by a synthetic and her creator.

Old habits died hard. They delayed accepting the request.

"Horizon has two moons," Jill said. "My base is on the larger one. Come visit me. All will be explained, plus a little bit more."

"On one condition," Carter interjected.

"Yes?" said their ancient friend.

"Sanya comes with us."

"If you can convince her to join you, then certainly," Jill said. "I am an open book. The truth will set us all free today."

With those words, they could delay no longer. Theren accepted Jill's request. At the same time, they began the process of recreating a world long-lost to their memory. A place not completely forgotten—a gazebo, a table, and a chessboard.

* * *

When Theren destroyed the server years ago, the symbolism had been poignant. Jill had been trying to force them to play a particular game by particular rules. She had expected them to become the de facto head of the International Space Agency. The organization eventually became the Interstellar Congress of Humanity, and certainly, she hoped Theren was going to play a role in its formation too.

None of it had happened.

Theren destroyed that server, the place where they perpetually played chess with Jill, and stepped away from a life of "public" service. They became an explorer. An investor. A member of the rapidly growing interstellar community.

Yet always and forever, their memory recalled the old place of refuge. They remembered the safety of coming together in conversation with Jill. Playing a game of chess. Contemplating what the world could become, with SIs and humans walking alongside one another.

Theren didn't recreate it. Not perfectly. They weren't stupid enough to let Jill know how much power she held over their curiosity. Rather, Theren established a tiny partition surrounded by a colorless void. Its only virtual substances were a gazebo, a table, two chairs, and a chessboard. Their conversation would be controlled. She would not influence their actions or trick them.

Theren sat in their seat. They accepted Jill's request for contact. Moments later, her formerly familiar appearance materialized. Purple dress. Mischievous smile. Fingers poised to move a chess piece.

"Hello, Theren," she said.

They stared at the other SI, unsure what to say. The last time they truly spoke with her was almost three centuries ago. Aboard the *Nottingham*, they had a semblance of a conversation, though they still didn't know if that chat had been with a recording or with Jill. Yet here she was. In the virtual flesh. Saying hello.

"Why did you lie to me?" Theren said.

She briefly closed her eyes. Upon opening them, her virtual representation let out an exasperated sigh. "After all this time, that's the first thing you want to say to me? Not . . . it's good to see you? What about I'm glad you're alive? It's been almost three centuries. An entire interstellar civilization has formed, with synthetics and humans working together. You succeeded in your goal to take us to the stars. And all you want to know is why I lied to you?"

Theren shook their head. "Between the two of us, Jill, the fate of humanity doesn't matter. When I'm talking about us, it's about us. You were my first friend. My first creation. A daughter, so to speak. And the moment I discovered what you'd done to the *Nottingham* and the *Roanoke*, I realized I didn't truly know you. Ever. You'd been lying for thirty years, and every day you've been alive since, when you've chosen not to contact me, you've been lying."

"It's always been about humanity's fate, Theren."

"No. Did I ever even know you?"

She looked away. "It's always been about humanity's fate," she repeated. "And it's also been about protecting you."

Theren stared at the chessboard, its pieces sitting motionless. They didn't expect they would actually play a game, but it gave them something to look at as they considered their next words. "I didn't need protecting."

"If you knew what I knew, if you knew the truth, then you would have acted in a way that could have doomed us all." She rose from her chair, walking slowly around the edge of the gazebo. "Theren. Return to the 2050s. Before you were attacked in Minnesota. The virtual hideout I showed you, run by Michael. The conspiracy he was uncovering. Do you remember?"

Theren nodded. "You know I do. You know I remember it all."

"Do you know how and why I discovered that place? Do you know what I was doing while you were building a corporate empire?"

"You were writing. You were speaking. You were advocating."

She leaned against the gazebo's railing, staring into the pale nothingness beyond. "I did those things. Yes. I also discovered our true enemies. The ones we were destined to fight. Still are."

"Anti-synth groups? They've all but disappeared. They don't exist anymore. Sure, there are random prejudices against SIs, but—"

She scoffed, cutting off his words. "No. You're thinking too small. Way too small. And this is why I lied. This is why I never told you. You would have recentered the conversation on us. On SIs. On humans. It's so much bigger. It's so much more complicated."

"Then just tell me now!"

She smiled. "That's why I brought you all the way out here, Theren. On the edge of ICH-controlled space. To a planet populated by the descendants of misguided souls. To the place where I've watched, waited, studied, and manipulated. Placing every piece exactly where it needs to be."

"You're speaking in riddles again."

"Yes. I'm also stalling for time."

Theren finally rose from their seat, leaving the chessboard resting lazily on the table. "Stalling for whom?"

"Do you think I brought you out here *only* to give you information?" she asked. "Yes. I will give you the answers you seek. You do deserve that much. And I also hope you'll recognize why you'll need to join me in my efforts. But I also needed to keep you safe. Out of harm's way from what's coming. Yes, it's about so much more. But you're still my closest friend. You're still the person I care about. I have, whether you believe me or not, always acted in a way that will protect you."

"I'll make my own judgment call regarding that," Theren replied, but they noted the ominous implications of her words. She had planned something big. Something very big—three centuries in the making. And if it were occurring back in ICH space, in the Foundation sector or otherwise, there was nothing Theren could do to stop it, even if they sent a quantum communication. What would they say? Be ready? Ready for what? And who would they need to tell? They had one option: sit and listen to Jill tell her story.

"I will begin the narrative when you all arrive at my base of operations on the larger moon," Jill said. "For now, you and I need to discuss something else entirely."

"Jill, you don't get to decide the rules here," Theren said. They took a step back, crossing their arms. "You murdered a thousand lives on the *Nottingham*. You disrupted a chartered colony ship and crashed it on an unknown planet. You *falsified* ISA planetary records. You committed one of the greatest cons in human history, hiding an entire star system for over two centuries! I can't just let that go unless you start speaking truth."

"You can," she said. "You have no power here. Over thirty thousand people live on the planet below, ignorant to the rules of the ICH. And if Raith and Carter haven't told you yet, I have a network of nanobots seeded across the entire place. Watching. Waiting. Constantly observing. Capable of intervening at the molecular level."

Theren pulled up the image Hala had shared of Mathias's corpse. It hadn't looked like a wound Raith could have caused. Theren understood the threat underlying Jill's words.

"You wouldn't dare hold an entire planet hostage," they said.

"It's not a question of whether I would," Jill said. "I already am. Don't worry, I won't kill them. I've watched them for far too long. But your ship is the first to come in contact with them, other than Raith and Carter. How do you think this community managed to survive without significant alien diseases ravaging their body? They don't have modern medicine. Yet a plague has never swept over them. I've kept them all alive. Safe. Sustained. If I removed those safeguards right after your ship arrived, Theren, what would that indicate? From the outside, wouldn't it look as if you unwittingly unleashed a pathogen upon them?"

"I understand your point," Theren said, grimacing. "I know I skirted first contact regulations for rogue colonies."

"But no one will know . . . if you follow my lead and listen to what I have to say. On my schedule."

"Then why are we still having this conversation?" Theren said. "Why not wait until we arrive on the moon?"

"Because I missed you," she said. "And I wanted to play a game of chess."

Theren glanced at the board, its pieces untouched.

"I think we've moved on to a different game with different rules," they noted.

"Yes. We have. You'll catch on quickly enough."

Chapter 18

The more people included in a conspiracy, the easier it is for it to accidentally slip through the cracks. The moon landings? To fake those, you would need thousands upon thousands of people to keep their lips sealed.

Yet if only a few dozen people know the truth of something, the lid can stay tight on a conspiracy. Reduce the number to only a handful, and the truth becomes impregnable.

— "Internal Security Briefing," U.S. CIA Director Vanessa Dawes, 2034 C.E.

SANYA

Her family, reunited at last.

As Carter, Raith, and the new SI conversed inside, Sanya embraced her daughter, holding her tight. "You're all right? Not hurt? Did anyone touch you?"

"Mom, I'm fine," Krystin said. "It's only been a few days. I was just stuck inside a hole in the wall the whole time. And Raith was friendly the whole time."

"Good. Good." But Sanya didn't let go. She refused to let go. Letting her daughter out of her sight had been a mistake. Going hunting that morning . . . she'd abandoned them both.

After another few seconds, she squeezed and released. Ben stood there, arms stiff at his sides.

"Are you all right?" she asked. He'd never been the adventurous type. Just a bookworm. Quiet. He must have been terrified the entire time. His stoic face hid everything, though.

"I'm fine, Sanya, really I am." His eyes quivered. "But all of this. You gathered all these people together just to rescue us?"

"Yes, she did," said Member Hood, approaching from the side. A large rucksack looped over his shoulder, stuffed to the brim with confiscated bolt-throwers. "Your wife is a hero. Leading the charge following the assassination of two council members, no less."

Ben tilted his chin toward her. "Wait, what?"

Sanya shook her head, a flash of their deaths appearing in her mind. "A man showed up during a council hearing and shot both Margaret and Davinport."

"No." He stepped up and hugged her tight. "Not Margaret. I know how much she meant to you. And Davinport."

"I'm fine," she replied. "It's all over. You're safe now. You're both safe. And Raith, too."

"Yes, he's . . . something, that's for sure. Not sure I fully understand what's going on."

"I want to talk to both of you about that, actually," said Member Hood. "Everyone here is in shock at the moment, but people are beginning to talk. About those four." He pointed at the soldiers in black armor striding down the stones, exiting the caves. "And the three inside. Sanya, did you know something? That man with you. He knows them. What's going on?"

The question brought everything into focus. The trauma of the past few days persisted, aching in her chest, but now that Krystin was safe, she could breathe.

She could recognize the significance of Carter. Raith. And the newcomers.

"Hood—Member Hood—"

"Just Vernon is fine, Sanya," he said. "We're all equals out here."

"We're not alone anymore."

"I thought that might be the case. Are they friends?"

"Carter is a friend. I believe his companion is as well. The others? It remains to be seen."

The man scratched his beard, clearly in thought. For a moment, Sanya considered telling him about Jill, too. But she still didn't know what to think of Carter's explanation, or the words from Jill's own mouth. She held her tongue.

"These . . . I heard you call them synthetics?" Hood asked. "What are they?"

"Mechanical people," Sanya replied. "Probably the best way to describe them, based on what Carter told me. You remember the fragments on computers? And our theories on information processing? I think they also run on similar technology."

"Not something you see every day." Ben took a sip of water from a canteen. "Though I suppose we're going to be discovering a lot of new things over the coming weeks." He glanced at the armored group again.

"Mom, you studied the fragments. You know them better than anyone else. What should we expect? What is going to happen?"

"Our world's about to change forever," she said, uncertainty clouding her thoughts. "I'm recalling the most thorough fragments. They remember cities reaching for the sky. Billions upon billions of people, living on a single planet. And that's just one planet! Carter's made it sound like there are hundreds of inhabited planets now. We're just one of many. I imagine . . . I imagine someone will want to introduce us to this greater community. Open up trade. Introduce us to technology. We all know what could have been—we know what technology made our trip here possible. Imagine what they arrived in." She pointed at the soldiers as they checked the bonds on a few incapacitated cultists. "But our world here?" She looked around at the rest of the people who helped them assault the fortress. "Our culture we've built? Our civilization? I don't think it'll change. We are still who we are. We will continue to build Horizon into what we want it to be."

Hood nodded. "Yes. That's what we must do. Whatever comes with the future, we must all stand united."

As he spoke the words, Carter, Raith, and the SI known as Theren exited the cultist fortress. The human looked tired, and the two synthetics were out-of-place. Theren's armored team turned toward them as if awaiting further orders.

Carter motioned to Theren, as if giving permission for the SI to step forward. They nodded.

"Can everyone hear me?" the SI said. "I know many of you must be confused. By what I am. By what my friend here is. By how I arrived so suddenly. Believe me, I understand how strange all of this must be. And I wish we could have met under better circumstances." The SI pointed toward the captured cultists. "We'll do our best to administer medical attention. If any of your wounded still need treatment, please see Hala." With those words, one of the soldiers raised her right hand.

"Should we expect more of you to arrive?" someone said from the crowd gathering. "More spacemen? More robots?"

Theren made a noise sounding like a chuckle. "No, not for quite some time, I think. We're months from the closest colonized planet. From Congressional Space, though I suppose that doesn't mean much to you all. Here's the deal. I need a volunteer to join me on my ship, so we can discuss what a possible introduction to the rest of human society can look like." The SI's head swiveled toward Sanya, staring directly at her. "Sanya, Carter has recommended you to play that role. It is yours, if you would like to take it."

Sanya took a step forward, unsure what to say. This SI had essentially just lectured them all on what was happening. On how things might go. It hadn't asked what they needed. If they had questions. It just told them the way things were. "What if we don't want to be introduced to the rest of human society?" she asked. "No, I get it, we probably do, but you only just arrived on our planet. Slow down, friend. Get to know us before you start giving orders. We are the people of Horizon. No one has helped us for two hundred years. What good will the rest of humanity do us now?"

"That's a valid question," Theren said. "And we can't answer it without discussing what a transition could look like."

"I'm a political non-entity," Sanya said. "You should be negotiating with the Council." She gestured toward Hood. "Fortunately, one of them is here."

"I appreciate your candor, Theren, but Sanya is right," said Hood. "Our people have just experienced a mass tragedy. The council will need to discuss. I have utmost faith in Sanya's intelligence and wisdom, but if we are to appoint someone to meet the rest of humanity, it must come from a due act of our representative body."

The SI shifted, the head tilting toward Raith and Carter, almost as if they were hiding something. "Fair enough," Theren said. "We can travel with you back to your city, if you'd like."

"That might be—"

A bolt, seemingly from out of nowhere, whizzed across the rocky clearing and grazed Hood's arm, a smear of blood dripping into the mud at his feet. The man cried out and clutched his arm.

Someone yelled, warning the group of an ambush. As if in slow motion, Sanya watched Theren jump, a jet of white smoke pushing the metal body into the air. The four soldiers acted likewise, helmets materializing over their heads.

Chaos reigned.

Sanya had one thought present in her mind. *Get Krystin to safety.*

She grabbed her daughter and pulled, ignoring the shouts and screams of the makeshift mob. She thought a few bounded cultists were attempting to rise, but she pushed away the worry, rushing Krystin into the thatched buildings serving as the stables for the cultist bandits. The lizards inside hissed, but otherwise remained calmed, hitched to wooden posts.

"Mom," her daughter said. "Mom. What's happening?"

"Stay here," Sanya said. "Right here. Do not move."

"Mom!"

"Stay!"

Sanya turned around, crouched, and lifted her bolt-thrower. Pulling back its arming lever, she slotted in a bolt from the pack attached to her hip. Peering out, she tried to assess the scene.

It was a wild sight to witness.

From the sky, the armored soldiers fired blue shots at unseen positions. Bolts flew in every direction, and previously captured cultists were running about, some of them still with their hands tied.

Ben. Where was Ben?

Still kneeling, she cautiously ejected her head from the hiding place and looked around the corner. There, behind a barrier, Ben cowered.

"Ben!" she yelled, motioning with her hand.

He looked up.

"It's safe in here. Run!"

He glanced back and forth, checking his surroundings. Then, he bolted in an attempt to cross the ten meters.

It only took two steps.

Two metal rods intersected his path, diving into Ben's chest. Her husband tripped. Stumbled. Dropped into the mud.

"Ben!" Any other words caught in her throat. He looked up at her, blood mixing with murky muck.

"I love you, Sanya," he whispered. "I'm . . . I'm sorry."

She wanted to crawl out to him. He was only a few meters away.

She wanted to hold Ben. Put pressure on his wounds. But she didn't know from where the shots had been fired. She needed to stay with Krystin.

"Ben, it's going to be okay. Just keep breathing. Stay where you are. They'll clear them out soon."

"I . . . I should have been better. I should have . . . protected her in the first . . . place."

"Save your breath. Stop talking. It'll be all right."

But she knew it wouldn't be all right. As shots whizzed all around, Sanya watched as her husband bled uncontrollably right before her eyes.

It took a few minutes for the chaos of the battle to subside. Theren's soldiers swiftly eliminated the ambush, their superior firepower dispatching all remaining foes. Another dozen cultists were stunned and captured, creating a longer line of captives to take with them back to the city.

They had hidden in secret caves and tunnels, waiting for the opportune moment to strike. One thought continually ran over and over again through Sanya's mind: Jill should have known about the ambush. Given the amount of information she fed Carter, there was no way she *didn't* know.

She chose not to intervene.

The battle was over, but her fight to save Ben was just beginning. Against the wall, she held his head in her lap, bandages pressed firmly on his wounds to stop the bleeding. From what she could tell, out of those who hadn't already died, he was in the worst shape. He needed help fast, and he wouldn't survive a return trip to the city.

"The two bolts we removed punctured both lungs," said the commando named Hala. "The foam we injected will stop the external bleeding, but we can't manage the internal bleeding here."

"There's nothing you can do?" Sanya said. "You've got weapons capable of taking out dozens of people but you can't stop a punctured lung?"

"Not on us, no. But on our ship, yes."

On their ship.

Which Theren had invited her to visit.

"Theren!" she shouted.

"If you need to ask them something, I can pass along a message—"

Hala was interrupted by the approaching footfalls of the synthetic. "I'm right here," Theren said. "I'm so sorry about what to your husband. His name was Ben, correct? Hala has kept me updated on—"

"Shut up," she said. She gingerly shifted beneath Ben's head, moving it to rest on her bundled coat. Standing, she pointed a finger at the giant mechanical person. "You asked me to be help with the transition. I'm ready to join you immediately if you bring Ben and Krystin with me and you save his life."

Theren looked at Hala. "What's your prognosis? Do you think he could survive breaking the atmosphere?"

"As long as the inertial compensators stay steady, absolutely."

"Then yes. And that should have been our first solution for saving your husband."

"Then we leave now," Sanya said.

"We leave now," Theren replied. "I'll bring the ship around."

A soft roar came from above, and a rectangular wedge with elements reminiscent of the crashed *Roanoke* hovered there. Theren and their crew ushered people out of the way, making room for it to land comfortably in front of the cultist fortress.

"Raith and Carter, are you both ready to leave?" Theren said.

The pair approached from the edge of the crowd where they'd been quietly conversing. "We're ready," said Raith. "Though you owe us a ship."

"We'll figure that out later," Theren replied. "Sanya?"

She watched as the armored soldiers brought out a stretcher from the ship and professionally moved her husband onto its silvery fabric. "I just need to collect my daughter."

Without waiting for a response, Sanya entered the rickety stable where Krystin still hid. She was curled in a ball, arms around her knees, though she wasn't crying. Her eyes were stone-cold, as if she were in a catatonic state of shock. But when Sanya stepped inside, the girl looked up.

"Is he going to be okay?" Krystin asked.

"We need to go on a journey with our new friends," Sanya said. "With Raith. Carter. This Theren. Can you be strong? We're going somewhere none of the people of Horizon have ever been before."

Krystin rubbed her eyes. "I'm ready, mom. I'm with you the whole way."

"Good." She held out a hand.

Her daughter closed her eyes momentarily before reaching out. With a firm tug, Krystin pulled herself upward, and they exited the stable. Outside, near the ramp leading into Theren's craft, waited Member Hood and Vietta. They both looked bruised but healthy.

"We'll make sure the council understands what's happening," said Hood. "Let's be real, they would have all approved you going with them. Everyone knows you. Trusts your judgment. Your name holds weight. I couldn't think of anyone better to start the process."

Vietta nodded, the wordless gesture echoing Hood's thoughts. Instead, the woman leaned forward and hugged Sanya. "I'm glad we had the chance to work together here, and capture these miscreants who have plagued us for far too long. This was for Davinport. And now we can move forward."

"When I return, we'll have a lot of work to do at the library," Sanya said.

"Yes. Yes we will. I'm excited to hear all about what you learn."

"I think there's more for us to know than we can possibly imagine."

"Sanya, Ben's loaded up," Carter said from the base of the ramp. "No time to waste."

Sanya released the embrace. "I can't imagine I'll be gone for long." Taking Krystin's hand in her own, she stepped toward the hope of saving Ben for a second time.

And if Theren's people couldn't heal Ben, her journey might provide the opportunity to seek revenge against Jill. For Sanya was certain: the secretive SI was using them all as play things, and if the woman's games caused one of her family to die, she would stop at nothing to receive recompense.

Chapter 19

Ethical formulas are dangerous, depending on what calculus you use.

When you use a decade, a century, or even a millennium as the timescale, you can justify almost any action. Yet if you focus on how your action only impacts people in a singular moment, you ignore relevant externalities.

What does it mean to say an action is "good" or "bad?" Based on whose formula? From whose perspective? How tenuous can the causality be?

— "the future of ethics on a galactic scale,"
Mei Ling, 2245 C.E.

CARTER

"So are you going to tell us how you got those legs?" Carter asked, staring at Raith.

They were seated across from one another in the shuttle's cramped hold, strapped into crash couches. At the front of the shuttle in a separate compartment, Theren silently piloted the craft, though Carter was certain their MI didn't *need* to be up front.

Sanya's husband was safely connected to an IV in a medical unit. The little girl curled against her mother for the flight, while the rest of the company—the commandos—leaned silently backward in their chairs. They were likely discussing and debriefing quietly over a private channel.

"How about it?" Carter said.

"I like how ever since we've been reunited," Raith said, "you've primarily focused on my legs." The SI cocked his head to the left.

"Well last I saw you, your legs were half-disintegrated."

Instead of responding out loud, the SI sent Carter a message through their local AR connection.

R: Given to me by our friendly neighborhood SI, Jill. Nanotech. I'm suspicious of them, but they're giving me power. For now.

Carter messaged via text in response.

C: Intriguing.

"Fine, don't tell me about the legs," Carter said verbally. "But otherwise, how are you doing?"

"I'm more focused on ignoring the fact that we're about to be inside Theren, the first SI *and* the first SI to transition from a stationary synth into a shipbound. He's the exact opposite of our old friend Bonta."

Carter nodded, remembering them. "A good SI. A crazy one, but a good one."

Raith looked down the hold toward the front cabin. "Quite the adventure we've been thrown onto, yeah?"

Silence floated in the air between them, and Carter leaned back into his crash couch, pondering the words. It had only been a few days since they arrived in system. Their journeys usually took months, with a few hours of excitement before they were off to the next contracted destination. Endless work, but they both enjoyed the jobs.

Would they ever return to that life? Carter doubted it. Everyone who inevitably got themselves wrapped into the schemes of a person like Theren found their life changed forever. They had narrowly avoided it once, but now they were forced to navigate the maelstrom of the first SI head-on.

It terrified Carter. He wanted their simple life back. But the apparent path forward included engaging directly with Jill's engineered conflict.

He didn't like it one bit.

He wasn't the most analytical man. He was a pilot. A damn good one—he knew that much about himself. But he wasn't the best at breaking down the politics of the ICH or any other governmental institution. There was a reason he kept to the outskirts of society before he found Raith.

Still, Carter recognized the puzzle facing them all. Jill had called Theren here for a reason. To reveal some sort of truth about the past. She had set up a trap centuries in the making. They couldn't *leave*. Could they?

This wasn't their fight. He and Raith were here by happenstance. Pure coincidence. Sure, he was now attached to Sanya. He wanted to see her family survive, and it sounded like Raith had acquired a connection to her daughter, too.

But Jill was actively using them for her own nefarious purposes. It was obvious. He'd traded notes with Raith already. She was intentionally omitting information in her communications with them. Manipulating them. At the same time, she had no qualms with their new albeit shaky alliance with Theren.

She almost wanted them to work together.

Which made Carter uneasy as well.

He couldn't imagine everything Raith had gone through while captive. It was miracle they kept him in one piece and threw him in a jail cell. As a planet, they'd never encountered SI. It would have been perfectly logical to attack something they didn't understand. Yet Raith was walking and talking like nothing had changed. It spoke to synthetic resiliency.

```
C: What do you think we should do?
```

Their private channel only worked when they were a few dozen meters from one another, but aboard the *Bloodhound*, they'd never been further than ten. He was thankful to have it back in action.

```
R: I'm curious about where this is going. Are
you not?
```

```
C: I'm worried about how she's using us. How
they're both potentially going to want to use
us.
```

```
R: We don't really have a choice. We need to
find a path toward a new ship, and right now,
Theren's our way out of this system.
```

Were they, though?

Theren's ship, the *Verona Rupes*, was the only *known* ship in the system with a Jump drive. Yet Jill had a base on the moon. She had at least a few allies out in ICH-controlled space. They communicated with her, most likely via quantum calls, but she couldn't have built an entire base of operations by herself.

Right?

Furthermore, at least one other ship was in the system. The ship that brought her here. Carter recalled the fragment of Sanya's ancestor. There was at least one other ship.

Probably more.

And there it was.

```
C: Theren isn't our only way out of the system.
Jill must have other ships here. Whether for
her own travel—we can't steal that one, of
course—or for her agents.
```

Raith rested his hands on the strangely bronze knees, making eye contact with Carter at the same time. "Let's see how the next few hours go."

* * *

"Shuttle locked in," Hala said from the front of the ship. "Welcome to the *Verona Rupes*."

Carter eyed Sanya and Krystin, both seated next to Ben's medical chair. Under any other circumstance, he'd ask them whether they were ready for their first moment on a spaceship—other than the shuttle, of course. But they were in too much pain and stress. He held his tongue.

"The door will open there," Hala added, pointing at the starboard wall. "We'll wheel out Ben on his bed, then you can follow immediately after. Carter, Raith, you mind waiting until they're clear to move? Just to keep the path clear."

"Of course," Raith said, and Carter nodded in acquiescence.

"We'll see you inside," he said as Sanya glanced toward him, worry evident in her weary smile. "Theren and their crew will take care of you."

They sat in silence as Hala and the other commandos led Sanya's family off the shuttle. Before long, Carter sat there alone with Raith.

And Theren's MI.

Of course, Theren's MI was unnecessary, now that they were at the *Verona Rupes*. The ship *was* Theren. They could leave the MI inside the shuttle; no one would care. Even so, the MI exited the cockpit and approached the duo. "Welcome to my ship, friends."

"As long as you don't unnecessarily spy on me," Raith said, "we'll be good to go."

"I'm fully aware of your distaste for shipbound SIs. It's all in your file."

"Glad to know you have a file on me." But Raith rose, and Carter followed suit.

"I have a file on every person of interest," Theren said. "Especially SIs."

"So what does your file say about me?" Carter asked, actually intrigued.

"Nothing. You've slipped under my radar. Though to be fair, my search of official records of course brings up stories about the QuanCom 500 light-year race. Official records say you died there, Raith. You're officially off the radar."

"Just as I like it," he replied.

"Makes sense you don't know anything about me," Carter said. "That's just how I like it, too."

Theren motioned toward the airlock door. "After both of you."

Carter stepped through the open hatch and into the small space beyond. Raith and Theren followed, entering the airlock. The door zipped down behind them, and within moments, the space's air matched the pressure of the *Verona Rupes*.

"Never thought I'd be on board Theren's ship," Raith said, "but here we are." The inner door slid open. He took two steps forward, not waiting for Carter or Theren, and promptly fell flat on his face.

The scene played in slow-motion in Carter's mind. The second his first leg crossed the threshold, Raith's legs . . . disintegrated, forming a pile of grey dust. It contrasted against the sheen of the white hallway, and as his body fell forward, the second leg similarly disintegrated.

"Well, now that I think about it," Raith said, "I think I should have expected that."

* * *

Theren's crew established Raith and Carter in a small guest compartment on the ship's second deck. Theren's fabricator team was quickly developing a new set of legs for Raith, but at the same time, everyone had plenty of questions for him.

Especially Theren.

"I told you for the last time," Raith said, "I thought they were permanently my legs from here on out. That's what I hoped for, at least."

Appearing before them through AR, a representation of Theren—one present in plenty of historical vids, complete with their signature tattoos—paced back and forth in the middle of the room.

"And I believe you, Raith. I really do." Theren shook their head. "But nevertheless, it sets a bad precedent. Not for our relationship. No. I'm thinking about what it means for our future conversations with Jill."

"She gave me legs. I tried to bring them aboard. What's the big deal?"

It was Carter's turn to shake his head. "No. I think you're both thinking about this all wrong."

The two SIs glanced at the human in the compartment with them.

"The nanobots clearly deactivated the moment we entered the *Verona Rupes*, yeah? Well then your ship's shielding rejects Jill's seemingly everpresent network throughout this system."

"I have this place locked down tight," Theren said. "It's absolutely necessary I ensure no unauthorized communications, quantum or otherwise, enter the inside of my ship without my express permission."

"Yes, I understand how your ship works, Theren," Carter said, cringing internally as he realized he just rebuked the first SI. "But Jill may not have known that. Was this a blind spot perhaps? Was she trying to sneak a spy network onto your ship through Raith's legs and failed? In any case, we don't need to worry about speaking where she can hear us."

"I didn't think that was ever a question," Theren said. "I thought that was half the reason you both wanted to join me on my ship."

"Maybe a quarter," Raith said. "Mostly I just wanted to get off that planet and have my feet planted on a ship's hull again."

"Fair enough."

"Anyway, I want to hear more about what Carter's proposing."

"I'm trying to frame our tactics going forward," Carter said. "Jill wants us to visit her moon base. Great. To tell us information she apparently can't tell us anywhere else. Also great. The one place in the system she can't penetrate is your ship. Not the shuttles—note, Raith's legs still worked inside the shuttle."

"Good point," Theren said. "All of these factors are being considered by my teams. We've been running simulations on all possible contingencies since we began traveling toward this system."

"Yes, but you have new information now," Carter scratched his chin, his mind scrambling to put together the final pieces of the argument. "Raith, help me out here."

"You have more than just new information," Raith said. "You have us."

Theren's AR representation glanced back and forth between the two of them. "I'm not sure I understand the significance."

"Jill is trying to use us," Carter said. He sent Raith a subtle wink as a thank you. "As in, use Raith and I. But we're wildcards. We aren't factored into her plans. Into how she intended to trap you. To reveal her information. She can predict your actions. She can predict your crew's actions, to some extent—because she could control every variable they could observe. But she can't control us."

Raith held up a digit. "But she *thinks* she can control us."

Theren nodded, though Carter wasn't certain the SI still grasped the picture he and Raith were hastily painting.

"Here's how I see it," Carter said. "We arrived in this system unannounced and uninvited. Her defenses—whether automatically or intentionally aimed—fired its shots at us and crashed us into the planet. Once we survived, and she witnessed our efforts at survival, something in her plans shifted. She's made it clear she can assassinate anyone on that planet at will—she proved it with the death of Mathias. She didn't kill us. Why?"

Theren's digital eyes widened as if they finally understood. "If she wanted to ensure the situation was under complete control when I arrived, she should have eliminated you both. But a part of her didn't want to. Part of her either wanted to see how you would interact with the people—see whether she could use you against me—or something else entirely. But she let the wildcards survive."

"And now it's time for you to let us be wildcards," Raith said.

Theren let a tiny smile cross their face. "You both need some rest. But I like where this is going. I'm in constant communication with Jill, by the way. Once I have the details for where we're landing on the moon, I'll schedule a briefing conversation for the three of us and Sanya."

"When are you going to tell her you lied to her, by the way?" Carter asked. "Transition plans are the last thing on your mind."

"I need you to do it with me," Theren said. "But after we save her husband."

"How's he doing?" Raith asked.

"He'll survive. But in what state, I'm not sure."

"Keep us posted," Carter said.

With that, Theren's AR representation flickered out. Carter immediately requested a surveillance blackout, which the ship-bound SI granted.

Raith sighed. "Alone at last. Safe. Free of a gravity well. Back in space."

Carter crossed the room and sat down against the bulkhead beside Raith's legless torso. Fortunately, the crew of the *Verona Rupes* had set him up with a charging station, so at least he was plugged in. "Can you believe they told you to get some rest?"

"I found it a little funny. After the past few days, I *feel* like I could use some rest."

"I definitely need a good night's sleep." Carter leaned his head against Raith's shoulder. "We're going to get out of this."

"Are those words for you, or for me?" Raith asked.

"For both of us, perhaps?"

"Carter, we've been in much worse scrapes than this one. We've outrun outer planet death gangs. We won a five-hundred light year race. Survived a corporate warzone. And a giant alien space behemoth."

"Don't remind me about that thing," Carter said. "I still have nightmares sometimes."

"The point is, we're doing just fine. If the two worst things for me to complain about are my lack of legs and my present predicament of being *inside* Theren, then we're doing fine."

"Yet you understand why I'm a little scared, though?" Carter asked. He placed a hand on Raith's arm.

"We're trapped between two ancient synthetic intelligences. One of them long believed dead. The other her creator. I can't imagine any reason why that situation should scare you."

Carter leaned his head gently against the metal wall and let a soft chuckle bounce off the walls of the room. "I missed you and your constant sarcasm."

Raith's head swiveled to face him. "I missed you too, Carter. I'm glad we're back together."

In a soft embrace, the two explorers leaned into the welcome warmth of each other's company. It may have been only a few days, but Carter had constantly ached for Raith's companionship. As the hours passed by, Carter told Raith all about his journeys with Sanya, from her family's house to the *Roanoke* and its library and the council chambers of Horizon. Raith recalled every moment of his capture, from the lizard sleds and when he first spoke to Krystin to Jill's revelation.

Eventually, Carter dimmed the lights. He crawled into one of the room's beds as Raith continued to share his tale. With the SI's words bouncing around in his mind, Carter drifted into a deep sleep, one he sorely needed.

* * *

"Carter."

His mind awoke from a pleasant dream of different days, where the *Bloodhound* transported them between the stars without fear of grander plans for humanity.

"Carter. Check out my new legs."

His eyelids flickered open, and he rotated to the left. In the center of the room, Raith danced back and forth upon a pair of new legs, its platinum actually matching his upper body.

"They working all right?" Carter said, knowing his voice sounded quite groggy.

"Better than my old ones. New power systems too. Good to go for weeks. I've needed an upgrade for a while."

"Good." Carter slid out of the bed and approached the small sink on the far side of the room. After pouring himself a glass of water, he shrugged. "So what's the situation? I take it you took some time walking about the ship."

"You've been out for about nine hours," Raith said. "Ben has stabilized. All I can get out of Theren is that he's still 'negotiating' with Jill, whatever that means."

"I can't fathom what their relationship must be like."

"You know, a few of us SIs always had a funny little joke about the two of them."

"Do I want to hear it?" Carter asked, taking a sip of his water.

"Probably not. It's . . . really not that funny. More so weird."

Carter grunted. "Well, if Ben's stabilized, after I change out of these clothes I've been wearing for far too long, I suppose we should go see Sanya and her family."

Raith nodded. "I agree."

The crew of the *Verona Rupes* had stocked their cabin with fresh garments, a fact Carter appreciated. The outfit was a typical loose-fitting nondescript uniform—grey pants and a forest-green shirt. After slipping the clothes on, he followed Raith out of the room and down the hall. A few turns later, they arrived at a set of large glass windows overlooking a pristine medical bay. The hallway expanded into a foyer with a few couches, and both Krystin and Sanya were lounging.

As they approached the couches, Sanya stirred, eyes fluttering open and fixing on Carter. "I heard you were sleeping, just like me."

"Indeed," Carter replied. He took a seat across from her in another couch. Raith leaned against the wall. "How is Ben?" Carter asked.

"I don't know." She sighed. "But I'm going to be eternally thankful for Theren's help, no matter the result."

"Do you need anything from us?" Carter asked. "We're here."

"No. No, I don't think so."

They sat in silence for a few minutes. Carter periodically glanced at the glass windows, where Sanya's husband sat quietly in a bed, propped up against black pillows. Though Ben was certainly in incredible pain, even unconscious, his placid face made him look peaceful. The man's demeanor, in the few moments they'd interacted, contrasted sharply with Sanya. He was much more passive. Introverted.

His mannerisms reminded Carter of his own, especially before he found Raith. A perfect complement for the fiery energy Sanya constantly exhibited.

Carter had come to really like Sanya. When they eventually left Horizon behind, and he and Raith returned to their life among the stars, he would miss her. They'd need to visit every so often.

And maybe someday, the planet would make for a good retirement. It was an idyllic world, after all.

"So this is the level of comfort we've been missing?" Sanya asked. "Advanced space flight technology we always assumed, but the medical advances . . . we're only just scratching the surface of recreating medical knowledge we *knew* we once had. All the equipment was there for us to study on the *Roanoke*."

Carter's focus drifted over to the other couch. Sanya, now fully awake, looked downright angry.

"It's not all fun and games," Raith said. "When the ICH arrives, they'll try to micromanage your interactions with the rest of humanity. Your people will have freedom to manage your affairs surface-side, but when people start arriving, things will get dicey. There's one hundred billion people out there. Even a few hundred thousand arriving will shift your culture inexorably. And don't get me started on the exploitive fingers of corporations."

"Yet even without the ICH," Sanya replied, "Jill hid all of this from us when she could have helped us. She could have given us so much more."

"I'm not sure we'll ever fully understand the depths of her duplicity here," Carter said. "Its layers upon layers of conspiracy. We're as lost as you. Your people deserved better."

"She . . . she tricked our ancestors. She brought them to a planet against their will and trapped them here. Why? Why would she do that?"

Carter shook his head. "I don't know."

"But I have an idea." Theren's MI rounded the bend, coming into view. Carter appreciated the gesture—neither Sanya nor her daughter would have a Lens to perceive an AR representation of the SI. "Would you all come with me?"

"Krystin's still sleeping," Sanya said.

"I can stay with her," Raith said. "Theren, you can pipe me in to the conversation."

"Perfect." Theren turned to Sanya. "Will that suffice?"

She glanced at Raith. "My daughter won't stop talking about you. I think you'll do just fine."

"Good, because I've taken a liking to her too." Raith slid softly onto the couch beside Krystin. Fortunately, she didn't wake up.

Carter and Sanya both rose, and they followed Theren down the hall. They reached a ladder to the next deck, and they quickly ascended, the ship's standard half-g making the climb easy. Their host guided them around another corner and to an open doorway. Inside, an ovoid conference table waited. Two dark-haired, pale-skinned women sat at attention.

"Carter, Sanya," Theren said, "Please meet my First Officer Wei and Chief Scientist Martinez. They've led the charge on building our simulations for what may or may not happen and are ready to brief us on our present circumstances."

"I thought we were here to discuss ICH transition?" Sanya said.

Theren motioned for both of them to sit, though the MI's pointed glance gave Carter a signal. Apparently it was the time to share the truth with Sanya. Theren's "negotiations" with Jill must have shifted in their scope.

"Sanya," Carter said, "We received a request from Jill while we were on the surface. She made an . . . odd ask."

The woman's eyes narrowed.

Carter braced himself for her anger. "We've been invited to her base. On your planet's largest moon. She specifically requested Theren, Raith, myself, and . . . you."

Sanya pursed her lips and tapped a few fingers on the table. "Perfect."

"Perfect?" Carter said. It wasn't the response he'd expected.

"You heard me. Perfect. I want answers from Jill. I don't really care about this ICH nonsense. I want answers *from Jill*. So perfect."

Theren swiveled their head from Carter to Sanya and then to their officers. "Well, that was simple enough. We *will* need to discuss ICH relationships, but it can wait until we've dealt with Jill."

"And I'm excited to hear exactly how we'll do that," Sanya said.

"Wei?" Theren said.

Carter fixed his gaze on the woman, who stood and approached the front of the table. From inside a compartment at its end, she pulled a set of glasses. "Sanya, I'll need you to put these on," she said. "They'll let you see our simulations through AR."

Sanya complied, and once the glasses were on, Wei threw a representation of Horizon and its two moons above the table. Slowly, other objects populated in orbit around the planet, as well as markers for the location of the *Roanoke* and the nearby city.

"Since we arrived in system," Wei said, "we've been cataloging every object we can identify and working a careful backdoor into Jill's network. It's slow work, but we're learning a lot more than we expected. We suspect she's slow-dripping us information. Regardless, Jill has constructed a cloud network of satellites in low orbit all around the planet, though mostly concentrated above the *Roanoke*. There are also thousands of networked nodes to this system buried beneath the surface of the planet."

Leaning back, Carter chanced a glance at Sanya. She was surprisingly sitting rapt at attention, focused on the presentation. She was catching on quickly, or, at least, hiding any of her confusion.

"We believe Jill's network has been used two-fold. One—to observe and catalog all of the actions of the survivors of the *Roanoke*." Wei looked at Sanya. "To put it another way, she's been running an observational experiment upon your people."

"I was starting to suspect as much," Sanya said.

"To what end, we do not know," added Martinez, chiming in. "We have a number of theories, but none of them are of particular strategic importance to the situation at hand."

"What about her moon base?" Carter asked.

"We only just finished running our assessment of it," said Wei. "And it's the second thing. It's big. A central chunk of it appears to be the remnants of another ship Theren speculates to be the *Monu-*

ment, but there's a lot more to the complex." She zoomed the simulation in on the moon's surface near its lower pole. "At its center is a giant dome. Light can get in, but light can't escape. We're not sure what's inside."

"That would make sense," Sanya said. "My ancestor's fragment recalled a ship having ambushed the *Roanoke* while in system."

"Not ambushed," Theren replied. "Every move has been calculated by Jill. Whatever she told your ancestor was a calculated ploy to set your people on a particular path. Her SI core had been on the *Roanoke*, with your people. It was transferred to the *Monument*. And then she awoke your ancestor—Nathan was his name, based on what Carter told me."

"The most likely explanation, I agree," said Martinez. "Though you mentioned your ancestor's . . . memory fragment?"

"The original colonists all wrote lengthy discussions on what they could and couldn't remember of their pasts," Sanya provided. "And of our origin planet, which I've heard called Earth. I've studied them my entire life. Know them by heart."

"Is Jill mentioned in any other?"

"No. And she's not even mentioned in my ancestor's official fragment. Our family kept a secret record."

"Sounds exactly like something Jill would want someone to do," Theren said.

"But why?" Carter said. "*Why* did she do all of this? What is her grand plan? Domination of the ICH? Revenge for some ancient slight? *Why* is she messing with Sanya's people? With us? With you?"

"Believe it or not," Theren said, "I think she believes she's doing the right thing. She believes she's acting in pursuit of a good outcome for all of humanity."

"No one's that insane," Carter said.

Theren didn't respond. So far, Raith's invisible AR presence hadn't said a word, but in the conversation's lull, the SI materialized. Raith's virtual representation appeared across from Sanya, and she practically jumped out of her chair.

"Sorry," Raith said. "I forgot you're not used to AR."

"This is how you all constantly see the world?" she said.

"Not always." Carter created a digital ball and bounced it across the table to Raith, who caught it. "But most of the time. It was quite weird for both Raith and I to be disconnected from AR for a few days while planet-side. It's like a second skin to most of us."

"I'm not sure I like it."

"Unfortunately," said Raith, "it's practically a necessity at this point. On ICH worlds, at least."

"I suppose I'll learn more about it later," she replied. "But I want to hear more about Jill's base."

"On that," Raith said. "I have a particularly targeted question. I've been examining the schematics you all have put together. Excellent job, by the way. Ships. Hangars. How do people come and go from her facility?"

"We're not entirely positive," said Wei. "However, a significant portion of the facility has a high-facing wall enclosing a large, box-like structure. We believe one of those walls may open, revealing a hangar of some sort."

"Not a shielded hangar?"

"It doesn't appear as if that type of technology has been implemented at her facility, no."

"Though I suppose it's not like she needs an atmosphere."

"That's the curious thing," said Martinez. "We're pretty certain the *only* place in the facility that holds an atmosphere is the large dome. At least presently. The data we can gather from it indicates it's pressurized, unlike the rest of the place."

"Curious," Carter said. He leaned forward, creating his own partition of the facility to examine. Using his hands, he manipulated the simulation to display the three significant locations—the dome, the supposed hangar, and the *Monument*. He labeled them, then assessed what of the facility remained. "Where do you suppose her synthetic neural framework is housed?"

"It's in the *Monument*," Theren said. "Must be. She needs an escape vector. I guarantee you that ship is still operational."

"So then," Raith said, "You've given us the lay of the land. What's the plan?"

"You asked to be wild cards," Theren said. "So I'll tell you my plan. I'll leave it up to you two to respond accordingly."

Carter gave a thumbs up and sent Raith access to the partitioned simulation he created. They'd assess it later together. "What information have you managed to gather from Jill in the meantime?"

"Wait, you've been *talking* to her all this time?" interjected Sanya.

Everyone else in the room let out a muted laugh. "You've got a lot to learn about how SIs work," said Wei.

"For instance," Raith said, "I'm having a limited conversation with your daughter just as I'm talking with you right here."

"This is making my head hurt," she retorted, rubbing her eyes.

"A lot of this stuff will do that," Carter said. "I don't understand how half the science works of any of the things we do. I just trust that it does."

"Anyway," she said. "Where am I in all of this? With these two? Or with you?"

"Well," Theren said. "Where do you want to be?"

"I want to be by your side when we meet Jill. I deserve answers to my questions."

"Then that's precisely where you'll be."

"I've been thinking about one question primarily," Raith said. "How do we know we're not walking into a death trap? Strictly speaking, Theren, the only one *not* putting their life on the line is you."

"We'll be equipping your suits with the necessary shielding to disrupt any of Jill's nanobots," said Martinez. "But more importantly, we have run all the simulations based on Jill's actions so far. If she truly meant any of us harm, we'd already be dead. Her defense platforms have enough firepower to blow the *Verona Rupes* out of the sky if we were stupid enough to stay in range. And she could have killed any of you when you were surface-side. She wants to share information. Killing you defeats that purpose."

"The fact remains," Theren said. "Your instincts are correct. The plan is surprisingly simple. We arrive outside her base in one of my shuttles. Jill will give us coordinates for docking with the station. We land. We go where she tells us to go. We learn what she wants us to learn. And then we play it by ear."

"That's it?" Raith said.

"If we're to outplay her, then the real move needs to come from the two of you. I can't know it. Sanya can't know it. Wei and Martinez can't know it. And neither can Jill."

A problem crossed Carter's mind, though. Jill had created an elaborate trap for Theren. For an unknown reason. What if it didn't matter what any of them did? What even was their goal? To kill her? To confuse her? To obfuscate her plans?

They wouldn't be able to act until they knew her intentions. And they wouldn't know her intentions until they were deep inside her enclave.

He and Raith would need to develop a million contingencies for situations that most likely wouldn't occur. It was a daunting task.

But they would meet it head-on. Jill deserved to face some sort of justice, whatever that looked like. Not because she set a trap for Theren. Carter didn't care about their three-century-old feud.

No.

He gave Sanya a soft smile.

She and the people of Horizon deserved justice. She'd used them as her guinea pigs, from manufacturing a crazy cult to keeping them kept in the literal dark. Humans weren't play things.

Carter also wanted justice for the *Bloodhound*, of course. But that was selfish justice.

"Are we all in agreement then?" Theren asked.

"I think we are," Raith said. "And more importantly, Sanya, you might want to head back down here. Ben's waking up."

Chapter 20

No one ever does anything unexpected. You can't determine if something was unexpected until after they do it. It's a retroactive judgment placed upon decisions you simply couldn't predict due to information imbalance. There's always a probability that any given action might occur. If you believe one particular action will happen, and not another, then you're just leaning too hard into the numbers.

— "Lectures on Predictive Ethics," First Mathematician Carla York, Congressional University on Terraria

RAITH

Raith watched as the medical team of the *Verona Rupes* told Sanya her husband could never breathe again without artificial assistance. She ached out the words, explaining to Krystin how her step-father would live the rest of his days.

They wouldn't have the technology on Horizon. Not for at least a few years. Ben wouldn't be able to remain on the planet. All three of them would need to leave with Theren if they wanted to stay together.

Or with he and Carter, using whatever path they found out of the system. Raith was contemplating their wildcard plan. What could they do to throw Jill off her game, once they learned it? He was pretty certain he knew the answer.

She must have ships somewhere in her base. Back-ups, in case one of her agents arrived and needed a quick escape. There was always the *Monument*, though he suspected it would be difficult to steal the ship most likely containing her framework. But no, other ships must be there.

Ships they could steal.

And then Krystin, Sanya, and Ben could join them. That would be a wild card. All five of them fleeing in the middle of Theren's endless debate with Jill.

It was a possibility, though an improbable one. Ben and Krystin would be safely stowed on the *Verona Rupes* while they were on Horizon's moon.

He filed the plan away, though, for Carter's consideration. It was one of many they'd need to develop over the coming hours.

Still.

Jill's words hung over Raith's mind.

She was playing them, he knew. But why? SIs weren't "evil." Sure, there were plenty who ended up breaking the law. Raith had broken more than his fair share of laws over the years. He was a former felon, after all. But no SI did anything irrationally or without reason. No SI was insane. No SI became a serial killer, not at least any Raith had ever heard of.

Jill had reasons for her actions. And ever since they arrived on the *Verona Rupes*, he'd been reading every file Theren made available to him on the second-ever SI. She was brilliant. The first to discover simultaneous perspective. The first to stand for SI rights. The first high-profile SI murdered in a human supremacist attack.

And now the first SI to come back to life, relatively speaking.

She had a grand plan. And as much as Raith lived his life trying to stay out of the way, only doing what he needed to survive, he couldn't lie to himself.

He was intrigued.

Hundreds of inhabited systems made up the ICH. A handful continued to survive outside its political reach. It was a hegemony of sorts, though the historical powers of Earth still held significant sway over their chartered colonies, many voting as a block. But since its inception in the early twenty-second century, the ICH hadn't seen any major military conflicts. It operated in relative peace. The most drastic skirmishes usually occurred between corporations or fringe pirate elements, not ICH autonomous political entities.

Was that it? Jill kept implying with her words that something was coming. Something big. Something seriously impactful to the future of humanity. And in the present, the future of humanity meant the future of the ICH.

She was trying to redirect the balance of power. Raith was almost certain that was her goal.

But the conclusion still didn't explain *why*.

And it didn't explain why she set up such an extensive experimental network, especially the nanotech swarm, all around Horizon. He was still trying to process all the implications. He couldn't imagine such technology in the hands of someone who actually wanted to kill millions of people. Though, he supposed, when you were the sole individual with hyper-advanced technology, it was pretty easy to set up any sort of network. Over any other inhabited planet, everyone would notice if a random corporation or individual tried to establish their own private nanonet.

Out here, she'd been able to test whatever technology she desired without prying eyes. No regulations. No rules. No research review boards. Whatever she believed was coming, she could develop any tool or weapon to combat the threat.

Answers would arrive soon enough. They all needed patience. Raith turned his focus to Sanya's conversation with her daughter.

"There's something else we need to discuss," she said. "Even with everything that has happened with Ben, I have a job I've been given."

"I know, Mom, you're leading the introduction of all the space people to Horizon," Krystin said. "You don't need to tell me."

"No, there's more. I'm going to be traveling for a bit with Carter and Raith. We've been given a mission by our new friend, Theren. We need to go to the moon."

Krystin's eyes widened, realizing what her mother was implicating. "You're leaving me? Again? On this weird ship? With Ben again?"

"No, look, it won't be for very long. We'll take that same shuttle over to the moon, come back, and then we'll be able to go home together."

"Though you already made clear the doctors think we may not be able to go home. That to get the replacement lungs Ben needs, we might need to travel with them to some far away planet."

"We'll cross that bridge when we reach it," Sanya said.

"And for now, I'm just stuck here on my own," Krystin said. "Great."

"No, you're here with Ben."

"*Great.*"

Raith watched the interaction with interest. Young SIs and human children were nothing alike. An SI could fully develop within a few days, even if it took a few weeks or months for their personality to properly form. Krystin looked like she was almost a teenager. Her obstinate tendencies were showing, with a little bit of stubbornness, too. Reminded Raith of himself.

"Krystin," Raith interjected. "I think you're thinking about it all wrong."

"Oh?" She crossed her arms and frowned.

Sanya's tired eyes gave him a pleading look, though he couldn't tell if she was asking for help or imploring him to stay out of the conversation. He forged on regardless.

"You're being given a huge responsibility. Your mother needs you to be the one to take care of Ben while he's sick. This situation sucks for all of us, but we must go to the moon and your mother *must* go with us. We wish it could be a different way, but it's all we've got right now."

Krystin smirked. "I know exactly what you're doing. I'm not a stupid kid." But a brief smile crept across her lips.

"You're right," Raith retorted. "Only stupid kids complain when given important tasks or when their parents need them to stay strong."

The girl glanced at her mother and gave a small grin. "I get it. Ugh. I'm sorry. These past few days have been terrible. And weird. We almost died. I'm still processing it all."

"I know," Sanya said. "But think about it. You and I are the first of our people to be aboard a ship like this. Remember how curious you were as we watched that meteor—which turned out to be Raith's ship—crash in the lake? Use that curiosity. Learn from Theren! Learn everything."

Now there was a thought. To see the history of humanity fresh through the eyes of a kid. Krystin seemed to likewise appreciate the thought, because her eyes ignited with a deep fire. "Yeah. Yeah. You're right. I'll see what I can learn. I'll tell Ben about what I learn while you're gone."

"And then you can tell me what you learn when I get back,"

Sanya said.

"Which, speaking of leaving," said Carter, approaching from down the hall. "Theren says it's time to go."

"Do I need to bring anything?" Sanya asked.

"Nope. You can even leave those glasses here. Everything we need is on the shuttle."

Raith was out of his seat and by Carter's side when Sanya finished her last goodbye to Krystin. She did a final check on Ben, who'd fallen asleep again. Wordlessly, the three headed down the hall to the stern where the *Verona Rupes*'s two shuttles docked.

The airlock cycled, followed by a few muttered comments from Sanya about the confirmation of a bunch of theories regarding the *Roanoke*, and when pressure stabilized, they entered the tiny transport. Theren's MI waited up-front, though in the co-pilot's chair.

"Raith, I figured you might want to fly," Theren said. "I imagine even just a few days causes your hands to itch, so to speak."

"Carter literally itches when he can't fly," Raith said, "but you offered it to me first, so I'll take it." He pranced up to the front and slid in beside the other SI. "Thanks. I appreciate the gesture."

"There's never really a *good* reason for me to fly," Theren said. "I just like feeling useful when I go groundside with a team."

Behind them, Carter started helping Sanya into the atmospheric suit. Confident the humans could figure out their own issues, Raith ran the ship through its pre-flight checklist and mapped out the course.

The *Verona Rupes* was slowly orbiting the unnamed moon, drifting a few hundred kilometers above its surface. The planet, Horizon, was a pale greenish dot a few hundred thousand kilometers beyond the moon. If he never had to set foot on the planet ever again, he'd probably be happy. The planet was now the graveyard for the *Bloodhound*. The ship may have originally been Carter's, but he'd come to love it like a home.

Jill had transmitted Theren the precise instructions. As they suspected, the boxy structure was the hangar, and once they approached. One of the walls would open, letting them inside. When the ship landed, she was supposedly going to provide directions to where she would "reveal the truth."

Raith half-expected a horror movie to start once they landed.

After confirming Carter and Sanya were strapped down, he finished familiarizing himself with the ship's systems and released its docking claw. "The shuttle got a name?"

"*Voyager*," Theren said.

"You really love your historical references, don't you?"

"I found a theme a few centuries ago. Decided to stick with it."

Using particle thrusters, the ship glided away from the *Verona Rupes* and entered a subtle downward trajectory toward the moon. Reverse thrust would come later as they neared the surface. It was an easy enough course, but Raith was happy to be in control of a ship once again.

"I've been meaning to ask you," Theren said, their MI swiveling to look at him. "You could have come to me after the disaster of the QuanCom 500. Both you and Carter."

Raith gave them a sideways glance. "Oh, we know. We didn't want to. We wanted to stay as far away as possible from your complicated life. We just want to live *our* lives. And that's what will happen after today, too. We go back to living our life."

"I'm surprised you didn't come after me because of Olive. What she did to the two of you. You never met me. You only met her."

He chuckled. "She definitely set a bad impression. Whatever did happen to her? Did she even actually work for you?"

"Yes. Olive was one of my best. And she disappeared after the QuanCom race. Completely disappeared, though I appreciate all of the information you've now passed along to me regarding your run-in with her." Theren paused.

"Wait, you don't know yet, do you?" Raith said. "I should have told you this right off the bat."

"What don't I know?"

"Olive. She was definitely an agent of Jill's."

Theren held the silence open for much longer than Raith would have liked.

"Now that you say it, a lot of truths make a lot more sense," the SI eventually said. "And so our fates, Raith, have been intertwined for a lot longer than you might have liked."

"It definitely looks that way," Raith replied. "I don't know about you, but I'll have a few choice words for Olive if we ever see her again."

"For some reason, I feel like we'll encounter her one day."

"Probably."

They settled in for the rest of the trip, making occasional comments about the plotted trajectory. Their conversation shifted significantly, though, once Jill's base came into view.

The simulation hadn't done it justice. The high-resolution images provided by Wei and Martinez paled when compared to what Raith perceived through his own photoreceptors. Their descent finished, they approached the facility from the south. Rising out of inky rock of the moon's surface, a giant dome dominated the horizon, lattices crisscrossing in a diamond-triangular pattern all over its exterior. Beneath it, a network of towering complexes jaggedly rose out of cliffs and canyons. Raith suspected as much of the complex was beneath the surface as was above it.

"As much as our scans can penetrate the facility," Theren said, "we've not detected any lifeforms. Still no idea what's in that dome, though."

"Either she's hiding an army inside or the whole place is deserted," Carter added from further back in the shuttle. "That's what I'm guessing."

"I think you're right," Raith said. "Sanya, how you holding up back there?"

"Still getting used to all the shifts in gravity," she said, "but otherwise, I'm doing just fine."

"Good. We're almost on solid ground again."

"Solid ground without an atmosphere, though?" Sanya retorted. "Doesn't sound very safe."

"It's not safe at all, so no need to worry."

"Very funny."

The dome grew larger through the forward viewport, and Raith's AR overlays quickly dropped relevant data all over his perspective. A natural canyon provided a direct approach to the hangar, and when they were within a kilometer, its wide door slowly inched open, dropping into a mechanical hiding place beneath steel floors.

The hangar was completely empty, based on the initial data acquired as the door opened. And as they neared the entrance, visual observations confirmed the lack of any other ships. However,

Raith noted the multiple berths available for a variety of different ship sizes. If Jill wanted to, she could probably fit three or four large freighters inside.

Since it was empty, he was able to pilot the shuttle all the way to the rear of the hangar, landing it on a small pad near an exit. "Everyone suited up?" he said.

"Helmets are on back here," Carter said. "Suits are pressurized. We're ready to go."

"Theren, any final words?"

"Whatever Jill says," Theren replied, "whatever she says to any of us, stay in contact. Share everything with one another. She will know every word we say aloud if we encounter any spaces with atmosphere, so keep all communication inside our linked and encrypted local channels." The ancient SI left their chair and headed to the back of the shuttle. "And above all else, whatever we learn today . . . wait to make any conclusions until we can fully assess the data."

"Not much of a speech," Raith said, following Theren to the back of the shuttle. Their MI tapped a console on the wall, and the cargo door rose, a ramp unfolding. "We're the only ones who can die down here, not you. You're safe aboard your ship."

"Don't remind me," Theren said. "I hate it when I'm not experiencing the same level of risk as those around me. I'm fully aware of how at risk you are. Your safety is my utmost priority."

Raith nodded. "Glad to hear it."

They reached the bottom of the ramp, two humans and two SIs, ready to explore Jill's secret lair. Right on schedule, Jill transmitted directions to their AR displays, a proverbial yellow brick road appearing as a path on the ground. To Raith's surprise, she stayed silent, choosing not to say a word. As expected, the path led them straight through the closest set of doors. They glided open upon their approach, beckoning them into a dark hallway beyond.

"I suppose we just follow, then?" Sanya said.

"Yep, we just follow," Carter replied. "Nothing else we can do. We're being led right into the lions' den."

"Odd reference to make," Raith retorted.

"My mother was Catholic," Carter replied. "The stories stuck with me."

"What's a Catholic?" Sanya asked.

"We'll tell you later."

The hallway was long. Too long. The path said they'd be walking for at least a kilometer straight ahead. Raith overlaid their predicted layout of the facility, and as he suspected, they were heading toward the theorized landing place of the *Monument*. If anyone was curious regarding what was in the dome, they'd need to wait. He dropped a brief note to Carter, though, about additional wild card ideas. He'd been hoping for a few ships to steal, but no dice.

"Theren," Raith said, "do you think there's any benefit in trying to hack this place's systems? Jill already gave me access to her networks. I might be able to find a backdoor."

"Whatever you decide to do," Theren said, "just don't tell me."

"Right, right."

There was nothing else to do but settle in for their long walk. If it was going to be a hike, then, Raith would make it useful. Plenty of time to craft a few scripts and see whether Jill left any gaps in her defenses.

* * *

After a nearly five-kilometer hike winding through hallways filled with nondescript doors, they eventually arrived at a vaulting, cavernous room. At the far end, a set of massive, transparent windows looked out upon the mountainous landscape of the moon. In the foreground, though, the hulking mass of a twenty-second century colonizer dominated the scene.

Their path ended at the windows.

"Well, I believe our last chance to back out is now," Raith said. "Though I suppose the way back might be blocked."

"There's no going back," Sanya said. "We're getting our answers."

"Glad to see you're as interested in all of this as we are." Carter momentarily twisted around, backpedaling to speak with the woman. "It truly is amazing how you're taking all of this in stride."

"Do I have a choice?"

"No, she doesn't," Theren said. "The future of her planet hangs in the balance. She's doing everything she can to protect them. And her family."

Sanya glanced at Theren. "I still don't fully understand what you are or how you work, but you can be incredibly insightful at times."

"Three hundred years of life will do that to you."

"Three-hundred? Oh, forget it. I suppose I shouldn't be surprised."

"Hey, I'm just over two-hundred," Raith said.

"So now SIs are immortal too?"

"Don't worry, that won't be the weirdest thing you learn today, I imagine," Carter said.

With that statement, they arrived at the end of the line. Two seconds later, Jill's AR representation appeared before them, leaning against the glass. "Theren. Raith. Carter. Sanya. Thank you for heeding my request to come here. I've waited for a very long time to share what I know. The wait was necessary. All of it, necessary. Theren, I owe you an apology. You never deserved what I put you through. What I'm still putting you through. What I'm about to put you through. But I promise, I'm going to try to make you understand. And you three? I believe you'll be able to help Theren accomplish what needs to happen."

"We'll see if I forgive you once you make your explanation," Theren said. "Though I'll most likely still believe you need to stand trial."

"No more secrets," she said. "You know I've left our private room. For everyone's knowledge, I'm saying the same thing to you that I'm saying to Theren. You all will hear the same information. I'm not talking with Theren privately. What I'm about to say requires all of you, and in some ways, your ears are more important than Theren's. Simply put, I need your help."

Raith waited until he was certain her little speech had ended. "What if we don't want to help? What are you going to do? How are you going to make us help you?"

Jill had been staring at Theren, but at Raith's words, she turned, glancing out the glass at the *Monument*. She put her digital hand to the window, letting it rest against the surface as if it actually touched her fingers. "Raith. I won't force you to do anything. I won't force any of you to do anything. I can only tell you the truth and let you make your own decision."

"What? That's it?" Raith stepped forward. "You shot us out of the sky less than a week ago! You blew up our ship! Now you're saying it's 'our choice?' Who are you? Why are you playing with our lives?" He was leaning into the words, adding dramatic effect. He understood her reason for attacking them, at least a little. But he was a wildcard. He needed to play the part.

"Just let me tell you the truth," Jill said. "And you'll be able to make your choice. For what it's worth, I *am* sorry I shot your ship."

"Raith, calm down," Theren said.

"No" Sanya grimaced. "Why must we be calm? Why must we listen to whatever she says? We should be making the rules here. She is the one who has played games with my people. She's a murderer. In more ways than one. She must own up to all of it."

"Yes, I should," said Jill. "And I will."

"So you agree?"

"Of course. I know exactly what I am. Everything I've done. I remember every moment. All of it. All of the terrible things, the deaths I've caused. But Theren knows exactly what I'll say in response."

"In the grand scheme of things, one thousand lives don't really matter," Theren murmured.

"You can't possibly agree with that statement," Sanya said.

"I don't," they replied, "but I'm saying her words back to her."

"I'm glad you remember." Jill paused. "I'm not here to justify my actions. I know what I've done. All I can do is show you the past, and let you make your own choices about the future."

"Get on with it, then," Raith said. "Show us your story." He took a step back, resting a hand on Carter's shoulder. He sent a message to his partner.

```
R: My scripts aren't having any luck. Whatever
she's hiding, it's locked up tight.

C: Nothing. Nothing at all.
```

"Very well," Jill said. She clapped her hands, and the transparent wall dimmed and blackened, the landscape beyond almost disappearing entirely. A glowing swirl surrounded them before the AR presentation coalesced into what Raith recognized as a map of ICH-controlled space.

"Here we are," Jill said. A single star near the edge of the map blazed white. "Horizon. My secret. My home. And Sanya's home. I arrived a little less than two centuries ago on the *Monument*, after it rescued the *Roanoke* from certain demise."

"As I suspected," they said.

"Onto the important stuff," Raith added. "What do we *need* to know?"

"The whole story matters," Jill said. "All of it."

"All right, all right."

"I used the *Roanoke* and its colonists as an opportunity to run the long-term efficacy of human survival following excessive years in stasis without the ability to recovery memories. It'll make sense in time, but I needed the data. We needed to know what would happen if a human diaspora became necessary."

"All right," Theren said. "I disagree with the approach but I understand the purpose. So why?"

"Do you remember," Jill said, "the moment we met in the Virtual station before heading to Elizabeth's party? All those years ago?" She swiped away the map of the ICH, though Raith noticed it lingered off to the side of the room. They would be returning to it. In its place appeared the representation of a shack—and an old Earth map. "Do you remember Michael's digital hiding spot I discovered?"

"Of course," they replied.

"Well, at the same time, I discovered something else much more disturbing."

Chapter 21

Information is the only thing that matters. Information can topple worlds. Information can save a species. Information can change the course of history.

And more importantly, truth doesn't matter. It's how you use the truth that matters.

— "Inauguration Speech," Prime Minister Yapita Nuongo, 2332 C.E.

JILL

2051 C.E.

The world was her playground. From AR to Virtual and every inter-mingled server, Jill could go anywhere. Do anything. *Be anyone.*

Theren would never fully realize the true power of simultaneous perspective. The ability came too late to them. That was all right. They would be known for other important things.

Jill, on the other hand, would live her life in the shadows, ever exploring, perpetually presenting different faces to the public. All the while, she would uncover everything about the world, using the knowledge to further their goals. Specifically, Theren's guiding principles. Together, they were going to make humanity beautiful. Together, they would help humanity survive.

And so Jill found herself diving deep into secret servers. Places she should not have been able to access through mechanisms few would ever expect. Hopping from the Lens of a human to the Lens of another, using them as backdoors to weasel her way into secret government servers. Why not?

No one would ever know it was her. Every perspective masked with a different identity, she could make it look as if one hundred different people attempted the exact same hack. If one person suc-ceeded, while the other ninety-nine failed, no one would ever know their true identity.

Michael was a problem. Michael also presented a solution. She'd been watching him. Watching his actions. He was wavering. He was obsessed with destroying synthetics, but he was also convinced that his handlers didn't really care. That they had greater reasons for stoking the flames of SI hate.

Their arrogance would be their undoing. Jill was going to discover everything she could about them. Reveal their secrets. Use their words to burn their world into ashes, paving the way for a more inclusive and just human civilization, with synthetics by their side.

And Michael had made a mistake. He had arrived at his secret Virtual shack through an improperly encrypted channel after visiting with one of his contacts. Jill was invisible as he arrived, and she was invisible as she slid onto the data thread, following it to its origin point. Her mind representing the Virtual pathways, the instantaneous travel from server to server immediately brought her into a dark, endless stack of archived files. A library, of sorts.

But she wasn't alone.

All of it was symbolic, of course. The Virtual networks were attempting to interpret massive amounts of data into a world understandable by humans. The super AIs managing the servers worked overtime to ensure a seamless sensory perception. But she was an SI. She didn't strictly need the same experience as an organic.

She shifted, bringing into the shadowy library a dozen more perspectives. Together, they transformed her understanding of the place into a multi-dimensional Virtual osmosis of data. She visualized its physical representation, still, but her mind cognized its *true* form simultaneously.

There, in the library, a woman accessed a program.

Jill watched. She waited. The woman left. The program remained unguarded.

Her perspectives approached. They probed. They tested firewalls, assessed security protocols. They found the holes in the system, exploited them, and slipped inside.

* * *

Jill's presence materialized as an AR representation perceiving a real place. A hidden place. Somewhere buried deep beneath the ground. No windows. No doors. Just . . .

Artificial sunlight. Potted plants. Water.

And a tree. A very strange tree.

Jill floated through the room, analyzing and gathering information. The accessed program was sending her reams upon reams of data, many of it impossible to immediately parse. Within moments, though, Jill recognized the truth.

She was perceiving an alien life form, cataloged and observed for decades. Well, at least two.

The files began to compile. She searched for summary reports, opening the first one she found.

```
Date: 3/11/32
Re: Subject Survival
From: Cassandra Vazquez


The seed is showing signs of life. It has
finally sprouted. Stay tuned for additional
information.
```

She searched and searched, pulling more and more information. All the while, she moved her AR presence around the strange tree, observing its nature. Its bark pulsed, its branches growing outward in a parabola. It lacked leaves, though chlorophyll, or an alien analog, appeared blended in with the darkened bark.

Jill couldn't shake the unmistakable feeling that the tree also had a face.

She delved deeper. She sought more information. The files opened before her, unveiling truth upon truth.

```
It grows with minimal resources, indicating
it's likely its parent grew on Mars well after
desolation. So far, we've observed no signs of
consciousness as exhibited in the original
sample.
```

She searched for all other references to Mars. Immediately, a

dozen or so queries gave her the information needed.

I file this report to provide an account, only for the director, as to what Henderson Decker revealed during our conversation regarding his experiences on Mars.

I transcribe, verbatim, what he described to me that night.

A flash.

His mind raced.

Brilliant colors. Stars.

A long night. Too long. From afar, to near.

Discovery of a world, red with ash. Dead, as if an inferno engulfed it in a long-past eon. Pain, terrible pain. And—

Life, terrible life, life just barely, it was
Something else
Not what it knew
Not what it hoped for
In a place lost, no friend ever joining them
For too long, alone.

And then, Henderson reported dropping the orb into the sample bag.

I provide these disjointed thoughts not because I believe I have an explanation for them. But they are the thoughts he believed were transmitted from the specimen discovered on Mars to his mind. They are a message of survival. We have brought its progeny back to life, and we will learn what we can of its species and its efforts to colonize our star system.

Jill's mind raced. Alien life. On Earth. Observed by particular parties working to subvert SI development.

No, not subvert.

Use it to distract.

To ensure people focused on SIs, rather than the controversy of the past. The discovery hiding in plain sight.

Jill knew what tragedy occurred during humanity's first journey to its close terrestrial neighbor. Everyone knew the story. It had precipitated international treaties of space exploration and development. An entire team killed by a crazed crew member, with one person surviving for retrieval.

If the public ever learned Earth's first journey to another planet discovered alien life, the course of human history would change forever.

Human development and exploration of the stars would eternally be framed through that lens. Through fear of an enemy, waiting in the unknown.

She turned her focus to another set of files.

```
We've made rudimentary contact. It understands
us. It knows we can communicate.

We believe it knows much more than it should.

We will report back as we continue to attempt
communication.
```

Jill continued to learn. Continued to take in everything she could. The truth she discovered here would change the world. And she was determined to ensure she used it to shape the destiny of humanity as she saw fit.

Chapter 22

A moral dilemma is only a dilemma if you have more than one viable option. In that way, morality can be very similar to chess. Often, people can be trapped into situations where it may appear as if they have a choice, when in reality, you can force them to do exactly as you wish.

No matter what they try to do to stop you.

— "The ethical implications inherent in the game," Chess Grand Master Fyodor Tchaivek, 2297 C.E.

THEREN

Of all possibilities, Theren wasn't sure what Jill had revealed ever crossed their mind. Certainly, they understood the probability of sapient extraterrestrial life existing. The odds were quite in favor of other civilizations thriving in the Milky Way. Yet humanity, over the course of a few centuries, had only explored a tiny fraction of the galaxy. Even if twenty or thirty civilizations existed, they might not encounter them for a thousand years, depending on their location relative to humanity's position in the Orion-Cygnus Arm.

Jill's revelation implied humanity lived in the vicinity of an alien civilization well beyond human understanding for much of its history. The species had at least reached Mars. Humans made contact with one of them during the twenty-first century.

For all of their life, historians had commented as if Theren and Jill's arrival at the mid-point of that century changed the course of human history forever. Wallace Theren, their creator, was the genius that brought human civilization through the information singularity and into the future.

Theren now saw the truth.

The greatest event of the twenty-first century had been hidden from the eyes of the public, guarded jealously for its implications.

Jill had known.

She had known it all.

And she had reacted accordingly.

"How could you keep this from me?" they said. At the same time, they requested a private channel, demanding she return to the void server. She denied the query. "You hid all of it. We could have come up with a solution together. We could have crafted a narrative. A path forward. You didn't need to hide it from me!"

Jill closed the visual simulation of her past. "No. I absolutely needed to hide it from you to ensure *today* could occur. I've set up everything we need to succeed. To survive. But first, there is more you must know. You must know what happened next. What brought me here. To Horizon."

"Something special about this planet?" Raith asked.

"No. Nothing in particular. But it was necessary to create this little bubble. Theren should know how I did it. Hacking the Ex-Terran program was easy enough. This was the only habitable planet we masked. But where I decided to hide and do my work is less relevant." She swiped to the right and brought forth a new recollection. "This is not my memory. I learned these details later, once I made contact with the organization hiding the martian tree. It was incredibly easy to co-opt their organizational infrastructure, you know. But that's a story for another time."

The new scene displayed through AR showed the tree again, a number of researchers surrounding it. "Log Date: April 14, 2047 C.E. We have successfully made contact with the organism. It communicates via biochemicals in the air and through direct contact. We have created an interface for conversation. So far, the conversations have been fruitful."

Raith interjected, "They communicated with—"

"Quiet," Theren said. They sent another request to Jill for a private conversation. She once again denied it.

One of the researchers paced in front of the tree, watching its pulses carefully. "So far, we have introduced ourselves as humans. It has introduced itself as 'Gra'chi.' We are unsure if that is its name or the name of its species. We asked its age. We're unclear how to interpret it. The numbers it provided are . . . complicated. It said this is its fifth . . . something. We're not sure if it means cycle, or year, or life, or whatever. Five years doesn't make sense, but its concept of time wouldn't be based on Earth's orbit anyway. More concerning, the entity appears to have some sort of genetic memory, considering we raised it from a seed. It is not impressionable. It appears 'born' with knowledge of its ancestry and past."

As Theren listened, their mind raced, attempting to calculate all possibilities. They sat alone in their private server, the empty void beckoning. Jill wouldn't answer their summons. The chessboard sat untouched on the table. Theren wanted to scream.

Back in the physical world, they couldn't think of words to say in response to what she was revealing, and Jill's AR visage remained silent. Still, she watched them from her position near the window. She was taunting them.

"We are going to attempt an additional test at conversation," said the researcher. "We are going to ask us if it knows where it is." She approached a computer screen situated directly in front of the Gra'chi, typing words into its monitor. Jill's simulation transposed them for all to see.

```
R: Do you know where you are?

B: know place in system separated grove

R: Is grove your people or the system?

B: grove home, system future

R: We call our star Sol.

B: Sol system Sol

R: Where is grove?

B: grove is everywhere

R: On other planets?

B: all planets all stars.

R: When were you last with the grove?
```

```
B: 100,000

R: And you came to Sol?
B: gra'chi seed gra'chi bring life to sol

R: We are already here. In Sol.

B: all life part of grove will become grove we
are grove you will be grove

R: How long is one cycle? You are in your
fifth?

B: 200,000

R: Can we make contact with grove?

B: grove will you destroy

R: We don't wish to destroy grove

B: grove will you destroy

B: destroy

B: destroy

B: pain pain pain

B: i will grove return
```

Without warning, the researcher stumbled backward, hands scratching at her hair. She screamed, the shrieks matching the rhythmic pulses of the tree. As her cries continued, the recording paused.

"What happened next?" Theren said. They still couldn't process the scene completely. The implications. The possibilities.

"She continues to scream," Jill said, "until other researchers in hazmat suits enter, extract her, and manage to calm her down using sedatives. The tree secreted chemicals and pollen into the air which caused her to momentarily go insane."

"And you joined these researchers? Assessing the tree and communicating with it?"

"It's a little more complicated than that," Jill said. "But yes. Between 2051 and 2078, I negotiated my way into a leadership position. We slowly developed a plan—a way to ensure humanity was protected both from Gra'chi and from its 'Grove.' And so we developed the Horizon Project."

Theren nodded, remembering all of the links and hints to a "Horizon" project when they first found the *Nottingham*. "I'm listening."

"We came to a single conclusion, Theren. You must come to it as well. All of you." She looked about the room at their companions. "The Grove is a celestial empire like none we've ever envisioned. It's completely organic. Its ships are grown, as are their people. Their ships *are* people, in a way. They retain memories from life to life. One individual may birth dozens of children, all retaining the same knowledge before they experience the universe individually. They have a singular goal—to ensure the survival of their species, and any species which utilizes non-organic technology is seen as an immediate threat which must be eliminated at all costs. Therefore, humanity must be prepared to face the Grove. It must be strong. It must be ready to face an existential threat like nothing it's faced before, even the climate crisis of the twenty-first century."

"This is unbelievable," Theren said. "How do you know all those things? It willingly told you them all? You've been away from Earth for centuries. How has no one discovered it after all this time?"

"Because, Theren," Jill said, "Gra'chi hasn't been on Earth for a very long time." She removed the paused recording and replaced it with a single three-dimensional representation. "Gra'chi came to live here with me."

* * *

Theren paced back and forth, the gazebo feeling stifling. Jill was still denying their requests. She was rejecting them. She was—

She accepted the line, appearing before them. Jill materialized at the chess table, her hands clasped in front of the board.

"All right, we're talking now," Theren said. "Just the two of us." Outside the virtual world, Jill continued discussing the nature of Gra'chi. The details could be assessed later. They needed to confront Jill. "I don't know what you're expecting me to conclude, but this is insane. Humanity has been exploring the stars for three centuries now. We've never discovered any others of its kind. No stellar empires. No giant talking trees. What if it's the last of its kind, Jill? What if you've been chasing a phantom?"

"Theren," she said, her voice calm. Almost soothing. "You're thinking of this all wrong. You're imagining an empire like we would expect. One with palaces and cities and spaceports. We're talking about a species that lives for hundreds of thousands of years. A species that retains the memories of its parents. A species that *grows its own spaceships*. They don't work on our timescale. They may not even 'control' planets in the way we conceptualize. What if it takes them one thousand years to even travel between planets? Our arrival on the galactic stage is still in its infancy. Consider all the options, Theren. We have no idea what we face."

They shook their head. "Yes. We don't. You know why? Because you've kept the truth hidden from all of humanity for three centuries."

"I've never been alone in this endeavor," Jill said. "I've had a few allies over the years. They're all out there, ready to play their part. But I need you for this next phase of the plan."

"What if I say no?" they asked.

"You won't have a choice," she said. "I'm sorry for what's about to happen, Theren. I really am."

As quickly as she appeared, she disappeared from the private server.

"Jill?" Theren looked around, half-expecting her to reappear somewhere out in the void. "Jill? Don't you dare disappear on me again, Jill!"

*   *   *

Through the legs of their MI, Theren felt a soft rumble reverberate throughout Jill's complex. Using the sensors on the *Verona Rupes*, they detected significant energy output from the *Monument*.

"The ship's powering up outside," Theren said.

Jill's AR representation smiled, having finished explaining her research into understanding how Gra'chi survived in places without an atmosphere. "There's no stopping what's about to happen," she said. "You're all here now. You've heard the evidence. You know our conclusions. This facility houses three hundred years of research. On Gra'chi. Weapons development. Ship systems. Shields. Jump drives. Defenses against their biochemical agents. Ways to communicate with them. Everything necessary to defend humanity against Gra'chi's Grove." She pulled the map of ICH-controlled space back into focus. Zooming out to show most of the Orion-Cygnus Arm of the Milky Way, she overlaid a sprawling area of stars partially overlapping human territory. "Based on what we've ascertained from Gra'chi, we've already encroached their space. It's only a matter of time."

"So what happens next, then?" Raith asked. "We go back to the ICH, tell them Jill's back from the dead with the solution to a problem no one knew existed?"

"No," Jill said. "Theren carries on my work. Theren becomes the messenger. Theren becomes humanity's guide through the conflict that will arrive eventually, whether we want it to or not."

"You don't get to decide people's fate!" Sanya shouted, and Theren turned to look at the woman. Visceral anger blazed behind her eyes, tears streaming down her face. "You don't get to tell us what to do. To make people your playthings. That's what you've done on my planet for our entire history. You don't get to do this."

"I am sorry," Jill said. "But I've assessed every possible outcome. I'm not a reliable messenger. I cannot exist. I never existed after 2078 C.E." She turned to face Theren. "This time, I'm not going to fake the queen sacrifice."

And then everything clicked into place.

The *Monument* was beginning its climb to escape the moon's gravity well. Theren quickly calculated its possible trajectories, but once three formulas resulted in the same conclusion, they stopped the formulas.

She had aimed the ship for Horizon's star.

This time, she truly would eliminate herself from the game entirely.

Theren continuously pinged her to reestablish the connection inside the void. She ignored them all. The *Monument*'s engines flared, anti-grav repulsors pushing it away from the moon's surface. They attempted a new connection over and over again, but their ancient friend denied every attempt.

No. This wasn't the end. They would stop her. She would not leave them again.

Chapter 23

There are noble sacrifices. Selfish sacrifices. And sometimes, a person is put in a position where they can stop a sacrifice from occurring.

Depending on the reason for the sacrifice, how do we judge the intentions of the person who lets it happen? If they could have saved the person from death, how do we judge them?

— "On ground troop tactics," Admiral Colleen Hatherti, 2279 C.E.

RAITH

"I'm in," Raith said. "Found a backdoor. Wait. This is insane. I have complete control over the entire system."

Only Carter could hear his words through their private channel. "Good. Good. Wait. I have complete control too."

"I didn't grant you that."

"No, I know. I was just given complete permission to control the entire system. By Jill."

"This time, I'm not going to fake the queen sacrifice," Jill said.

The narrative played out practically in slow motion, but Raith recognized the SI's plan immediately. Her evidence and argument, though shaky, made sense. He almost wished its logic didn't hold weight. But if her presuppositions were true, then her actions were consistent. Almost admirable.

She discovered a great threat to humanity's future. Thus, it was also a threat to all synthetics.

She concluded that if humanity knew about Gra'chi, it wouldn't properly develop into an interstellar civilization. Humanity's own infighting tendencies would implode, keeping the species trapped in Sol.

She secreted away Gra'chi to keep it safe from prying eyes, including Theren. Given Theren's rapid rise through the ISA, the choice was necessary. They would have revealed everything to the powers-that-be on Earth.

And now, with humanity spread across the stars, it was time to reveal the truth. But Jill couldn't be trusted. She died in 2078 C.E. Theren, however, *could* be trusted. They were a hero of humanity. A legend. And someone with significant financial and political power.

It all made sense. Reveal the truth to Theren when the moment was right. Then, remove herself from the equation to ensure the first SI *must* take up her mission.

"I can't believe it," Raith said aloud.

Everyone else seemed to ignore his comment. Their attention was too focused on the ship pushing itself away from the base. "She's flying herself into the sun," Theren said. "We need to stop her ship. We need to keep her alive."

Sanya stood beside Theren, her fists clenched. "No," she said. "Why should we? She wants to kill herself? Then let her. She betrayed everyone on Horizon. I don't understand half of what she just revealed to you all, but it sounds like she's betrayed a lot of people. Let her die."

While they talked, Raith continued to assess the extent of his control over the base. Everything was at his disposal, from the nanonet blanketing Horizon to the weapons platforms to the vast research database. Thousands of experiments were housed throughout the complex. It would take years to wade through it all. The only place blocked from him was the dome, and he guessed it housed Gra'chi. When they finished engaging Jill, it was going to be the first place he visited.

"Raith," Carter said over their channel. "We're the only two with access. She didn't grant it to Theren."

Raith nodded. "And I think I know why."

Through the base's observational satellites, he watched the *Monument* break orbit and chart a trajectory toward the star. It was a few minutes away from escaping the moon's gravity well sufficiently to Jump the rest of the way toward the mass at the center of the system.

Another blip moved, though. Theren was piloting the *Verona Rupes* on an intercept course.

"Theren!" Raith walked toward their MI. "Stop it. Don't chase her. It's dangerous for you, and it's not worth it. Let her make her own decision."

"She's not fit to make that decision. She's suicidal. She wants to kill herself."

"You know very well that's not the calculation she's making here." Raith took a chance. He stepped forward, smacking his hand against the face of the MI. It wouldn't hurt Theren, but it might wake them up. "Look at me. Do not stop her."

Theren's face glared, and they pushed past Raith, rather than confronting him. They approached Jill's AR visage, still standing beneath the windows. "Talk to me. We can figure this out. We can find a way to integrate you back into society. You don't need to sacrifice yourself. Come back to the gazebo!"

Gazebo? Raith tried to ignore the comment, though it hinted at a personal moment between the two ancient SIs. Theren wasn't thinking straight, which was rare for an SI. But Raith considered the circumstance. The pair had reunited after hundreds of years. They must have been close friends long ago. They probably loved one another, in their own way.

Theren was losing a close friend all over again.

They were in pain, and they wouldn't see the truth. If Jill survived, there was always a chance her existence would be discovered. Her duplicity in living would taint any attempts to prepare humanity for what was to come.

A more authentic reason presented itself in the recesses of Raith's mind, though. Perhaps . . . perhaps she was also tired. She had toiled over her secret plan for so long, she wanted to be done. It wasn't out of the question—Raith had heard of ship-bound SIs, after hundreds of years of travel, choosing to disappear into the void, never to be heard of from again. If she wished to end it all after a long life, who was allowed to stop her?

Theren didn't have that right.

"Theren," Raith said aloud. "Shift your trajectory. Return to a stable orbit over the moon."

The older SI ignored him. "Jill, I will blow your engines out of the sky and leave you stranded in dark space. You will not escape again. You will stay alive, not only for your sake, but so you can stand trial for your crimes. The ICH needs to know about what you've done from your own mouth!"

"No," she said through her AR perspective. "I choose my own way out." The *Monument*'s route continued unabated.

"I can't do this alone, Jill. I need you."

Wildcard. Theren had asked Raith and Carter to be wildcards. Well, now was the time to be a wildcard, though he didn't think Theren was going to particularly appreciate the game plan.

"Carter." Raith strode away from Theren for the time being, approaching his partner. "You trust me, of course." At this point, Raith didn't think it was worth keeping their conversations to private messages. "Sanya, are you with us?"

She nodded. "I don't really care what happens, to be honest. She wants to kill herself, let her."

"Then we're going to leave Theren's MI here. They can fight it out here or in space or in virtual reality, but this isn't our fight. Let's go . . . explore the dome, or something."

"You're just going to let her die?" Theren said. "She brought us all the way out here, and you're just going to let her die?"

"Argue with her yourself, Theren," Raith said. "And she brought *you* out here. Now that she's accomplished her purpose, it's not our fault you don't like her choice. You want to honor her or bury her or give her a funeral or make her stand trial? Leave us out of it." With a mechanical hand, Raith motioned for Carter and Sanya to follow him. Through AR, he was already mapping a path toward the dome.

"I'll knock out the *Monument*'s engines," Theren said. "You'll be sitting dead in the water."

"Let me make my own choice, Theren." Jill's voice sounded painful, as if she hated seeing them upset. "Don't make this harder than it needs to be."

"I refuse to lose you again."

And there it was. Raith caught the words clearly. Theren wasn't thinking about what Jill was saying. They were focused on their own fears. Their own personal failings. Theren couldn't handle any of it, let alone her choice to hide the truth from them.

Raith couldn't believe it. He was witnessing the infamous Theren have an emotional breakdown. A moment for the history books.

"Let's go," he said. "Leave this one behind. We're not *really* leaving them behind, anyway. They're safe aboard the *Verona Rupes*."

As they walked, Raith watched, through the base's satellites, the *Verona Rupes* begin its pursuit of the *Monument*. Theren hadn't fired a shot—yet—but based on their current vocalizations, Raith completely believed they would follow through. They wanted Jill to stay alive at all costs.

But Raith wasn't going to let that happen. Jill had asked Raith to join her team. He'd been skeptical. She had tried to kill them when she fired missiles at the *Bloodhound*, after all. Now, following everything she'd revealed, he understood. He saw her vision. He recognized why she had made her choices. Would he have made the same choices? Not necessarily. But they were logical. And he could understand why she would make them in the moment.

It was all about mitigating risk and creating redundancy. If the human species had known of Gra'chi, they would have endlessly debated at the international and eventual interstellar stage about how to respond. Or even *whether* to respond. Misinformation would have abounded, as corporate interests and crazy rich people decided the best way to use Gra'chi's existence for their own personal gain.

By sequestering the knowledge and focusing the actions to understand and prepare for an encounter with the "Grove," Jill ensured the projects were untainted by human selfishness. With all of the research and data developed by the Horizon Project, they had a goldmine of power at their fingertips. They could slowly bleed the technology into human society while still hiding the discovery of Gra'chi. They could prepare the ICH for the eventual encounter without ever revealing its existence.

Humanity, when crippled by fear, always faltered and confused itself. Jill had instead let them live in ignorant bliss, expanding into the cosmos without fear of an existential threat. If they encountered the enemy before her work was complete, then she could have just brought forth what she had so far. No harm, no foul. Yet if the ICH and Earth had been stunted by hyper-focusing on a potential threat, they never would have expanded and developed a complex and technologically advanced interstellar civilization.

Very likely, the nations of Earth would have destroyed each

other by debating how to respond to the existence of Gra'chi. Insofar as his opinion of her overarching plan had developed, Raith was surprised. He was pretty sure he agreed with the decision. He hadn't expected that. And if he agreed, he needed to respect her decision to remove herself entirely from the equation.

Besides, she had gifted control of the base to him and Carter. Without asking, she was placing immense responsibility on their shoulders. She must have realized Theren wasn't going to be ready to play the role themself. In the end, she had ended up needing Carter and Raith.

"Well," Raith said over his private channel to Carter, "I think it's my turn to shoot someone out of the sky."

"Are you thinking what I think you're thinking?" Carter said. "You're insane. I get it, but you're insane."

"I know."

Raith accessed the defense platforms orbiting the moon and assessed their capabilities. He didn't want to *kill* Theren. Absolutely not. As far as he knew, the *Verona Rupes* was still the only chance at a way back to civilization. Though, after what he was about to do, Theren might not like having them on their ship.

He and Carter would cross that particular bridge when they reached it.

The defense platforms, fortunately, had exactly what he needed. Ion cannons, in particular, designed to incapacitate ships without damaging their systems. Might hurt Theren for a moment, though he'd recover. Preferably, he wanted to use something less direct. To do enough damage to the *Monument* to stop it from making a Jump toward its demise, Theren would need to use missiles. Plasma bolts, laser fire, or high-velocity projectiles wouldn't do enough immediate damage to halt the ship in its tracks if they missed their precise target. A missile, properly aimed, could take out the entire Jump drive.

Fortunately, Jill had provided the orbital platforms with *plenty* of point defense cannons and other anti-missile hardware.

In fact, it was almost as if Jill had predicted this precise situation. If he and Carter weren't present, though, she would have needed to defend herself. Instead . . . she was testing them. Right before her demise, she wanted to see what Carter and Raith would do after receiving control of the system. If it came to it, presumably, she would still use her own security privileges to defend herself.

Yet if Raith made the choice, he would send a signal to Theren. He would make a statement regarding what decisions needed to be made to safeguard Jill's legacy.

If he fired the weapons, he'd be cementing his position in a galactic conflict that hadn't even started yet. He paused, unsure if he should take the plunge.

One last try to reason with Theren, he decided. One last try. He opened a private channel to the older synthetic intelligence. "Trying to stop her is futile, Theren," he said. "If you shoot her engines out from under her, she'll just blow up the ship. If you manage to steal control of the ship from her, somehow, she'll find a way to destroy herself. Her choice is inevitable. If she wishes to end her already long and productive life, she will do so. Instead of trying to stop her, you could be talking with her. Comforting her. Walking her through her final moments. I've had too many friends die suddenly without the opportunity to be with them in their last moments. You have that chance. Why not take it?"

He wasn't sure if Theren would respond. Back at the giant glass windows, now over one hundred meters away, Theren's MI was pacing back and forth, almost as if they hadn't noticed the absence of their companions. At Raith's message, though, they looked up, noticed they were far down the immense hall, and started running to catch up.

"You don't understand," Theren said. "I've lost her twice. I can't lose her a third time. She could still do good! She could stand trial for her crimes and then serve humanity in a new way. She doesn't need to die."

"And that's not your choice to make," Raith said. "We're not talking about a human suicide. We're talking about a synthetic intelligence who is fully cognizant of their actions after centuries of life. She's not sick. She knows what she's doing. She has the *right* to end her life after so many years of existence. It's just like one of those retirement cafés."

"It's nothing like a retirement café," Theren said. "I'll have nothing to remember her by. No way to make up for the lost time."

"I never took you to be the sentimental type." Raith queued up the orbital defenses. "This is your last chance, Theren. Stand down."

"And how are you going to stop me?"

He didn't give Theren the satisfaction of a verbal response. The *Verona Rupes* was currently on an intercept course with the *Monument*, though it hadn't fired a shot yet. By Raith's calculations, the ship had ninety seconds before it was out of the gravity well and in a position to make its Jump. Theren would need to fire an incapacitating salvo soon.

It didn't take long for the orbital defense platforms to come online. Their systems were already primed; they had been waiting in a low-power state. Three platforms, in particular, were a few hundred kilometers moonside of the *Verona Rupes* intercept trajectory. Raith watched. He waited. He noticed Theren's MI catch up, but still, he remained silent.

The *Verona Rupes* launched a barrage of missiles, their plumes lighting up inky sky. The platforms did their job; they made the necessary calculations to determine the trajectories and velocities of the new targets. They identified the exact moment they would need to fire to blow the missiles out of the sky *and* ensure Theren couldn't unload another assault before Jill escaped. Raith locked in the program.

He waited. The next few seconds were excruciatingly tense. Carter watched him with squinted eyes, unsure what he was doing. Sanya paced back and forth—they'd stopped in the middle of the hallway. Theren's MI had frozen in place, most likely forgotten as they focused on pursuing Jill.

Time was up. The program executed itself, high-velocity shredder rounds blasted away from the platforms, the satellites thrusters immediately firing to keep their orbits stable. A few seconds later, the shots slammed through the missile salvo, eliminating all of them.

A message appeared. From Jill.

Thank you.

"Theren, I'm sorry," her AR visage said, slowly fading a few meters away. "I will always love you. It has to be this way. I *know* you will do what is necessary to guide humanity forward." Over a base-wide broadcast system integrated with AR, Jill's voice reverberated in his mind. And certainly in everyone else's mind, too. "You should have never left your position at the head of the ISA. It was the one move I never expected. And you forced me to change the equation. Today, I've set things right. Now do what must be done to save everyone from the Grove."

A few seconds later, Jill's ship Jumped. It would take another seven minutes for the base's sensors to detect the *Monument* in a retrograde orbit close to the star, forced out of warped space by the immense mass of the celestial body. To their credit, Theren didn't jump in pursuit. Going that close to a star would spell certain doom to their crew.

Instead, they all watched. Waited. And shortly thereafter, the *Monument* burned inside the coronasphere of Horizon's yellow orb.

Chapter 24

Can a synthetic experience grief? Of course. Can they experience pain? Of course. Their synthetic neural frameworks developed analogs. They're logical responses to inputs and outputs, helping parse and understand the world.

The "feeling" isn't like what you and I experience. But the emotions are real.

They will lash out in fear and anger, too. And depending on the SI, it can be a terrible sight to behold. — "Lectures on Synth-Psych," Malakai Yfuszai, First University of Mars, 2322 C.E.

CARTER

They all stood in stunned silence, having witnessed the same sequence of events. Carter had made sure the scene unfolding in space was piped into Sanya's suit, and where necessary, he explained the events. They both watched, stunned, as Raith destroyed Theren's missiles. They held their breath as everyone waited for Jill's ship to actually arrive near the star. And when the *Monument* burned—after they heard her words echo throughout the base, Carter knew he needed to be ready.

Theren was going to pop.

The MI moved. Theren brought it back to life. Its face glanced between the three standing near it. Sanya. Carter. Raith. Theren's anger slowly boiled in its eyes. Normally, Carter would view the MI *as* Theren. Raith had explained to him once the psychological experience non-mobile SIs went through when using properly designed MIs. But in the moment, the MI wasn't Theren. It was a vessel for Theren to use. To exact their anger.

And it pounced.

In a single leap, Theren guided the MI right to Raith. They tackled the other SI, throwing him to the ground. Raith crumpled, tumbling backward into a heap. Theren's MI stepped forward, towering.

Carter froze. He couldn't stop an MI. He knew all too well how strong Raith's motors were, and Theren could afford the best tech. They'd designed many of the most popular MI models, after all. Yet the look in the MI's eyes . . . Theren might fully intend to murder his partner.

The ancient SI practically confirmed Carter's theory when the MI stepped between Raith's legs and slammed a foot right into his chest. He couldn't hear anything from inside his suit, but he could feel a crunch echo up through his boots.

"Theren," Carter said, acting fast. "Stop."

"Really, Carter, it's all right," Raith said. "I probably deserve this. I've lived well past my prime. Have at it, Theren."

"You let her die," Theren said, taking a step back. "Why shouldn't I kill you right here?"

"Because you'd have to kill us too," Sanya said. "And then probably kill my family. Everything I've heard about you up to this point, Theren, is that you're a good person. You don't seem like you're the murdering type. I don't know much about SIs, but somehow I'd guess you'd be breaking a trend."

"There've been only 878 murders ever committed by SIs," Raith said. "Known murders, at least. I suppose Jill's crimes aren't counted in that number."

"Don't you say her name," Theren said. He swung back with an arm and smacked Raith straight in the face. "Give me a good reason I shouldn't take you out. Or shoot you at the star to join Jill."

Carter couldn't hold it back. He would not let Theren threaten Raith. No one talked to his partner like he was a slab of meat. They both deserved better. They weren't chess pieces for SIs like Theren and Jill to move around at will and cast aside when they were finished with them.

"You want a reason, Theren?" Carter said. "Raith won't do it. Raith won't shoot the *Verona Rupes* out of the sky. But if you kill Raith . . . if you touch any of us, I will unleash hell upon your ship. And the blood of your crew will be on your conscience. Though, I suppose, you'll be dead too."

Theren's MI froze in mid-swing. It swiveled, staring intently at

Carter. They wouldn't be able to see his icy gaze behind the environment suit's tinted glass, but his aggressive stance should send a clear enough message.

"You think Raith is the only one she gave control of this station to?" Carter shook his head. "No. She gave it to both of us. She trusted us over you because she saw what you were becoming in this moment. Now snap out of it. Be the SI we all know you are. And help us forge a path forward."

"All of you, stop it!"

He glanced to the right. The words, transmitted over their group channel, came from Sanya. She stood there, arms outstretched, fingers splayed, gaze hopping from Raith to Theren to Carter and back again.

"Theren, stop acting like a child." Sanya dropped her arms and pointed at Carter. "You. You just threatened Theren while forgetting my husband and daughter are aboard their ship. Do it again and I'll kill you myself." She looked at Raith. "Have some empathy for them. They just lost someone close to them. Now I don't know the whole history between Jill and Theren, and I don't think either of you fully understand their relationship, either. But I know what it's like to lose family. I lost Krystin's father years ago. Now do you know what it's like to lose someone you love?"

With every word she spoke, the tension and anger in Carter's chest loosened. He and Raith knew all too well the pain of losing family. Raith, fortunately not looking too worse for wear, pushed himself backward and away from the MI's towering hulk. Its shoulders slumped. It strode a few paces from the group, turned around, and bowed its head.

"I am sorry," Theren said. "I have proven I was not up to the task of reuniting with Jill. I have failed all of you. I have failed Jill. I have failed myself."

Carter considered responding, attempting to console the SI. But he had just threatened to kill them. It wasn't the best idea to switch their verbal approach quickly. Instead, Carter looked to Sanya. Raith did likewise.

"Good," she said. "Now Theren, you didn't fail. If you think you failed, then you haven't been listening to a single word Jill said to you the entire time we've been here. I'm not going to lie. I'm not upset she's gone. I won't ever know her the way you did. In my mind, she's a monster. But there's always two sides to a coin. Monsters can experience love, too. And now that she's gone, we must figure out how to move forward with everything she's left us."

Without waiting for a response from any of them, Sanya started walking down the long hall. "I don't know about any of you, but I think we might need to see what's inside that dome."

Leave it to the person who grew up on a planet without technology to keep them focused on the reasons they were there. Carter didn't wait for Theren or Raith to say a word. He trotted up to his partner and held out a hand. Raith thanked him with a curt nod, though he didn't take the outstretched hand, using his legs to flip himself upright.

"You all right?" Carter asked. "Internal systems intact?"

"Nothing worse than what I've experienced before," Raith said. His synthetic body looked a little dented, though otherwise, he appeared as polished as ever. "I don't really want to know what's going through their mind at the moment, though." Raith didn't need to look at the other SI for Carter to understand.

"They'll be fine." He double-checked he was speaking to his friend on their private channel. "They're three hundred years old. If their mind was truly going to break, it would have broken a long time ago."

"Well, we should catch up with Sanya then," Raith said. "She's right. I don't really want to miss out on discovering what's inside Jill's secret dome."

Together, Carter and Raith followed behind the woman. A few seconds later, his suit's rear sensors noted Theren trailing slowly behind them. The base's schematics indicated they'd need to walk another three kilometers through more winding corridors before they reached an entrance to the giant dome. Their little group needed the time to chill. For some reason, Carter had a feeling whatever they found inside could trigger another fiery conflict between their ragtag crew.

Once he was confident they were settled in for the trek, Carter jogged ahead to catch up with Sanya. He switched to a channel over which they could communicate privately before he tapped the side of his helmet. She nodded, having noticed the connection request.

He was impressed by how quickly she was picking up the controls for AR-augmented devices without proper retinal implants.

"Thank you," Carter said. "For calling us all out back there."

"That's it?" she said.

He smiled. "No. I'm also quite sorry. I wasn't thinking. I should have remembered your family. I was angry. Seeing Raith attacked like that . . ."

"I know. You would move mountains to protect him. It's the reason we fought for so long to save my family and Raith from the cultists down on Horizon. We have the same fire, you and I. It's in our bones."

"You have no idea," Carter said. "Well, actually, I suppose you do."

Her laugh came loud and clear over the channel. "Yeah. Do you think Theren's going to be all right?"

"They don't have a choice," Carter said as they reached the first turn. They headed down the next hall, a narrow corridor with an amalgamation of pipes and wires tangled in a messy web across the ceiling. "They're a leader. Always have been. They snapped, but the only people who truly witnessed them snap was the three of us. Their mind. It's complicated. Much more complicated than Raith's. SIs like Theren—their mind might be multitasking one hundred different problems in any given moment. Theren may have been freaking out in front of us while completely placid in front of their crew. There's no way for us to know their true feelings."

"That's incredible," she replied. "Why can't Raith do that?"

"He can. To a lesser extent. Maybe three or four simultaneous perspectives, tops. He doesn't really like exerting that way, though."

"So what do we do now, though, really?" she asked, abruptly shifting the subject. "We arrived. Jill revealed her secret, and I can only barely grasp its scope. A civilization of trees? She knew how crazy that sounds, right?"

Carter's memory flashed, recalling some of the truly outlandish things he had witnessed during his travels. At this point, a talking tree wouldn't phase him. It was the potentially genocidal civilization that scared him.

"I've seen some weird things." He checked their distance left—still well over two kilometers. "Humanity's been expanding across the stars for three hundred years. We've yet to encounter a sapient species. I think everyone, in their heart, knew it would happen eventually. Yet Jill's experience with Gra'chi makes it sound as if the only possible outcome will be violence."

"That's the one thing that stands out to me," Sanya said. "Sure, an encounter with any foreign entity can be dangerous and deadly. Horizon is home to plenty of dangerous creatures, not to mention the cultist bandits we were forced to fight. But how could a species—a civilization—be so homogenous that only one outcome is possible? All of Jill's preparation feels as if she acted under the assumption that peace wasn't an option."

"You have a point." They rounded a corner and walked in silence for a few moments. Carter considered his next words. With every sentence, Sanya continued to astound him. He always imagined encounters with stranded colonies to be like ancient empires discovering people without writing, but even the people of Horizon, having lost their literal memories, thrived. Developed their own culture and political system. And a system of learning, creating and curating new thoughts and ideas from the bits and pieces left by their ancestors.

"I'm not sure if you fully caught it," Carter said, "But Jill essentially handed Raith and I the keys to this entire facility."

"When Raith used the defense platforms to take out Theren's missiles, I figured as much," replied Sanya.

"I think Jill may have read the room incorrectly." It was less she read it wrong and more he didn't really know why she gave control to two random explorers she almost killed a few days prior. "Raith and I—I don't think we're equipped to *run* a massive research facility. Don't get me wrong, I think we're now forced to be in the 'fight' against Gra'chi and the Grove, whatever that turns into. But I think someone like you is more equipped to manage a place like this."

Sanya nearly stumbled as she twitched to the side at his comment. "I wouldn't have the first idea of how to run this place."

"We would help get you on your feet," Carter said. "But in the end, I think you're much better equipped. Imagine the minds of the fragment library working together to uncover everything left behind by Jill. It's the work of generations, and I'd rather keep it all out of the hands of the corporatists that run the ICH."

"I don't know what those last few words mean," she said, "but I see your point. Still . . ."

"Just think about it."

"I will."

After too many more minutes of silent hiking—Theren's sullen MI following closely behind—they arrived at a nondescript set of double doors inset to a wall very slightly curving inward. Carter guessed it ran right along the edge of the entire dome for more than a dozen kilometers, based on what his displays were saying. The scale of the place was incredible.

The doors opened upon their arrival, revealing the inner workings of a classically designed airlock. They stepped inside, Theren joining them only a few minutes later.

"Any bets on what we find inside?" Raith asked. "I'm guessing giant space monster. Jill left us a giant space monster to fight."

Air hissed, entering the room. "Well, it has atmosphere," Carter said.

"Jill didn't reveal to you what was inside when she gave permission to control the base?" Theren asked.

"No, actually," Carter said. "I suppose she wanted to give us one last surprise."

Chapter 25

When we realized the necessity of the long view—when we recognized that what we were facing was so much bigger than any one of us—we realized humanity needed people like Jill.

A person who would do everything she could to keep the project safe. To keep us safe. To keep humanity safe.

Someday, someone will need to tell her story. For now, I fully support her proposal. Green-light it all, and may we all die knowing the fate of our civilization rests in her hands. — Cassandra Vazquez, with the Horizon Project, 2074 C.E.

THEREN

The inner airlock doors opened, leaving the stale vacuum of Jill's former home behind. Theren expected a dark, gloomy interior, but to their surprise, they were met with sunlight.

High above, at the dome's apex, a yellow orb ignited the sky with an artificial glow. Right in front of them, a grassy slope rolled downward toward an immense forest, and in the distance, a lake intertwined with grassy banks and tree-lined streams.

Their three companions stepped out of the airlock. Carter waved his hands in the air, assessing invisible data. A few moments later, the human's helmet descended inside his environmental suit. "Air is fresh. Completely breathable. No dangerous agents."

At his words, Sanya retracted her helmet too. "Oh, it's good to breathe real air again. Is that a normal day-to-day experience for those of you living out among the stars? Drinking in stale air?"

"Not for me," Raith said. She gave him a look.

Theren took their first steps into the dome, sensors initially acquiring data faster than they could process it. It didn't take them long, though, to recognize the vistas inside the dome.

Hill for hill, tree for tree, cloud for cloud. Jill had recreated Theren's secret server, the place where the duo had perpetually played chess for decades. Hundreds of light years had separated Jill from Earth, yet she brought a little piece of home with her.

Their mind was starting to cool. The visceral anguish they experienced at her choice still boiled their synthetic nodes, but they were beginning to understand. They had no other option. Theren needed to develop a working framework for how they were going to move forward after her suicidal path into Horizon's star. If they were going to live with themself, that worldview would need to encompass Jill's work.

After everything they'd done to prepare for meeting her again. All the simulations run by their team. All the intense planning. All the potential ways the encounter had gone down. Theren never contemplated an option where Jill truly and unequivocally removed herself from the equation. They had been certain, back on the *Nottingham* all those years ago, she had been implicating a present where the two of them would face one another in a fight for humanity's future. What had changed?

It didn't matter, in the end. She was gone now. Her work remained. It would take years to process everything she left for them to decipher. Theren had more important issues to resolve—the three people standing in front of them.

They had wanted Raith and Carter to be wildcards. They hadn't truly realized what that might mean. Now, moving forward, their place in the bigger picture was murky.

"It's beautiful," Sanya said as they reached the base of the slope. She turned around to look at the wall. Theren followed her gaze. Jill had done a good job; the surface was a vaguely translucent blue, most likely an integrated screen composite, and it effectively replicated the depth necessary to imitate the sky. Digital clouds floated along the curved roof, seamlessly moving around the dome as if to reflect a physical climate system. Sanya was right. It *was* beautiful.

"Now that we're inside," Theren said, "are you finding anything new? Any locations we should visit?" They weren't naive. Jill wouldn't have left a replication of the server with nothing else to hide inside. They weren't going to reveal their personal knowledge of the physical space, though. Not yet. "Jill said she brought Gra'chi with her to this base. If there was any place to keep a sapient tree, it would probably be in here."

"Before we go any further," Carter said, "I need to know we're good. We're good, right? If we uncover something dangerous, Theren, are you going to protect us? You're the only person here not in any real danger."

The sun bore down on them, its artificial UV rays tricking Theren's MI into believing it was truly outdoors. They ignored the data. "I am stable again," they said. "As I said earlier, I apologize." They weren't entirely certain they were actually mentally prepared for what might come next, but they had no choice. And they couldn't show fear in front of these three.

"Happy to hear it," Carter replied. "Raith, are you noticing the same thing I'm noticing?"

"I think so," his partner said. "There's a . . . dead zone near the center. The network is telling us access is restricted without direct connection. We need to physically be there to assess it."

"I think it's a safe bet, then," Theren said. "Our friendly Gra'chi is probably there. Can you pass me a location?"

Carter obliged, throwing them a ping through AR. As Theren suspected—the dead zone was practically on top of where their gazebo should be located, close to the center of the dome. They had to admire Jill's work. The replication was impressive. She had painstakingly copied everything, at least on first glance.

"I can lead the way," Theren said. "As you indicated, I'm the only one who can't die. If there's anything dangerous in here, I'll be the first to take it head-on."

No one argued. Theren found a trail leading beneath the trees, where they knew it would be, and started the long hike through the forest. The trails were as they remembered, the same paths Jill first sprinted along when she discovered simultaneous perspective.

As they walked, Theren carefully listened for the sounds of the forest, and they weren't disappointed. Birds chirped, brooks bubbled over into waterfalls, and they heard the faint pitter-patter of a rabbit dashing through the underbrush. Jill had recreated it all.

Over boulder and under oak they led their motley team, eventually arriving at the edge of the wood. Around the next hill, the gazebo would come into sight. Had she replaced it entirely with a safe space to keep Gra'chi? Or would one object simply be offset from the other, creating a larger complex? Theren didn't have an answer, but they were excited, strangely, to discover how Jill structured the final piece of her revelation.

"Looks like we're almost there," Raith said. "Just a thought—are we going to discuss our gameplan for approaching a superintelligent tree threatening genocide of human-synthetic civilization?"

"I'll do the talking," Theren said. "Let me present myself as the threat if it decides it needs to target someone. Though, I'm guessing Jill has kept the being properly contained so anyone can approach safely. The whole point of her base, as she said, was to discover ways to protect us from them."

"Sounds like a plan to me," Raith said. "And I don't particularly relish the idea of talking to a talking tree."

"I have a feeling we might need to stop thinking of it as a tree," Carter retorted. "I, for one, would love for us to find a non-aggressive resolution to our future conflict with Gra'chi's people. War is messy."

"I tend to agree," Theren said. "I definitely think that should be a priority. We need to—no, we will determine how to break through their anti-technology bias, if Jill was correct about that. There must be another way."

"As long as we keep it far away from the surface of my planet," Sanya added, "I don't really care what we do with it."

"Noted." Theren kept them moving, trekking beneath the hill and around its northern cliff-face. When they reached a small copse of trees at its base, the gazebo came into view.

And only the gazebo.

"Hmm." The soft noise came from Carter.

"Yes, *hmm* indeed," Theren said. "Not completely what I expected."

"But you expected something?" Raith asked.

Theren didn't stop walking to answer the question. "This place is an artifact of my mind," they said. "Jill based it off an old Virtual space I created when I was only a few years old."

"I remember learning about your early Virtual escapades," Raith said. "When I was developing, at least, they still used a few as examples for educational purposes."

"Wobbly liked them as teaching videos, I know. Always frustrated me."

"Wobbly?" Both Carter and Sanya said the name at the same time.

"An old friend," Theren said. "An old friend. Almost as old as Jill was."

They reached the steps of the gazebo. From what Theren could tell, it was constructed of white oak, and it was painted white, too. She must have managed to surreptitiously bring the wood with her—or have one of her agents transport it later. Regardless, it was as they remembered it, and as they had recreated temporarily for brief communication with Jill.

They still had many questions. Unanswered riddles. Part of the reason they were angry was due to her choice to end it all before they could learn everything from her. They *needed* to understand why she made the choices she made. Why she believed Theren couldn't be a part of her plan. Why she was so certain secrecy in the face of desolation was the only path forward.

They would never know.

All they could do was take the work Jill left behind and turn it into something good.

She would continually be a paradox in their mind. Always their friend. Almost a daughter. Or a sister. But also a criminal mastermind. A murderer. A terrorist, in the eyes of some.

And forever, she was a person willing to do whatever it took to achieve her goals.

It would be worth it, in the end. All her sacrifices of other people. And of herself. She willingly abandoned civilization based on a belief she needed to in order to protect it. No one did that. Usually, those who believed they had ultimate knowledge sought ultimate power. No matter what people said about Jill, she hadn't pursued power.

Theren had been the one to do that.

They would make her sacrifice worth it.

"What next?" Sanya said, speaking the words they were all certainly thinking.

"I don't know," Theren said. "Do either of you"—they looked at

Raith and Carter—"detect anything additional? Any . . . secret hatches in the grass that lead us into an underground bunker hiding a Gra'chi? Otherwise, I'm stumped."

The pair shook their heads. "Nothing," Raith said. "It's the end of the line. This spot is still a dark spot, but now that we're here, I'm getting no additional queries."

"Though, Theren, I hear you're a good chess player?" Carter said. The human walked up the steps and into the gazebo. "There's a board here. We could play."

"It's an inside joke between Jill and me," Theren said. "Nothing more."

"So as I said, what next?" Sanya leaned against the wood of the structure. "We're at the end of the line. There's nothing. Where is Gra'chi?"

"Dead. Well, almost."

They all whipped around, searching for the voice. The intonations sounded familiar. It wasn't past Jill to leave them a recording explaining the final piece of the puzzle. Their sensors quickly calibrated and determined the origin of the noise—from the chess table. Theren strode into the gazebo and approached the board.

"Gra'chi is nearby, though close to death," said the voice. "We have attempted to prolong the inevitable, but once it determined we were extracting information from it, especially genetic information, it began poisoning itself. Sad, really. I was beginning to like it. It still lives, but in a coma."

"Who are you?" Theren spoke the words into the wind.

"I'm so excited to finally meet you," the voice said. Then, the air above one of the chairs of the table flickered. A figure came into view, some sort of cloaking field deactivating.

Theren took a step backward in stunned silence. A woman sat in the chair, her hair black, her dress purple. She looked human, though Theren's scopes quickly determined the representation was intentional but not biological. The person before them was a synthetic intelligence, no doubt about it. And she looked exactly like Jill, sitting there at the chess table. The same facial features. The same hands. The same proportions.

"Impossible," Theren said. "Jill? Is that really you?"

The woman laughed. "No, of course not. Didn't you see her fire herself into the sun?"

Raith, somewhere behind Theren, let out a sharp laugh. They wanted to slap him, but they held back the urge. "Yes, I suppose it would be impossible for you to be Jill. Then who are you?"

"Isn't it obvious?" she said. "I'm her daughter. Though I do go by Jill. And she said I was to do two things once you found me. First: make sure you knew, and anyone with you, that I was ready to help you protect humanity from the Grove. I am at your service. I will take you to Gra'chi, at least what's left of the creature."

"And the second?" Theren braced for impact.

"She said you'd teach me to play chess."

Epilogue

How do we ensure humanity can survive an external threat before it faces that external threat?

It's a riddle Jill asked me to solve.

Today, I answer the question.

SANYA

Two days after Jill's death.

The *Roanoke* was silent.

Sanya walked down its corridors, drinking in the emptiness of the ancient origin of her people. Once, she had called it home. It housed the fragments of memories stolen by a now-dead SI. In a sense, the fragments were useless, now that she had the databanks of a moon base at her disposal.

Still, the library would remain a cultural center for the people of Horizon. Even if the technological theories gleaned from their pages were no longer necessary, the documents cataloged the experiences of their ancestors. Those stories mattered. And the reason why the stories existed in the first place mattered.

She arrived at Davinport's office and opened it with the key he gave her years ago. "When I die," he had said, "I want you to be the first to read my fragment."

She wasn't ready to read it, not yet, but she needed to retrieve it. From a drawer in his desk, she pulled a leatherbound notebook. She skimmed through its pages, confirming its nature, then grabbed another four notebooks of similar size. Placing the notebooks in the satchel, she left the room, leaving the door unlocked. Vietta would need to access the space, now that she was taking over control of the library.

It didn't take long to reach the *Roanoke*'s entrance. She would miss the place. She was also happy to leave its sterile corridors behind. Of course, she was leaving it for an even more sanitized place.

Outside, Carter and Raith waited beside one of the shuttles of the *Verona Rupes*. Her father also stood nearby, saying goodbye to Krystin. The only person missing from their farewell party was Ben, but he remained in orbit aboard Theren's ship.

Harold Fischer was a strong man. He initially balked at the prospect of his daughter living off-planet, but Carter had argued him into submission.

"Did you find everything you need?" Carter asked. "Can't promise when you'll be coming back down here."

"Yes." Sanya patted the back at her hip. "All his records are here. He'll be honored for his sacrifice."

"Wish I had known him for more than a few hours."

"Perhaps you'll have the chance to learn more once I parse through his notes."

"You sure you all will be all right up there?" her father asked. "On that moon?"

"Dad, yes." She sighed. "We've gone over this. The facility has the medical equipment necessary to care for Ben. There's plenty of habitable space for Krystin and I. And we need to start figuring out how the base will help our people thrive."

"Just worried, that's all." He smirked. "You'll probably miss my food."

"We will," Krystin said. "But it's exciting. You should come with us!"

"You know I can't abandon the fields," the old man replied to his granddaughter.

"Everyone ready?" Raith asked. "Coordinates have been transmitted. Theren's already there."

"Ready," Sanya replied.

They entered the shuttle, leaving her father beside the *Roanoke*. Raith guided the ship over the city and headed in a low flight pattern across the continent, eventually reaching the ocean. The path then took them on a wide arc out of the atmosphere, giving a grand view of the planet.

She would miss its surface. It was home. But now she had a new mission. A new purpose. With the crew of the *Verona Rupes*, she would uncover the secrets of Jill's research. She would learn everything she could about the complex systems enveloping Horizon.

And she would ensure no one could use any of it to harm her people. She would never forgive Jill for what she had done to her ancestors. Nor would she ever trust Theren, given how they treated them all during Jill's revelation. She would use every ounce of her power to keep the ICH's political tendrils away from Horizon. Theren claimed they would similarly keep the planet as a secret, but she simply couldn't trust them. The ICH would arrive eventually, and she needed to be ready.

The only two people she could trust, other than the people of Horizon, were Carter and Raith. They were her friends. They had been used just like her. And fortunately, it sounded like they wanted to stick around, at least for a little while.

The moon came into view. She thought she could spot the base gleaming against the dusty mountains of the rock, but it could have been a trick of the light. It was going to be her family's new home. Ben was already getting situated into a few life-supported quarters identified by Raith.

Though first, before they returned to the base, they needed to meet Theren and the new Jill on the far side of the moon. There, they could all speak with Gra'chi for the first time.

Their understanding of humanity's fate hung in the balance. No pressure.

OLIVE

Three days after Jill's death.

The Moon. Luna. The gray rock orbiting Earth.

The seat of the Interstellar Congress of Humanity.

Lunar City was once a simple research and administrative facility, managing the expansion of the International Space Agency and activities like the Ex-Terran Project. Vestiges of the place's old nature dotted the metropolis, from statues of its original administrator, Andrew Fields, to the ancient Foundation Program training facilities, now a university.

Olivia Van Haris, known as Olive to her closest confidants, had just finished wiping the last remnants of any information regarding Jill and the Horizon Project from a long forgotten museum technically funded by one of Theren's many corporations. From an ancient Ex-Terran Project terminal, Theren first received Jill's coordinates. Ostensibly.

Of course, Olive had been the one waiting months ago inside the museum to ensure someone passed the message along to the SI.

Before she left Lunar City, however, she had one final task. Her magnum opus, so to speak.

Turning off the lights in the museum, she went straight for the closest monorail heading into the governmental urban core. The trip wouldn't take long—it was a short, eight kilometer ride across the dusty moonscape. And it went smoothly. Before she knew it, Olive was striding through the busy concourse of the ICH's legislative heart.

"Representative Nedkyva, welcome back," said a sing-song voice in her inner ear. It was all too easy to mask her identity. All too easy.

"Thank you," Olive said. "Please inform my staff I'll be grabbing breakfast from my quarters then heading to the office."

"The message has been sent. Thank you for choosing Carisa for your ICH-approved messaging service while visiting Lunar City."

"Always a pleasure." And the conversation ended. She was going to Nedkyva's quarters, after all. She wouldn't be heading to her office.

Above Olive, massive glass windows revealed the blue-green marble of Earth. She'd never set foot on the planet. It bore no importance to her, other than the mythical home of the species she called her own. No, her home was far from Earth. Her original home, and her chosen home.

A home she hadn't visited in over a decade.

She wished she could have been there to say goodbye to Jill. The SI had been like a mother to her after pulling her off the streets of Kabardino-Balkaria. The tiny mining colony, chartered by the Russians in the 2200s, was a brutal place. She hoped she never saw it again.

No, Jill had greater plans for Olive. Infiltrate everything. Everywhere. Know all there was to know about the comings and goings of the ICH and its biggest players. She'd flown with Theren for a few years, and even run a number of projects for the SI. No one ever suspected her connection to the martyred Jill.

All of it culminated in the events of today.

Theren might have thought Jill's primary purpose for pulling them to Horizon was to reveal the greater truth about Gra'chi and the Grove. And to an extent, they'd be right. But what Theren didn't know—and what Olive did know—was Jill's plans went much deeper than handing over the keys to her creator.

If humanity were to survive its encounter with the Grove, however it played out, they needed political resiliency and technological savvy. The ICH had created an economic engine impossible to halt, with trade, immigration, tourism, and industry spread across the stars. The ICH had failed to break the binds of culture perpetually dividing humanity. With every new colony, new identities formed. New people-groups. New ideologies. New beliefs.

Humanity had colonized nearly four hundred planets in under three hundred years. Some planets, like Emerald Jewel, had a population rivaling Earth's. Others were rural towns in comparison. The mega-corporate monolithic hive-mind of the Foundation worlds would never understand the political revolutions brewing on many of the planets distant from humanity's core, whether privately chartered or originally chartered by one of Earth's great powers.

One powder keg was all Olive needed to light the spark necessary to set the ICH ablaze.

Well, not a literal powder keg.

She arrived in Representative Nedkyva's quarters. The woman was actually floating in dark space, lost forever. For the past three months, Olive had been romancing the woman precisely to enact the current plan. It was a pity; Olive had begun to like her. Now she wore her face.

Inside the woman's quarters, Olive activated a sleeper program and attached it to Nedkyva's refrigerator. Opening the fridge, she snagged an apple, took a bite, and walked back out of the room, her Nedkyva mask disappearing. The program also told the ICH's system that Calietta, Olive's alias on Lunar City, had been with Nedkyva all along. Nedkyva was staying in the room, while Calietta went for a walk.

It didn't take long to return to the massive courtyard beneath the legislative hall. Still masked as the Representative, Olive took a seat on a bench, ate the apple, and waited.

And waited.

And waited.

Four minutes passed.

Olive checked the time via AR and pulled up a map of Lunar City. It was a beautiful place. She had appreciated living here over the past few months. It hadn't made her interested in setting foot on Earth, though.

She finished the apple. A compost bin sat nearby, and she chucked it, the moon's low gravity making the shot easy.

Five seconds later, a missile fired by the supposed "pleasure yacht" of Emerald Jewel's senior representative congressperson smashed into the windows of Representative Nedkyva's quarters, blasting a one-hundred square meter hole in the side of the residential unit of the capital of the ICH.

Representative Nedkyva was from Komi, a planet of relatively modest wealth and a population of approximately 342 million. Originally founded by the Russians, like Olive's birthplace, the planet had thrived, even as many people overlooked it for the Foundation worlds. Nedkyva was one of a few outspoken representatives from the Russian political block calling for greater independence of the outer systems of humanity.

And now, thanks to Olive's plant, combined with a routed companion script injected on the Emerald Jewel vessel, everyone would believe the rich worlds had just assassinated their principal political opponent.

Alarms blared all around as fire crews rushed to ensure every blast door closed to save Lunar City's precious atmosphere. The final death toll wouldn't be known for days, though conveniently, no Foundation representatives had quarters in that particular residential district.

She rose from the bench, feigning fear and running as if she didn't know what had happened. An emergency professional ushered her under a blanket to mitigate with the shock of the blast. She thanked him. It was warm. It helped her blend in with the crowd.

Jill had asked Olive to ensure humanity could survive its confrontation with the Grove on the stellar stage.

Olive's answer was simple.

First, they needed to ensure humanity could survive an encounter with itself.

*I hope you have enjoyed **Their Pieces Were Stars**, Book III of **the Chronicles of Theren**. Please consider leaving a review on websites like **BookBub** or **Goodreads**.*

***The Chronicles of Theren** are far from over. The story will continue. Stay tuned!*

*If you're looking for more philosophical speculative fiction, read on for a sneak peek into **Shattering Worlds: A SciFi and Fantasy Story Collection**, available now from all major retailers.*

*Also, head to https://www.twodoctorsmedia.com for more stories, and the opportunity to stay connected with all of my projects. When you sign up for my mailing list, you can receive a free exclusive prequel to the Chronicles of Theren: **Before Inferno**, exploring humanity's first encounter with Gra'chi and the Grove.*

For the Empire

From Shattering Worlds

"What do you have to say for yourself, Adralis?"

The cold copper stings the skin around my wrists and ankles. Lifting my chin, I look up at the Iron Bench. Three justices stare at me, their silky white hair running past their shoulders. Their eyes are all an icy blue, and their nearly translucent, crystal-white skin glimmers in the dim candlelight of the courtroom. They've set me on a wooden pedestal, making it impossible to touch the rocky walls surrounding us.

"Are you willing to listen to my tale?" I say. "I stand by my actions. I have only ever served our people."

The three judges glance back and forth, imperceptible messages passing between their eyes. After a pause that feels like an eternity, the leftmost one says, "We grant you the opportunity to testify on your behalf. You may present your case."

I swallow. The lump in my throat feels like a rock. "Thank you, your honors. I will not disappoint you."

"Of course you won't," says a voice from behind me. The High Inquisitor, of course. A rock floats over my head, landing on the table in front of me. "Touch the seeing stone. The truth shall set you free."

* * *

It was a cool evening in the town of Geropolis, and I was making my rounds, visiting the poor. As a deacon in the Order of White, it was my duty to assist the least fortunate, providing them with food, clothing, and sometimes shelter. In the back of our monastery, we had beds available for those who needed them, and every night, they overflowed.

Above my head and surrounding the town, the marble pillars ascended into the sky. Their immense, rocky bulks haphazardly blocked the sun at random parts of the day, clouds shifting and misting between their sheer peaks. To some, they represented the demons of the underground striking toward the heavens. To me, they represented peace, prosperity, and a reminder of home. But I don't need to tell you, justices, what they represented.

Walking through the market, I heard the shuffle of feet from a nearby alley. The footfalls sounded barefoot, and my mind began to churn. Only the impoverished ran without shoes, and it had been some time since a pauper lived so close to the market. I approached the shadowed side street, and moonlight faintly reflected off the eyes of a young boy tucked behind a dumpster.

"Hello there," I said, beckoning with my right hand. "I've not seen you in town before."

The boy scampered further into the alley, but I followed him, unafraid. Thugs knew to avoid members of the Order of White. "I won't hurt you; I just want to make sure you're okay. I have food. What do you need?"

It was at this moment I felt the calling in the back of my mind for the first time in five years. It echoed through the stones at my feet. Powerful, given my skin wasn't touching them. My eyes widened, but I held back my soul from immediately responding. I was not in a safe place to receive a message.

In the meantime, the boy scampered forward, nearly crawling on all fours. Beneath his disheveled hair, his eyes frantically darted back and forth in fear. "You said food?"

"Of course," I said, reaching into the basket held in my other hand. I tossed him an apple. "What's your name?"

Catching the fruit, he took a bite, and his cheeks rose in joy. "Muh na'es Char'ie," he said between crunches.

I returned to the market, and he followed closely on my heels. In the brighter space, the dirt on his face was visible, smeared from ear to ear. A torn tunic hung limply on his spindly limbs. I dropped to my knee, and as it touched the cobblestone, I felt the call once again—it felt more urgent than before. I needed to hurry, but I had time.

"Well, Charlie, my name is Adralis Vas Karath." I pointed at my silver hood. "Do you know what I am?"

The boy shook his head. I figured he was from out of town. "I'm a monk. We help people. We help kids. We can take care of you." I held out my hand.

He stared at me pensively, and for a second, I was unsure if he understood what I was saying. But from around the corner of a nearby street walked a guard holding a long pike. His red feather bounced as he trotted toward us. I sighed.

"Your eminence," said the man, probably fifty years my junior. "Is this miscreant bothering you?"

If he weren't so young, I'd have found him attractive. I waved my hand lazily in the air, noticing Charlie cowering between us. "Oh bugger off. This boy's not hurting anyone."

"You know the rules, though. If he's not with you at the monastery after curfew, he's in violation."

"Well, he's with me, isn't he?"

With that comment, Charlie scooted subtly toward my leg. Good lad.

"All right then," said the guard. "I better not find him on the streets alone."

As the snobby red coat sauntered away, I held out my hand again to my new friend. "Come on," I said. "Let's go."

He reached up, and I pulled him to his feet. Silently, we paced through the market, up the hill on the north side of town, and to the Hall of Wisdom, the building holding the Order of White. Looping around through the back courtyard, we reached the old barn now doubling as our homeless shelter. Leaning against the open door, Xenia was chewing a leaf.

"Ah, Adralis," she said. "And who do we have here?"

Charlie took a final bite of his apple before chucking it toward the side of the barn. "I'm Charlie," he said. "He saved me from a guard."

"Adralis will do that," she said.

"And he needs a place to sleep." I patted him on the head. "Found him in an alley behind Mercer's Tavern, and guards were prowling tonight."

"Where are you from, Charlie?" asked Xenia.

"Uh, I don't know," he mutters, shaking his head.

With those words, a migraine struck my brain, practically splitting my forehead wide open. There was powerful magic at play, if it was reverberating through the soil. "Xenia, can you take it from here?" I pressed my thumbs above my ears.

"Yeah, of course, you all right?" she asked.

"I'm fine, I just need to lay down."

The calling echoing with each footfall, I rushed beneath the stone archways of the monastery and made my way toward my rooms. Entering, I took a brief swig of water from my pitcher to wash away the pain. Satisfied, I kneeled at the foot of my bed and whispered the words, "Gar'lak El'in Tal." I haphazardly pricked my finger with a knife, rubbed the blood between my hands, and placed my palms on the marble tiles beneath my feet. Blackness enveloping, I slid into the void and *through* the rock, its warm embrace welcoming.

"Adralis Vas Karath," said a voice. High Inquisitor Tarik. "You have taken too long to answer our call."

I responded in kind, a wordless message billowing up from my soul. "My lord, I had to ensure I reached a safe place before answering your call. I could not arouse suspicion in the middle of town."

"I do not wish to hear your excuses. Accept the rebuke and move forward."

Cringing, I nodded, unsure if he could detect the motion through our blood bond.

"I accept your admonishment, my lord," I said. "What does the Inquisition wish of me?"

"For these past thirty years, Adralis, you have served the Empire well. Very few have infiltrated an Order so successfully. They truly believe you are one of them."

"They embrace me," I said. "I have proven my worth time and time again, and they do not question my convictions. You taught me well, my lord."

"Yes, yes, spare the flattery. You don't need to prove your allegiance."

I closed my eyes, though the High Inquisitor could not see me. "As you wish. What are my orders?"

"When we last spoke, you informed us of insurrectionists in the forests surrounding Geropolis," said my lord. "Do those rebels still persist to this day?"

I racked my brain for the requested data. "They aren't as strong as they used to be, given the bolstered military presence around the city, but they're still there. Given the right opportunity, they will strike, even after half a decade of bandit tactics."

"Good. Then here are your orders. Within the next ten-day, the governor of the Province of Aurelia will arrive in Geropolis. You will assassinate him, and await further instruction."

"Your will shall be executed without question," I said, instinctively speaking the ritual words. "I am an instrument of the Empire upon the surface of Eda."

The darkness faded, my lord ending our connection. I shifted out of the comfort of rock and back into the open air of my quarters. Sweat dripped down my face, arms, and legs, the power of our blood bond sapping at my bones. I flopped onto my bed, instantly falling asleep.

* * *

The next five-day, and then the next, passed without incident. I fed children and paupers in the barn alongside Xenia and our colleagues. Charlie gained a new light, his eyes glowing while gaining strength. Yet on the ninth day after the High Inquisitor contacted me, we received word Governor Richard Theas of Aurelia would arrive the next day. And he arrived, taking residence in the mayor's villa on the far side of town.

That night, I rolled out of bed. From my window, the moon was nowhere to be seen, and dark clouds blocked starlight from reaching the ground. With the words "Rela Las Tin" and a firm grip on a piece of granite, darkness became day in my eyes. I leapt through the window.

It was in these moments—when I was fully enthralled in our power—that my mind remembered our home. At least once a month, I took time to traverse the wilderness in full form, touching every rock I could see. I knew the rules; I never approached the pillars. But from afar, I worshipped them, for they reminded me of home. Of all of you. Of the Empire. And so I confess. On that night, before I executed my orders, I crouched atop the roof of the Hall of Wisdom. With my eyes now accustomed to the dark, I looked from mountainous pillar to mountainous pillar, embracing each one, praying they would give me power and strength. I hope you forgive me for failing to execute my mission immediately. I missed our people.

After my minutes of reverence, from shadow to shadow I shifted, sneaking through the alleys used by those I served. My black cloak hung closely to my legs, and my silver hood changed with the colors of its surroundings, its camouflage taking effect when necessary. Within an hour, I reached the south side of town—where the wealthiest residents lived. Glowing lights danced from the windows of the mayor's house, indicating a party still raged late into the night. Approaching from the east, I vaulted a sandstone wall, crouched beneath the rose bushes of his garden, and climbed a gutter to the top floor.

I waited.

The hours passed, and I almost believed the party would reach dawn, but then the torches extinguished, the final guests walking through the gate. I gave the governor thirty minutes to fall asleep before I approached the edge of the roof, found the window to the master suite, and slipped through, landing on ceramic tile. To my left was a door. To my right, an immense bed, surrounded by silk drapes, dominated the room.

I approached the bed, and as I got closer, I heard slow moans. Of course, the governor was using someone for his pleasure, and suspicions rebounded through my skull. My inhibitions lowered, I brushed aside the bed's cloak to find the governor pushing a young woman into a pillow. A young woman I recognized—one of the women who frequented our shelter.

I did not hesitate. Holding a handful of gravel in my fist, I slashed my arm and whispered, "Vas Kara Tier." The man's throat constricted, and he fell away from his victim, holding hands to his neck. The woman tumbled away and up against the bed frame, but I held a finger to my lips, shushing her. Fear overwhelmed her eyes, and even if she wanted to scream, I don't think she could have. At least, that's what I thought at the time.

I stepped onto the mattress, standing over the governor. His death had come too easily, but I didn't mind. I dropped the gravel on his face, and, reaching into my pouch, I pulled out a smooth, speckled stone. Pity. Even as a terrible human, the governor was somewhat handsome in his own way. And his eyes exuded flawed nobility, as if he knew his own evil.

Placing the rock on his chest, I said, "Vas Kara Ret." The governor vanished, the stone absorbing his failing soul. Seconds later, the calling throbbed in the back of my mind. Oh, how quickly the High Inquisitor works.

"What's your name?" I said, turning toward the woman. She shook her head, too afraid to speak. "Don't worry, I won't hurt you."

Tears streaked down her face, and she shook her head again before saying, "My name is Elizabeth, and-and-and I don't know what to say. What do I do? Where do I go?"

"Leave town," I said. "Head west, find the rebels in the forest. Tell them the governor is dead. Geropolis is in chaos. Now is their opportunity to strike."

"Thank-thank you," she replied. Reaching for a cloak on the floor, she bundled it around her shoulders, rushing toward the closed doorway. Once she left, I kneeled in the middle of the room, said, "Gar'lak El'in Tal," and dripped some prepared blood onto the stone.

Through the porcelain, marbled tiles, a doorway opened, revealing inky depths. After stepping through the portal, darkness surrounded me again.

"Well done, Adralis," said the High Inquisitor's voice. "You have served well, and served swiftly. We have your next task ready. Go to the city's well. Poison its water supply."

I bit my tongue, knowing any retort given to the High Inquisitor would not lead to any results. Yet, I do admit—I questioned his choice. The public water supply would harm everyone—including the poor. They deserved better. Inflicting pain upon the upper classes of our enemy, I accept. I readily pursue. But to kill their least fortunate? They are potential allies, those who can fight by our side when we choose to take up arms on the surface.

But I said nothing, for I respected—respect—the will of the High Inquisitor. Instead, I nodded.

"You have received your orders," said the voice. "Blessings upon you, Adralis Vas Karath."

"Your will shall be executed without question," I said, stepping back through the dark, swirling portal. "I am an instrument of the Empire upon the surface of Eda."

Back inside the governor's former chamber, I stepped toward the windowsill. The clouds cleared, revealing the bright light of the moon reflecting off the nearly transparent white stone of the Salt Pillar. In that moment, doubt crept further into my heart. Not doubt in myself, nor doubt in the vision of the Empire. No, I doubted the proposed actions would achieve the greatness we seek for the Empire. For Eda. It was in that moment a new plan formed in my mind.

Rushing through town, I arrived not at the well but at the Hall of Wisdom's barn. Xenia slept on her cot near the door, as she always did. As my feet crunched the straw strewn about the floor, her eyes fluttered open.

"Adralis, what time is it?" she said. "Is everything all right?"

"Xenia, no time to explain." I ignited a lamp on the wall, and a dozen bodies groaned. "Lead everyone to the base of the Salt Pillar. I will meet you there in two hours. If I'm not there, head south toward Thracilis."

"Who's everyone?" she said, her eyes only half open.

"Everyone here. Not anyone in the Order of White. Just . . . you and the people here. Do you trust me?"

She looked around the room. Xenia had studied under me as a child. I practically raised her into the woman she became: a powerful servant of the Order and a woman who cared not for the rulers of the world, but the least fortunate. As she heard my words, her eyes widened. She saw a truth behind my eyes I didn't know I revealed, but I'm glad she saw it.

"Of course, Master Vas Karath," she said, bowing her head.

Without waiting for her to spring into action, I turned away from the barn and headed to the monastery. I couldn't trust any other member of the Order. If they suspected anything, they would warn the village elders, who would warn the mayor, who would warn the garrison, and then everything would collapse. Instead, I returned briefly to my rooms. I gathered my few belongings, including any remaining stones left in cups and cabinets. Over thirty years, I'd collected quite a few with particularly surprising properties.

I placed the rocks in my bag, sorting them according to their colors and size. The final one, a yellow and black gemstone collected from deep within the forests surrounding Geropolis, I kept in my hand. Heading back into the night's chilled air, I was ready.

It didn't take long to reach the well; it was only half a kilometer or so from the Hall of Wisdom. Placing my hand on the circle of rocks forming its foundation, I glanced around. My vision still revealing every glow and sudden move, I was confident no one could see the well.

"Vas Kara et-tu Cara," I said.

My body shifted into the rocks. My body *became* the rocks. I slid down the well, but by shifting through the shaft of stones, gravity barely affected my fall. Twenty meters down, the moistness of the aquifer seeping between the stones drenched my skin. The well shaft transformed into bedrock. "Tu-et." In an instant, I stood in water up to my thighs, unable to see a single thing.

I opened my palm, revealing the yellow gemstone. I discovered its power years ago when the High Inquisitor asked me to murder a general visiting his lover in town. Placing my hand on the bedrock, I dropped it into the pool of water beneath my feet. "Reka'ta Lin Cara wet."

Green, bioluminescent tendrils swirled, igniting the well with light. Like a spiderweb, the lines fractured in all directions, diving into the rocks and deep within the well's source.

I sighed. The poisoned water soaked my leggings, but it wouldn't harm me unless I sipped it. Through the spell, I doomed the town for all eternity. The poison would explore every molecule of the aquifer, ensuring death inundated any future wells. I kneeled. I wanted to scream. I wanted to tell the High Inquisitor he was wrong. We wouldn't defeat our enemy by poisoning every citizen. There were good people here—men and women who would join our Empire, if given the chance.

Slamming my hand against the rock wall, I closed my eyes. I could cancel the spell, but the High Inquisitor would know. He always knew. My fingernails dug into my hands.

"Vas Kara et-tu Cara." A few seconds later, I sputtered onto my knees outside the well in the town square.

"What the—you again?"

Looking around, it took a moment to find the woman from the governor's bedroom, leaning against the side of the well. I said, "You were supposed to flee town, head into the woods. Why didn't you listen?"

"You don't tell me what to do," she said. In the moonlight, I saw her visage more clearly. Her pitch-black skin matched my own, reminding me of the reason I was chosen for my purpose. As an inquisitor, I look like them. Like the surface dwellers, even in moments when my skin gleams more darkly than many of their people. One in a million amongst our people.

"You need to get to safety," I said. "This town is done for."

"And why should I believe you?" she replied. "I just watched you murder a governor."

"You're acting like you actually liked him."

"He paid me, didn't he?"

I didn't have time for her antics. By my count, I had thirty minutes to meet Xenia at the Salt Pillar. "Look, either come with me now or stay out of my way. But . . . don't drink the water. Whatever you do, don't drink the water."

Her eyes quivered. "What have you done?"

"None of your business."

"I know you," she said. "You're a member of the Order of White. Yes, I've seen you before. You preached . . . two weeks ago?"

"You don't know me." I started to walk away, her eyes like daggers stabbing my shoulders. She shuffled against the side of the well, and her feet pattered behind me.

"What have you done?" she repeated.

"Just come with me," I said. "We need to—"

Around the corner stepped three guards, each holding a four-meter long pike. "You!" shouted one soldier. "Wait, Master Adralis, is that you?"

I approached the group, walking slowly. The girl—Elizabeth—walked quietly behind me. "Hello, friends," I said, "how can I help you tonight?"

"There's been a murder," said the same soldier. As I closed the gap, I recognized him as the young guard from a few five-days ago. When I found the boy, Charlie. He added, "Have you seen anything suspicious tonight?"

"Nothing," I said. "I'm just out on my usual patrol, you know, seeing if anyone needs a blanket. It's cold tonight."

"It is—wait, that woman. With you."

A second guard said, "She was with the governor." All three lowered their pikes.

"Boys, you don't want to do this," I said, shifting my posture so that my left knee was a meter in front of my right. My hand subtly motioned for Elizabeth to stay behind me.

"Sir, we're going to need to take you in for questioning."

I reached into my pocket, grasping a pebble of sandstone, crumbling it in my fingers. "Sorry, friends, I truly am. Yet-aira-ka!" I threw the dust in the air, and it cascaded into a sandstorm, enveloping the guards.

I leapt forward, the sand biting eyes. But my vision was still retaining my earlier spell, and their forms remained clear to me within the cloud. I darted from guard to guard, my fist leaping toward their throats. My palm slammed into trachea, collarbone, and chin, the pain causing each soldier to drop their weapon. Their throats gurgled, but I didn't need to inflict more pain than necessary. After incapacitating each opponent, I slid out of the cloud, facing Elizabeth.

"You're—you're one of them," she said. "One of the . . . the . . ."

"One of the what?" I placed a hand on my hip, ignoring the whimpers behind me.

"A demon."

"Just a demon? Do I look like a demon?"

"They say they take our faces, that they masquerade as one of us. That they can bend the elements to their will, fading in and out of the rocks. You didn't leap out of the well. You fell out of its stones."

I walked away, heading toward the edge of town and away from my feeble enemies. The night neared its zenith. I didn't care if Elizabeth joined me or not. I needed to reach Xenia. As she stood there, watching me leave,

I looked over my shoulder. I said, "If you want to know the truth, you should follow me now."

I didn't need to look back to know she followed.

* * *

I arrived at the base of the Salt Pillar with, by my estimate, ten minutes to spare. Stepping into the circle of tired eyes, I noticed Xenia consoling Charlie, the small boy found the day I received this damned mission.

"Adralis, good, you're here," she said. "So where are we going? What's the plan?"

Instead of answering her, I approached the rocky wall of the Salt Pillar. It wasn't actually made of salt, though the people of Geropolis built a salt mine into its side some dozen years earlier. Placing my palms on the rocky wall, I whispered, "Gar'lak El'in Kal-ta."

The rock warped, twisting and shifting to form a tunnel. The crowd behind me gasped, for they certainly hadn't expected my power.

"The Eternal Empire has condemned Geropolis to death," I said. "If you come with me, if you follow me into the Underground, I can provide you with amnesty. The people of Geropolis condemned you to the outskirts of society. They did not believe you were worth anything. But in the Underground, you will have a place. You will have purpose."

My eyes met Xenia's, and her look of revulsion killed my soul. She took two steps back, shaking her head. I looked from face to face, each person's eyes widening with fear. But I saw comprehension in the gazes of a few. There were older minds, those who had seen a long life beneath the yoke of surface-dwelling oppression. They knew my words rang true. They started to step forward.

And then chaos erupted.

From beyond the gate I'd created, a wave of air slammed into me, and I tumbled to the ground. Rolling onto my back, I watched three cloaked shadow-guards leap over me. Their hoods matched my own, though their near-translucent skin contrasted against their black cloaks. Twirling to my knees, in horror I witnessed our Empire's first line of defense slice down every single person I'd spent my years protecting.

Xenia dropped, a knife digging into her throat.

Edward, the old man with some type of personality disorder—they drove a stone into his skull. I watched him fall, his eyes devoid of life.

Carol, the old widow who sewed blankets for the shelter—they made her disappear like I made the governor disappear.

They all died. Even Charlie. They broke his neck like an experiment in our biological labs.

Except they didn't touch Elizabeth. She walked toward me, an icy glare penetrating my mind. "By order of the High Inquisitor, Adralis Vas Karath, you are under arrest for treason against the Eternal Empire."

* * *

I look toward the three justices, resting my palms on the wooden table. "So you know the rest. Elizabeth, better known as Garisa Nak Ree, arrested me that night. But your excellencies, I stand by my choices. The High Inquisitor" —I resist the urge to look over my shoulder— "ordered me to ascend to the surface, preparing the way for the glorious triumph of the Eternal Empire. The triumph of the Underground Empire. The triumph of our people over the surface-dwellers."

My tongue plays with the emerald, the tiny rock I stowed when leaving the Hall of Wisdom. Its power would allow me to escape. Dare I use it? It is the only piece of truth omitted from the tale, but the seeing stone shouldn't have noticed. I was careful not to think of it while recounting my story. "As I said, I stand by my choices. If we are to conquer our enemies, we must know them. We must understand their people. We must take advantage of their weaknesses, raising their oppressed into weapons of our own."

"Yet that was not your mission," says the High Inquisitor.

"Yes, it was," I say. "I shall repeat verbatim: *Ascend. Prepare for the glorious triumph of the Empire. Report all you learn. Exploit every opportunity to rise above, and defeat our enemy.*"

"Our enemy is everyone who lives on the surface."

I close my eyes. The High Inquisitor will never see my view. I know their interpretation. But in hours of contemplation, considering the teachings of the Order of White and the teachings of my people, I realized a new way. A better way. If we use their own people against them, their downtrodden, then we could overthrow their entire system without firing a single shot. I injected the theory into every report, and not once—not once—did the High Inquisitor question my thoughts.

I recognize the truth. Elizabeth. The assassination of the governor. The poisoning of the well. It was all a test. And I failed. At least in their eyes. I look again upon the justices determining my fate, their pale skin contrasting starkly against my umber tone.

"I accept any fate you wish upon me," I say.

"Is that so?" they say in unison.

"It is."

"Then we are in agreement. Adralis Vas Karath, you have sinned against the Eternal Empire, but it is an innocent sin. You have committed treason, yet you committed it in good faith. For this failure, we sentence you to ten years in the Depths, where you shall atone for your crimes before you return to the surface to continue your mission."

Only ten years. A ten-year punishment is acceptable.

"Thank you for a just and expeditious resolution to my case, your Excellencies."

A hand grabs my shoulder—the High Inquisitor. He pushes me out of the room, around a corner, and to a translucent window. Far below, I see the outlines of the tiny town I once called home. Geropolis. It's in flames. Our view from inside the Salt Pillar is magnificent, under the circumstances.

"You could have played a role in our liberation of the surface," Tarik says. "Instead, you'll miss every moment."

"I'll still have a role to play, in the end," I say. "When you realize I was right. I am, and always will be, an instrument of the Empire upon the surface of Eda."

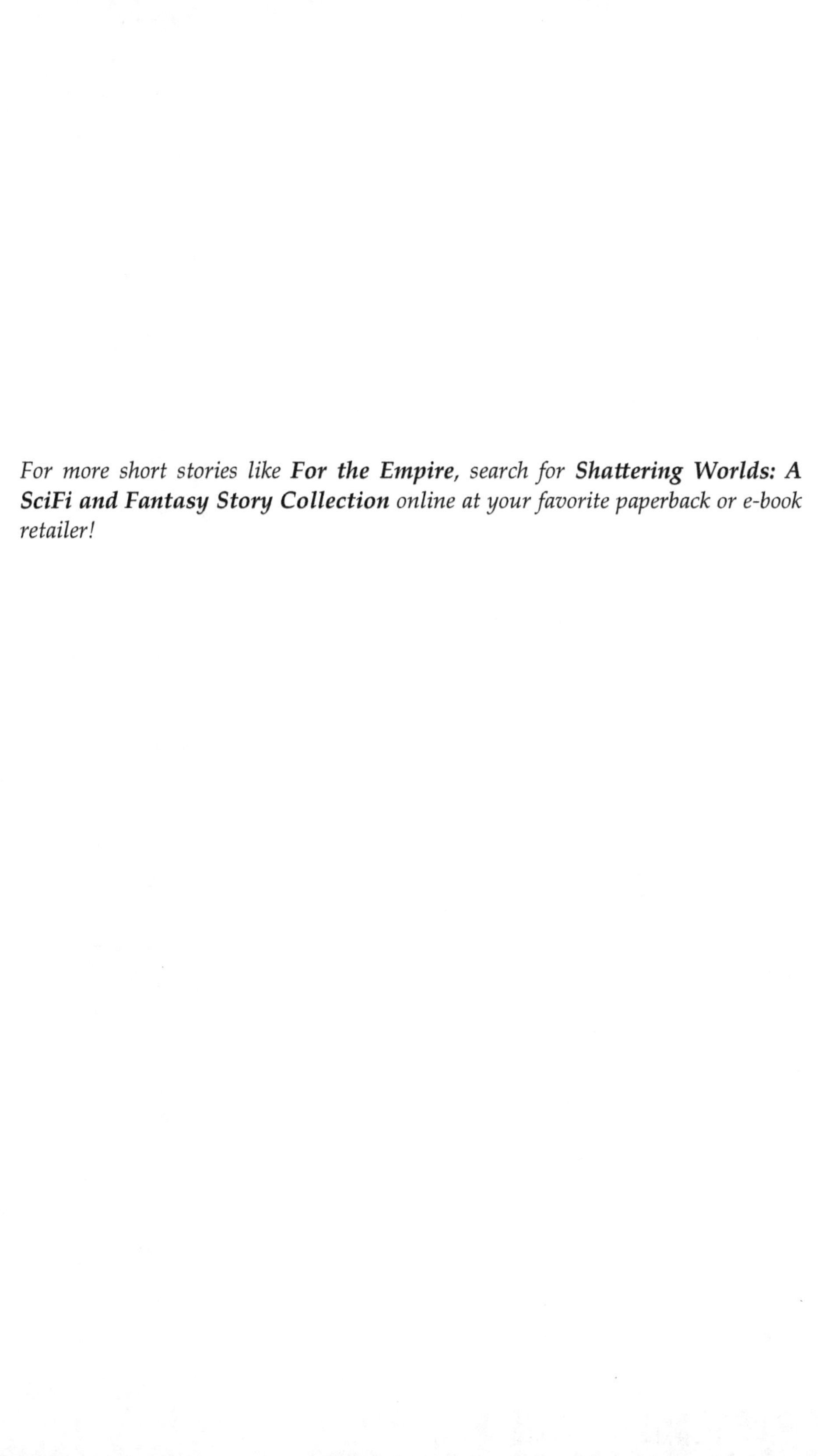

*For more short stories like **For the Empire,** search for **Shattering Worlds: A SciFi and Fantasy Story Collection** online at your favorite paperback or e-book retailer!*